CU00705867

"Cheating Chance is an aw
resent every single second th;
reading to deal with the incony
and sleeping. . . . . Cheating Chance is a must have for the
library of all m/m lovers, and it will place James Buchanan on
the list of authors you must buy!"

Bella, *Two Lips Reviews*
(www.twolipsreviews.com)

". . . The gifted James Buchanan lures you into the
networking within the legal systems and the progression of an
investigation, the emotional turmoil of a new relationship and
the motivations for murder. Cheating Chance is a well written,
realistic mystery blended with humor and sensuous love play
that keeps your emotions attached to the very end of the story.
I enjoyed this impressive and tantalizing story immensely."

Chocolate Minx, *Literary Nymphs*
(literarynymphsreviewsonly.blogspot.com)

". . . James Buchanan needs to hurry up and write more
about Nick and Brandon. I can't wait to see what the future
holds for these two intriguing characters and their troubled
relationship!"

Hayley, *Fallen Angels*
(www.fallenangelsreviews.com)

"Cheating Chance is a little dark sometimes, hot all the time
and very exciting. I love Nicky and Brandon. They're sexy and
fun and incredibly hot together. Cheating Chance is more than a
great story with two all around great guys who have amazingly
hot sex."

Nannette, *Joyfully Reviewed*
(www.joyfullyreviewed.com)

MLR Press Authors

Featuring a roll call of some of the best writers of gay erotica and mysteries today!

Maura Anderson	Storm Grant
Victor J. Banis	Wayne Gunn
Laura Baumbach	J. L. Langley
Sarah Black	Josh Lanyon
Ally Blue	William Maltese
J. P. Bowie	Gary Martine
James Buchanan	Jet Mykles
Dick D	Luisa Prieto
Jason Edding	Jardonn Smith
Angela Fiddler	Richard Stevenson
Kimberly Gardner	Claire Thompson

Check out titles, both available and forthcoming, at
www.mlrpress.com

Cheating Chance

JAMES BUCHANAN

mlrpress

This book is a work of fiction. Names, characters, places, and incidents either are products of the author's imagination or are used fictitiously. Any resemblance to actual events or locales or persons, living or dead, is entirely coincidental.

Copyright 2008 by James Buchanan

All rights reserved, including the right of reproduction in whole or in part in any form.

Published by
MLR Press, LLC
3052 Gaines Waterport Rd.
Albion, NY 14411

Visit ManLoveRomance Press, LLC on the Internet:
www.mlrpress.com

Cover Art by Deana C. Jamroz
Editing by Maura Anderson
Printed in the United States of America.

ISBN# 978-1-934531-08-2

First Edition
2008

CHAPTER ONE

Leather and velvet and PVC and brocade graced the patrons as they swirled through the cavernous building. People ebbed and flowed from sidewalk to bar to dance floor. Security guards swiped IDs through high-tech gadgets that flashed a person's age for all to see. Every color known to chemistry was dyed into at least one person's hair. Monitors repeated image after image of the grinning skull with its black tri-corn and tattered flag backdrop suspended above the dance floor. Promoters were already out stumping for votes on next year's city: Tampa, New Orleans or Vancouver.

Night two of Convergence 11 and Nicholas was dressed the only way he knew how: over the top. Slim-line trousers were almost painted on his legs. His long black hair broke across the shoulders of his deep-purple, velvet frock coat. It was a little unusual; priest's cassocks seemed to be the rage this year. Otherwise, Utilikilts and black paramilitary BDUs pervaded the venue for guys. And pirate hats were everywhere, what with this year's Convergence theme being pirates. Underneath his coat, a white silk shirt was constrained by a black brocade cincher. Only the boiz who didn't need anything cinched in around the middle ever wore cinchers, since anything extra got pushed out the top. A few extra pounds and you'd look like the girls with their overflowing tits. The requisite knee-high Doc Martens completed his outfit.

He was depressed, and not the I'm-too-cool-to-be-happy affected depressed, but really depressed. Two months before Convergence, his long-time relationship had imploded. Besides emotional fallout, it had left him stuck with a non-refundable, non-transferable, sixty-five dollar ticket and no chance of getting a roommate to split the costs of the room—at least no one he was willing to actually sleep in the same room with. Nick almost hadn't come, but shit, he wasn't going to let the breakup ruin this. Still, he'd bailed on the first night's event, and most of the afternoon's as well, and caught hell for that. Most of these people he only physically saw once a year. They were an extended, on-line family of sorts: offering career advice, mojo for hoped-for jobs, general banter and good-natured sniping. If dressing for clubs wasn't such an ingrained habit, he probably would have stuck with black jeans and t-shirts all weekend.

That said, here he was alone and listening to a really bad band. His crowd had gone off earlier in search of food. Eating just didn't sound like something he wanted to do. It would kill the buzz he currently had working. Drunk and depressed; if he had to be out, that was how he was going to be. He leaned against the rail separating the concert seating area from the dance pit and played with the brim of his top hat.

The music, if you could call it that, reverberated through the cavernous space. Shit, it was bad. Whiny and off key, all the crap that ordinary sheeple claimed Goth sounded like to them. What he wouldn't have given for a little Lycia or Die Form. The bleachers behind him echoed a tinny counterpoint to the off-tempo backbeat. A few people were making a half-hearted attempt to dance near the stage. The Los Angeles contingent swayed and caressed themselves like they were masturbating in their own bedrooms. Dancing for the local crowd consisted of feigned epileptic fits. Every level in between was represented in the thrashing throng. Most people, however, either stood between the dancers and the bleachers or sat off to the left in a darkened area crammed with mismatched couches.

Some chick in leather bondage pants and a black leather waist-cincher was crawling around on the floor. Nick smirked. He looked better in his than she did in hers. A voice came from off to the right, near the bar, "Hey, did you lose a contact or something?" Its tone was low, but commanding, self-assured. The kind that was quiet because its owner never needed to yell. A warm baritone, it swam under the throb of the music and grabbed Nick's attention. "Can I help you find it?"

Pushing down his half-specs, and peering at the speaker over the top of the purple lenses, Nick's eyebrows shot up. Wow. Biker-Goth...big time. Short black hair in a spiked pseudo-military, high and tight, and a boyish face all set on a tall, muscular frame. The guy was kneeling down, legs sheathed in riding chaps. Black jeans, black, tight T-shirt, biker boots and tats banding his upper arms completed a nice package. There was a damn fine ass in those jeans and chaps. Half a dozen piercings ran down the edge of one ear, but no spools. Nick wasn't fond of the spools look. It didn't feel right when you nibbled on someone if they had a plug the diameter of a penny stuck in the lobe.

"Maybe this will help?" Nick dug out his keys and flipped on the tiny Mag-Light fob. "What are we looking for?"

"A ring, silver, it has a two-thousand-year old piece of Roman window glass in it." She set her cheek to the floor and looked across the matte black surface. There were about twelve other rings on her fingers; how would she ever miss one? "I caught it on the edge of my cincher and it popped off. Shit!"

Biker boy looked up and rolled his eyes at Nick. They flashed blue in the light of the mag. "Are you sure it was around here?" He had a single ring in his left brow.

"No, I felt it slip off as I was walking from there," she pointed off towards the dancers, "to the bar here." The tiny pool of light crawled back across the floor from where she had come. Nothing. Others joined in the search, looking about their feet. "Man, if I ever find it, it's going to be squished with all these fucking platform boots." It was funny seeing a bunch of overdressed, gothier-than-thou people scrounging on the floor. Not unusual, just funny; most of the time people at clubs were just nice. A few uppity baby-bats had given the whole scene a bad name.

Some D.J. was spinning now; the music was a hell of a lot better. After a futile search, Nick switched off the pen light and shook his head, it was a hopeless cause "It ain't here, or someone's lifted it." Blue Eyes looked up Nick and smiled. That smile wiped any hope of rational thought from Nick's mind. The best he could manage was to mumble towards the woman, "You might let the security guards know. Things that get lost generally tend to wind up there."

"Yeah." The man who'd first caught his attention nodded, stood and helped the girl to her unsteady feet. "I agree." As she wandered off, he turned to Nick. "That calls for a drink."

Without thinking Nick shot back, "You buying?"

"Sure, but I got a better idea." He smiled and wiped the dust off his hands onto his ass. "It's almost last call. The bus back leaves in a few. Some guys I kinda know and I bought a bunch of booze this afternoon. You can come back to my room and have a drink there."

"Cheaper than three bucks a pop." A party in someone's room didn't sound too bad. It was better than drinking alone, and Nick didn't feel like going to bed just yet. He snorted to himself...drunk logic. "Sure, why not? My friends bailed for food when MonsterKiller turned out to be a dud. What you got?"

"Rum, vodka, and I'm sure something else, depending on what you're in the mood for."

Smiling, Nick responded, "It's almost two a.m. I could be in the mood for anything."

"Yeah, me too." Something was lighting up those blue eyes. Nick was too drunk to try and figure out what. With a velvet laugh, the guy murmured, "Let's go catch that bus." They joined the throng spilling through the doors out to the street.

Almost half the venue was waiting out on the sidewalk. A large silver tour bus pulled to the curb. The door swung open and a rail-thin man in a chauffeur's cap peeked out. "Shit. Y'all for this bus?" He shook his head at the roar of assents. After a moment of thought he added, "Hell, okay folks, if y'all can get everyone on the bus, I'll get everyone back to the hotel."

A cheer went up, and people piled on. Seats were double and triple-filled. Everyone was in a good mood, laughing, joking and commenting on the bands and DJs. Nick and his Biker Boy were halfway back, standing in the aisle. Someone passed a CD over their heads. Blue Eyes laughed again, bending down slightly to put his ear near Nick's. "You up for jamming in? Get a few more bodies on that way."

Nick turned sideways and slid closer. "Like this?" His butt was against a seat back, his leg wedged between Biker Boy and the armrest. A whiff of cologne drifted up from the guy's skin, warm and slightly musky. Best of all, he hadn't drenched himself in it. A cool shiver ran down Nick's spine. "So, are your friends meeting you back at the hotel to party?"

"Not that I know of." A private party, just the two of them? That was unexpected. It started Nick thinking that there might have been more than just the offer of a drink extended. A hand reached out and yanked the top hat from Nick's head. He grabbed for it and missed. It ended up resting atop a girl three rows down with fairy lights strung through her dreads. "Hey," the guy teased, "what the hell is she doing with your hat? I wanted that."

"Just the hat?" Shit, he couldn't believe he'd said that. He was way too drunk. When they hit the hotel he'd bail and go sleep it off.

Grinning, Biker Boy leaned in again. "Well, I might want those pants, too, or what's in them."

Holy shit! Too drunk and moving too fast, it was time to back this down a bit. "What if that's not what I want?" Nick's voice didn't back up his words.

"Oh." Another smile flashed. God, the guy smiled a lot. "Well then, we'll have to figure out what you do want."

The bus jerked into the street. As it moved out, Nick was thrown against the cute biker's leg. Oh shit, could the guy tell he was hard? He was pretty sure from the way they were talking that they were thinking along the same lines, but you could never really be certain. The ride back was a jumble of conversations and laughter. The CD had made it to the front and the ever-obliging driver had thrown it on. Someone's demo...but it was better than a couple of the bands had been.

His new companion was talking, or rather shouting, with the girl who'd snatched his hat. They and several others were rehashing the evening's entertainment, DJs, bands and the alleged talent search. Nick drifted in his own thoughts, watching the people on the bus. Most were really upbeat. Thrashes the hell out of the image of us all as depressed freaks, he mused. Then that voice was at his ear again, startling him. "By the way, what's your name?"

"What?"

"What's your name?" Biker Boy's lips were a little closer to Nick's skin than they needed to be. The caress of his breath lit up Nick's nerves like a chill coating frost, giving him goose bumps. "I want to call you something other than just Cute Guy." He whispered so low that Nick almost didn't catch it.

Nick leaned forward so he could be heard. "Well a lot of people know me by disdain99, but my name is Nick." The scent of the cologne rose about him again. The bus jerked to a stop...or rather it stopped and all the drunks jerked as no one had any balance. Nick slid against the seat and Blue Eyes slid against him. And what Nick felt sent chills down his back. This guy was as hard as he was.

Their hips were pressed together as the crowd righted itself. "Nice to meet you, Nick." The door whooshed open, and people began to spill from the vehicle. It would take a moment for the pressure to give this far back.

"So what's your name, or should I just call you mine?" He didn't move, didn't try and draw back. It was all Nick could do not to tremble as he savored the feel of the other man's erection. "Unless you want the Glitter Goth with Tinkerbell caught in her hair."

As the people nearest them began to exit, Nick had to turn away. From behind him, next to his ear came, "You could call me 'mine,' but my name is Brandon." A hand ran across the cheek of his ass and Nick tensed. "Sorry."

"Really?" Okay if he was going to bail he had to do it now. The moment he thought of it, he knew he wasn't going to. "I never say sorry when I mean to do something."

Brandon laughed, "Well, you know I've had a lot to drink." As if to punctuate his words, he missed a step and bumped Nick's back. They made the sidewalk without further mishap and stepped away from the bus. Small knots of people were gathered about. Some were making plans to get food, some were just saying goodnight to friends.

"Brandon...isn't there a joke in a movie that all gay guys are Brad or Brandon, or Steve?"

"You think I'm gay?"

Oh, shit, Brandon was giving off mixed signals like crazy. Nick shrugged and retrieved his top hat from the thief as she passed. "Just making a joke."

Tapping the topper as he sauntered off towards the lobby doors, Brandon seemed to just assume Nick would follow.

"Glad you got that back." Two seconds of indecision and Nick gave in.

As he caught up, he dropped the hat on Brandon's head. "There, you wear it." They were almost the same height. Bowing slightly, Nick teased, "Lead on MacDuff..."

"Where's my room key?" Brandon fumbled through his pants. "I can't find my key. I know I put it some place in my pants." He was smiling again. Smiling at Nick. A wicked light danced in his eyes and his tongue rode the edge of his teeth.

Fairy-light girl shoved her hands in Brandon's back pockets. His eyes went wide in shock. "Want me to help find 'em?" she slurred.

"Well, uh..." By the look on his face the last person he wanted help from was her. Brandon stepped forward freeing his pockets from her hands. "No, wait, I think I found it."

Nick watched, amused, as Brandon shook off the girl. As she wandered past, he half stuck his tongue out at her. She flipped him off. He turned back to Brandon. "So where are we headed?" They'd passed through the Nuevo-California décor of the lobby and were walking across a grassy courtyard next to the pool, toward a cluster of courts with guest rooms.

Brandon waved toward the building in front of them, "Somewhere round here." His voice was a little slurred as well. Brandon stumbled over a sprinkler head. "I might need some help finding it, Nick."

Nick wasn't quite to that point yet. "You a bit fucked?"

"Just a bit," was the reply. "But I would like to be more fucked. How about you?"

Nick couldn't believe Brandon had said the last part aloud. Maybe it was a Freudian slip or maybe he was just reading things into it he wanted to hear. They'd both had a lot to drink. "I ain't feeling no pain right now." Actually he was. His pants were tight, tighter than normal. It was one of the hazards of wearing such tight jeans. "What's your room number?"

"Would you like to?" The blue eye man laughed. "Feel pain? Or feel something else, maybe?" Brandon let the thought drop. "Room number is thirteen."

God, he hoped he wasn't reading things into this. Brandon had to be coming on to him. "Jesus, how many people did you have to beat off to get thirteen for a room number?"

"I had to blow the manager, and then some." Brandon laughed again. "Sort of." He headed up the stairs just on the other side of the court.

Alright, Nick wasn't reading things into it. "If it was the same guy manning the desk when I came in it wouldn't have been too bad."

"Yah, I know what you mean." Brandon was fishing in his pants trying to get the key out as they approached the door.

"Ya lose something down there?"

"Well, I can find something hard in there, but it might not open the door...at least this door." The electronic key appeared. "Maybe a different door?" Two green LED flashes and the lock clicked. "Come on in. Can I make you a drink?"

Surveying the room as he stepped inside, Nick responded, "Sure, what you got?" For a Goth Con it was a weird setting: sort of 50's Hawaii meets Southwestern pastel. Lots of fake bamboo and salmon-colored hyacinths. Bathroom and closet to the right, oversized armoire with the TV and mini-bar lined up with a desk on the left wall. Opposite the door was another one, set between windows and leading to a small patio. One queen-sized bed sat in the room...no roommate?

"What ya want?" Key, conference badge and spare change hit the sink counter as Brandon stepped into the bathroom.

Nick wandered past. He felt like a smoke and didn't want to just light up in someone else's room. "Got Coke?" When Brandon nodded, he added, "Make me a rum and Coke then."

"Sure, anything else?"

"Got tunes?" Clothes were thrown around. Almost all were black. A laptop computer sat on the desk amidst the convention clutter. "You brought work with you?" Nick asked the second question without waiting for an answer to the first as he pointed to the computer. Heading toward the balcony, he pulled a pack of clove cigarettes from his shirt.

The top hat landed on the bed. "No, just use it for surfing the web and email." Brandon's finger danced across the mouse pad and the screen cycled to life. "Mostly using it for listening to MP3s here, 'cause their wi-fi network sucks." When he hit the play button on the media player, a series of descending minor tones rained from the speakers. Then a reedy voice with a southern accent and full of hate broke. *Thou shalt not lie with mankind as with woman kind, it is an abomination. As God has said, and I myself will fight against you with an outstretched hand and with a strong arm, even in anger, and in fury, and in great wrath. This is a monstrous sin against God almighty!* A harder rock beat wound for a moment. *More than this nation needs air to breath or food to eat, this nation needs our message that God Hates Fags!*

Nick stopped dead in his tracks, one hand frozen on the patio doorknob. Aw shit, he was going to get his head beat in. Skinheads and the Nation were prevalent on the scene. He was too drunk and he'd misread everything. He was certain of it. Nick swallowed and looked back into the room. Brandon was kneeling in front of the armoire where the hotel fridge was. The only way out was over Brandon or over the bed. He wasn't sure he could manage either in his current state. The speaker screamed out, *You and every other sick Christ rejecter... You're going to hell!* A hard rock rhythm was giving a back beat to the sounds of distant battle, crying children and screams. *I'd like to explain that the reason that fags have to go to hell is that they can't repent and the reason they can't repent is that they're proud of their sin.* The music trailed off and a non-vocal industrial beat took its place.

Play it cool, casual. In as even a tone as he could manage, "What the fuck was that?"

"Just some industrial sampling," Brandon shrugged as he stood with a bottle of Coke in his hand. He snagged a couple of glasses by the ice bucket. "Some piece I found on a site lampooning the religious right. Downloaded a bunch of stuff at the same time. Like it?" He was mixing the drinks, not paying attention to Nick.

"It's a little harsh."

Brandon paused, startled by Nick's tone. "Yeah, I guess it would be if ya didn't know the context...That it's supposed to be satire on the whole right wing thing. Sex ain't good, but war, beating your kids, that kinds of stuff is fine." He went back to mixing. "Probably not the best first impression of my taste in music, huh?"

Nick let out the breath he didn't know he'd been holding. "Nope. Wasn't. I'll let you have a second chance though." Opening the door to the patio Nick drew a cig out of the pack. "Ahh, the smell of Goth in the evening...cloves."

"Need a light?" Brandon looked up and smiled again. Man, he had a nice smile.

Nick nodded. "Yeah, if ya got one." He stepped out onto the little patio, savoring the cool air off the ocean. Two lawn chairs and a cocktail table graced the small space. San Diego was nice; Nick had always liked it. This hotel was nice. Each room had its own little private patio with a half-wall capped by a rail forming the balcony. The ones towards the front were open to the parking lot. This one looked over the small beach and out onto the marina.

Brandon fished a lighter off the clutter on the desk and tossed it through the door. "Sure, here ya go. Can I have a drag?"

"Didn't bring any skirts...oh, you mean the smoke..." As Brandon walked through carrying two drinks, he traded one for the cig and took a swallow. It was stronger than the ones at the club.

Brandon took a puff and blew a smoke ring. "I have only one skirt, actually a kilt, but I prefer chaps." He dropped into one of the chairs.

"But do you wear it like a Scotsman?" Nick shot the comment into the night as he took a seat as well. "Chaps are cool...you ride?"

"I like to be ridden." Nick almost choked on his drink. Brandon laughed and handed the clove back. "Oh, you mean bikes, right? Yeah, I have a Harley-74. How 'bout you?"

"A crappy rice burner and a fix-up hearse." Nick was relaxing into the teasing. It had been a while since he'd teased like this. "Once I get through all the rust there may be a car under it. Bikes are rather sexy though. Guys who ride bikes are rather sexy."

"Even guys who ride rice rockets."

A lot of Harley riders didn't believe that the Japanese had ever actually made a motorcycle. Nick's tone was a little apologetic. "Hey, it gets me around, saves on gas, doesn't take up space in the garage."

"How's that drink? Need anything else?" As dark as it was outside, Nick couldn't tell if Brandon was smiling, but he bet Brandon was. "Let me have another hit off your cig."

One of Nick's boots was up on the table; the other knee was slung out to the side. Offering up the cig, Nick held it level with his bent knee so that Brandon would have to come in for it. "I could use another drink."

"You're not just blowing smoke now, are you?" Instead of just reaching, Brandon leaned forward and took a drag as Nick held it. He blew the smoke along the line of Nick's leg. It swirled near his crotch before dissipating. "Drink number two coming up; rum and coke again?" Rising and walking back into the room towards the mini-bar, the biker took off his shirt and tossed it onto a chair. "It is getting a little hot in here."

"It's the leather." Nick leaned over to look through the door. His pulse was keeping time to the industrial beat. Watching Brandon's half-dressed form move about in the dim light was intoxicating. Tats crawled from his arms across his back, lines weaving in and under each other in a dizzying labyrinth of ink. "It makes you sweat." He could still smell the leather from out on the patio. It blended nicely with the breeze, the cloves and the rum.

"Yeah, that and other things." Brandon leaned his trim frame against the doorjamb. He obviously worked out, but not to an extreme; enough definition to be model-sexy. "Here's your drink." He held it out and shook it so that the ice rattled.

Nick grinned in response as he took the offered drink. "Course velvet ain't much better." As he took the last drag on the clove, he added. "Want another?

"If you got one."

"In my shirt pocket."

Brandon bent down to grab the pack from Nick's pocket. "Is this it?" He fumbled around a bit stroking Nick's chest through his shirt.

"No, that's my sister's tit." He laughed. "Yeah, that's it."

"I thought that was a little hard." Brandon laughed as well as he pulled a smoke from the pack with his teeth. Leaning over, he chain-lit it from the dying ember still in Nick's mouth.

Damn, the boy's eyes were so blue. Nick could think of a thousand things he could do with that mouth if a cigarette wasn't in it. Instead he flicked his butt over the rail and sucked on an ice cube. "Still hot?"

As Brandon took a deep pull off the clove cig, he moved in close. "Always." His hands were braced on the arms of the chair as he leaned over. The nearness of him made Nick tremble. Taking the cig out of his mouth, he blew the smoke in between Nick's parted lips. "Adds new meaning to the term second-hand smoke, doesn't it?" Brandon teased and moved in closer. "Want anything else?" One hand ventured down to caress Nick's thigh.

Oh God, did he want something else. He couldn't breathe waiting for Brandon's lips to touch his. Nick's tongue was still cold from the ice as he slipped it inside Brandon's hot mouth. He could taste the cloves and the rum mixed with Brandon's flavor.

Brandon's hand slid up his leg, stopping briefly to toy with Nick's hard bulge. Desire was thrumming through his veins. Exploring fingers worked his shirt from under the cincher. They danced with his nerves. Fumbling with the buttons and trying to shuck the jacket and shirt without breaking contact, Nick whispered against sensuous lips, "You…out of those jeans. The chaps can stay." He was being silly. It was what happened when he got drunk.

"Anything you want." Brandon stood and unbuckled the chaps. One leg went up on the table. Then he slowly slid the zipper open down the outer thigh of each leg. The sucking sound of leather coming off too-hot a body gave Nick chills. Smiling down on Nick, Brandon started to unbutton the fly of his jeans and slide them off his hips.

"Crap, out here on the balcony?" Nick hissed.

"Sure, why not?" As the chaps slid from Brandon's legs, he flipped his head towards the marina. "Who's going to care—seagulls?" Fingers hooked through both his jeans and briefs, and inch by inch, Brandon revealed himself. His wicked smile darted over his lips the entire time. Brandon was enjoying putting on the show.

Damn, Brandon's dick was hard. Of course, so was Nick's. Oh man, the guy's cock was beautiful, thick and shaved. "True." That one word throbbed with Nick's desire. Brandon toed out of his boots and stepped out of his pants. Kicking them to the side, he grabbed the chaps and stepped back into his boots. "What are you doing?"

Laughing, Brandon fastened the leather about his legs. "You said you wanted me to leave the chaps on, didn't you?"

Nick swallowed and nodded. Oh, Christ, talk about fantasies. Brandon leaned over him again, kissing his chest, sucking on his nipples, fumbling with the fly on Nick's jeans. The claw of the metal as the teeth gave way echoed in the pit of Nick's stomach. "Is this what you want?"

"Oh, hell, yeah!" Nick could barely breathe, he wanted it so much. "That and everything else." His own fingers found the back zippers on his boots, yanking them off as fast as he could manage. As Brandon's mouth worked at lighting fires under his skin, he struggled to get his jeans down. Fuck, why had he worn something so tight? Another pair of hands joined in the effort, peeling the fabric from his legs.

Brandon knelt down before him. "Commando?" he teased. "That makes things convenient." Trembling, Nick watched as Brandon took his cock in one strong hand and ran his tongue along the tip. The touch bubbled Nick's skin. "I like the way you taste." Brandon's tongue traveled down Nick's length. Then he licked Nick's shaved sac. Nick wasn't as bare as Brandon, but he kept it all pretty clean. It made everything so much more sensitive. That strong hand was stroking his cock as Brandon pulled his balls into his hot mouth and began to suck.

"God, yeah," Nick groaned. "Suck on me." Brandon's tongue flicked across his balls and traveled about the area just underneath them. Nick was enjoying the ride. He liked having someone go down him. His last partner hadn't been especially giving. And God, doing it out on the patio where anyone might see them, it was thrilling.

"Tell me what you want." It took a moment for Brandon's words to register.

The thought of that blue-eyed boy pounding him made Nick shiver. "What do you think I want?" A hard, hot cock stroking his insides…Nick's blood pulsed with need. His skin tingled at the thought of it. "Oh shit, my wallet is in my pants."

Brandon paused. "What the hell do you need that for?"

Nick laughed. "No glove, no love, baby." He might have been three sheets to the wind, but he wasn't suicidal.

"Oh," Brandon's laughter tickled the base of Nick's sac. "We'll get to that later. Right now I want your legs back so I can see what you've got." Strong hands pushed Nick's legs apart and the explorations moved further down.

"Oh, Christ." It had been so long since anyone'd rimmed him. Nick spread his legs further and slid down in the chair until the cincher caught on the edge. Shit, he'd almost forgotten he was still wearing it. The tightness made it a little hard to breathe, but in a thrilling way. Brandon's tongue swirled around the entrance to his body. Everything burned with anticipation. He caught his right leg behind the knee and gave Brandon even more room.

Brandon's tongue forced itself into his tight hole. One hand reached up to grip Nick's cock, the other pushed his left leg back hard. Brandon was fucking his ass with that tongue and stroking him hard. The pit of his stomach froze. Nick couldn't remember when he'd felt anything this exquisite. "God, that fucking feels good," he moaned. Brandon probed deeper and faster, his nose pressed against Nick's body. Nick was pushing back against his mouth. He couldn't stand it. He wanted more. "Shit…you going to put something else up there?"

Rocking back on his heels, Brandon's blue eyes crawled over Nick's skin. The gaze was almost as erotic as the touches had been. "I don't know. What did you have in mind?" Brandon stood and looked down on Nick. He was stroking himself.

Legs still spread, cock weeping, Nick groaned. "What do you think?"

This time Brandon's smile was beyond wicked. "Then stand up and turn around." He jerked his head toward the ocean.

Nick's eyes went wide. "Over the balcony?" Down where they were was partially hidden by the low wall, exposed, but not too exposed. If he leaned over the rail anyone walking by would be able to see them.

"Yeah, over the balcony. I want to see your ass." A few moments of indecision and then Nick jumped to his feet. Closing his eyes, he grabbed the rail with both hands and leaned forward. Brandon's hands ran across his bare cheeks and traveled down his legs. Frost flowed wherever his lover touched him. God, he liked thinking of Brandon as his lover. Moaning and twisting as Brandon's hand spread his cheeks and Brandon's tongue found his hole again, Nick was in heaven. Desire screamed through his body as Brandon growled, "I want my cock in your ass."

"I want your cock in my ass," Nick begged.

He tensed as Brandon stood. As he leaned forward over Nick's back, he breathed, "Tell me what you want." His rock-hard cock pulsed against Nick's skin as Brandon pushed against him. The thin barrier of the condom, coated in cool gel, grazed his flesh. Fuck, when had Brandon put that on? "I want to hear you say it again."

"I want you to fuck me." The sentence was hardly out of his mouth before Brandon pushed into him, and Nick moaned the last of it. Brandon spread him so nice. Bigger than normal, but not so much it hurt -- how'd he get so lucky? The almost-pain sent shocks down his own throbbing length. Nick's cock rubbed up against the rail. He pushed back, taking all of Brandon inside.

Fingers dug into Nick's hips, and Brandon began pumping hard. His cock was deep inside Nick, hitting everywhere just right. It was so damn hot. Nick moaned, and Brandon thrust harder in response. "Like that?" he hissed.

"Hell, yeah." Nick bucked against him.

One hand wound into Nick's long, black hair, pulling his head back. The other pushed against the small of his back. Fingers locked into the laces on the cincher. "Fuck you!"

Nick was in ecstasy. Pushing back against Brandon's hips, raising one leg and resting it on the low wall just below the railing, he gave his lover more room. Brandon's dick drove even further inside. Rough stucco ground into Nick's knee as he was impaled. The pain from his scalp and his knee drove his senses higher. His mouth was open, his breathing ragged as he stared out at the night.

Withdrawing his hand from Nick's back, Brandon slid it between his legs and put a vice lock on Nick's balls. They were as hard as rocks. A low moan broke between Nick's lips at the touch. Releasing his sac, Brandon's grip moved to Nick's throbbing cock.

Nick cried out, "Fuck me hard," and lost himself in the pleasure. He didn't care if anyone saw. He didn't care if anyone watched. All he cared about was how wonderful it felt to have Brandon stroking him inside and out.

Brandon's voice was heavy with his own desire. "I'm going to fuck you so hard you won't be able to sit down for a week."

"God, do it!" Nick pleaded.

Brandon rode him harder and harder, driving his big cock so deep Nick thought that he'd be hurt. Not that he cared at this point. The strokes were burning up his balls and cock. "Fuck you, tell me what you want."

"Fuck me, make me come!" He couldn't believe how much he wanted Brandon. His blood was boiling over. His balls throbbed, he couldn't last much longer. The skin of his thighs danced. Every nerve was frozen over. "Come in my ass!" He screamed as his own orgasm rocked his core. Cream exploded across Brandon's hand, the rail, and splattered on the sidewalk below.

Still stroking Nick's cock, Brandon's fingers spasmed, and he yanked Nick's head back by his hair. "Oh, God!" sounded over Nick's shoulder as Brandon came.

"Oh man...fuck me, cream me." Leaning over the rail panting, Nick almost regretted the condom. What he wouldn't have given to feel Brandon's juices inside him; to feel Brandon lick the come as it leaked from his body. "Aw, shit," Nick moaned as Brandon kissed his back.

CHAPTER TWO

Denny's. Nick didn't think he'd ever been in one when it was actually light outside. It was a 'three a.m. after the club' kind of place. Screaming country chic in oranges and blues was muted to vaguely less nauseating hues through his sunglasses. He wasn't half as hung over as he'd thought he was going to be. Still, his stomach was a little off. Nick toyed with the food he'd ordered. So far the only thing he'd actually eaten was the toast. Brandon reached across the table and snagged a sausage off his plate.

"I didn't know we were at the sharing food point." More irritation than he'd intended snapped in his words.

"Well, you weren't eating it." Brandon shrugged as he chewed. "Didn't want it to go to waste."

The scent of Brandon's cologne rose from the T-shirt he'd borrowed. Nick woke in Brandon's bed at about nine; far too early considering when he'd fallen asleep. He couldn't believe what a little slut he'd been. And then, when Brandon had rolled over and smiled, he'd gotten excited all over again. Stroking each other in the bed had led to stroking each other in the shower had led to Nick on his knees sucking on that beautiful cock. While the water had run over his body, he had tasted Brandon for the first time. Brandon tasted so good. He'd licked the tip. He'd kissed the shaft.

He'd wrapped his lips around Brandon's throbbing dick and sucked him down hard. Brandon's fingers wound in his hair as Brandon pounded his mouth. And then, when he came, Nick had swallowed all that salty-sweet come. He never swallowed. Brandon made him act in ways he just wasn't used to. He liked the way Brandon made him feel.

Brandon stole another sausage link from Nick. "Thinking about something?"

"Yah." Nick gave a half smile.

"Bet I know what you're thinking about." Brandon's leg slid against his in the booth. Nick's pulse jumped. "Want to go back and put a little action behind those thoughts?" Delivered in a low-toned whisper, the question sent shivers up Nick's spine.

Did he ever want to! How did he ever land someone as hot as Brandon? Nick just wasn't good at the one-night stand thing, never had been. Convinced Brandon was just being nice in not trying to chew his own arm off; the first morning kiss had blown him away. It was hot. It was sexy. Thinking about it was definitely getting him excited. And already he liked Brandon, liked him too much to just fuck and run. It was uncomfortable not knowing whether someone else just considered you the weekend's entertainment. "Look, I got to tell you something."

"Damn, you're suddenly so serious, Nicky." Brandon grinned over his coffee. "What?"

"I just broke up with someone." He pushed the eggs around on his plate for a moment. "I just thought I should tell you."

"So you're rebounding?"

"Yeah. I guess." That's what made it doubly uncomfortable; not knowing if he was liking Brandon for himself or just because he needed to feel, well, needed.

"Okay. I can deal with that." Brandon picked up the check and looked it over. When Nick tossed a ten on the table, Brandon threw it back at him. Then he laid a twenty down. Standing and taking a last swig of his coffee, he asked, "Wanna go back to the hotel and rebound some more?"

They waded through the veiled stares of the after-church crowd to the parking lot. Black jeans, black T-shirts, big stompy boots, Nick's long hair and Brandon's tats and piercings weren't quite Sunday-go-to-meeting clothes. Add that to their height and build and Nick bet there were a few people more than a little relieved they were leaving. He resisted the temptation to flash a vampire smile back to the diners as they headed through the doors. Nature had gifted him with a set of canines that other Goths required serious dental work to achieve. Between his look and his teeth the people at work had dubbed him Dracula. If he had been a little less hung-over, a spook show might have been fun. Brandon's bike sat waiting for them. For the first time Nick noticed the California plates. "You're local?"

Brandon shrugged. "Sort of. From the hell of the nine-oh-nine. Riverside."

In Southern California area codes were shorthand ways of identifying things like lifestyle. San Diego was 619, and Nick had friends in West Los Angeles, the 310 specifically; a 909 area code was considered Hicksville. "What do you do in the boonies?"

Brandon just stared at him, weighing something in his mind. After a moment it seemed Brandon'd made a decision. As he grabbed the Smokey-style helmets from where they swung on the bars, he replied cautiously, "I'm a cop."

Nick laughed, "No, seriously." That was just a really bad joke.

"No… seriously, I'm a cop." Brandon's defensive attitude confirmed that it was no joke. "Riverside P.D. all the way. Been there almost nine years now."

Nick stopped laughing and swallowed. "I didn't know they let cops have piercings." Okay that just sounded stupid. Brandon was going to think he was a moron. He didn't have last night's excuse of being drunk.

"They do if you're vice. And answering the question you're just dying to ask…I don't date much, and I don't date local. I keep this part of my life pretty much under wraps. Job's risky enough without having to worry about some of the Neanderthals I work with." He handed over a helmet. "Okay, you did your honesty shtick, I'll do mine. Let's be clear, I'm not out. I don't ever plan on being out, not so long as I'm a cop. You okay with that?"

"I wouldn't have guessed that from last night." Wait, maybe he had. Brandon had seemed to be giving off mixed signals. That might be why. And why would he care whether Nick was okay with it? That was his choice. It would only matter if it was something long term…unless Brandon was thinking this might become more than just a one-night thing as well.

Brandon shrugged as he strapped the helmet under his chin. "I was pretty drunk. It's not like I expected to run into any of the guys I work with at a Convergence club event. I haven't done anything like last night in a long, long time."

"I don't do that on a regular basis either." Brandon's tone had implied that things were different for Nick. "Out, and acting like a slut, are two different things."

Brandon was smiling again. "I stand corrected. Your turn for the bio."

Almost apologetically, Nick answered, "Vegas." Nick's life was a lot more boring than Brandon's. "Electronic Services for Gaming Control." When Brandon shot him a look of utter incomprehension he explained, "I test slots and video poker machines as an agent for the Nevada Gaming Commission. We investigate allegations of cheating and that kind of thing."

"Like the Attorney General's office?" Brandon was resting his butt on the saddle, with his arms crossed in front of his chest. "Badges, sworn personnel and all that stuff?"

"Sort of." Nick shrugged; it wasn't the easiest thing to explain. "We're not affiliated with the AG, but yeah, I have a badge. I guess you could call it law enforcement. We're more like Treasury Department or BATF agents."

"No shit? That's pretty wicked." Brandon thought his job was cool? "Vegas…so you're only four hours away. And you just cut loose on a relationship." That wonderful smile flashed again. Keys spun on Brandon's finger as he stood. "You wanna pilot?"

"You fucking serious?" Nick had never ridden such a nice bike. It was all chromed out with wide, custom handlebars and saddle-style seat. The ride over had been pretty exhilarating, and that was just sitting on the back. He ran his hand over the black gas tank. Looking to Brandon as though expecting him to withdraw his permission, Nick swung his leg over and straddled the Harley. Brandon slid onto the pad behind him. "Man, this is one fucking, wicked bike." He was grinning like a kid on Christmas morning as he rocked it off the stand.

Brandon leaned in over his shoulder. "I figure if I'm going to let you ride me, I might as well let you ride my bike, too." As Brandon spoke, his hand dropped between Nick's legs.

Nick wasn't sure he could handle the bike and getting felt up at the same time. He swallowed. "I'd have guessed you as pretty much a topper."

"I like it all." A short squeeze punctuated Brandon's statement.

"Wow." The hand retreated, damn. "I don't…didn't get that end of things much. Jake didn't go much for that."

"Jake, huh?" Brandon's voice dropped to a near whisper as a large-boned tourist-type couple passed within a few feet of them. When they'd moved a good distance beyond, he continued, "And he wasted that big dick of yours?"

Nick blushed as he started the bike. "I'm not that big." The engine purred between his legs. Between Brandon and Brandon's bike, Nick was developing a raging hard-on.

"I think you're selling yourself short, Nicky." Brandon started singing in a bad, 80s pop falsetto. "Oh, Nicky, you're so fine, you're so fine you blow my mind."

He laughed. "Not like I haven't heard that before." Normally he hated being called Nicky. That's what his grandmother called him. But when Brandon said it, it sounded okay. "Mind if we go back to my room? I feel like the Whore of Babylon in last night's jeans."

"Only if you promise to act like it."

CHAPTER THREE

The Gaming Control Board headquarters skulked ten blocks north of the insanity of the strip. Electronic Services Division's lab was on the second floor of the Grant Sawyer Building, a nondescript five-story office building. The word laboratory implied clean rooms, sterile environments, and highly skilled technicians in white coats hunched over arcane equipment. It suggested acres of brightly lit spaces where great minds deduced the inner workings of mysterious machines meant to pick the pockets of the unwary.

The ESD lab was an unimposing room with, maybe, the floor space of an average Starbucks. Formica workbenches were littered with electronics. The guts of various slot machines lay strewn about the feet of intact models. Mixed in with those were a few of the field agents' laptops requiring upgrades or repairs. Sometimes it was hard to tell what pieces and parts belonged in the games and which ones belonged in the computers. Approved EPROMs, Erasable Programmable Read Only Memory chips, were kept in a set of industrial storage cabinets off to one side. Heavy-gauge metal screens and padlocks assured they were only accessed by those who had legitimate reason.

Electronic Services Division was the branch of the Gaming Control Board which examined, tested and recommended gaming devices for approval or denial within the State of Nevada. Gaming devices were inspected both in the laboratory and in the field to ensure continued integrity. When disputes arose between patrons and casinos about the functioning of a machine, the ESD would be called in to resolve them through analysis of device electronics and software.

ESD was responsible for pulling American Coin's license in the late 80s for putting "gaffed" EPROMs in their electronic poker machines. They had determined that the chips were rigged to never produce a royal flush, the highest payout possible. They'd also uncovered the "near-miss" phenomenon in the Universal Distributing Company slots. Any slot machine was capable of near-misses, where one tile of a winning combination would appear just above or below the payout line. That, in and of itself, was not illegal, just part of the random nature of the games. What Universal had done was program its machines to produce near misses instead of paying out. Those machines had been banned.

This week Nick was working in the lab. Most ESD agents did both lab work and field inspections. He'd been assigned to do the workups on a set of machines from a new manufacturer, Frontier Entertainment Services, Ltd. All the main players were former employees of bigger, more established, gaming companies. Workups meant hours of reading through source code, breaking down how the program randomly generated numbers, determined payouts and, most importantly, tracked money played so that appropriate taxes could be assessed. The cynicism of government employees pervaded the ESD. Those tasks had all been done months ago in order to gain Board approval of the programming.

Now that the first phase was over it was time to review the EPROM chips, the brains of the machines, to make sure they actually had the approved code imbedded in them. Thank God most of the key men at Frontier were old school. It made it easier. Really new companies were hell because they often had no clue of all the requirements. It wasn't favoritism. It was a knowledge that the big guys were going to run clean so that you were just looking for hinky shit. New guys would start monkeying with the programming while it was in the approval process and be all pissed when they had to start over at square one.

Nick needed easy this week. Brandon was coming. All Nick could think about was that Brandon was coming. He'd swapped out Friday for the Monday he was supposed to be off with another agent. And he'd wrangled a half day on Thursday so he could be home when Brandon arrived.

The final day of Convergence, he and Brandon had exchanged e-mail addresses. They'd spent all day Sunday with each other, missing the final night's costume party because they were tangled together in Nick's hotel room. But then Monday morning had dawned and things had to be over. Real life restarted at nine o'clock sharp on Tuesday. Brandon had kissed him, said "It's been fun, Nicky," and slid the scrap of paper with Nick's e-mail address into his pocket. Then he walked out the door.

All day Tuesday, Nick had snuck peeks at his personal e-mail account. Nothing. Wednesday he'd booted up his home computer before he'd even taken his morning shower. Nothing. Braving it out through Thursday afternoon, he'd sent a terse, "Hi. Just seeing if you got home alright," message. Friday came and went with no response. By Saturday, Nick figured he'd been blown off. Trying to kill the hurt, he went running, showered, did the laundry, and then worked on the hearse for a while. Sitting down to surf that night, there it was: Brandon's reply.

It took him a while before he could bring himself to open it. *Heya, Nicky!* Nick could almost hear Brandon's velvet voice as he read the words. *Forgot to tell ya, four days on, four days off. Worked Tues thru Fri this week. Slept most of today. F'n bastards. So yeah, sorry didn't reply sooner, got back fine to Hicksville. Assume you made it to Sin City without mishap. Sobered up yet? Still nekkid under those jeans? Been thinking 'bout what's in those jeans a lot.* Nick squirmed as his pulse raced to the lower parts of his anatomy. *Been thinking about what I want to do with what's in those jeans. I'd tell you about it, but I suck at writing shit like that down. How goes life at your end?*

Three hours later, Nick finally had a reply he was willing to send. He'd discarded most as too sappy or desperate sounding. That reply had started an e-mail correspondence comprised mostly of one-liners and terse rants about work. Finally they'd switched to IM. Four days on, four days off...when Brandon was off they'd stay up until well past midnight chatting. If Nick was off the next day as well, they kept it going as late as two or three a.m. Sometimes they just "talked." Life, outlook, bands and stupid people they met. Other nights they'd stray into sexual teasing and trying to get each other off.

The IM box had popped up on Nick's desktop two weeks earlier. BranCarr567, Brandon Carr, was inviting him to conference. *Hi!* Nick had typed. Then the message BrandCarr567 is now offline appeared. Shit. Then the door knock and BrandCarr567 is online appeared. A couple of seconds passed. Nick tried again. *Hey how's it going?* Brandon registered as offline again. What the fuck was going on?

As soon as he came back online a message appeared. *Argh! F'ing computer freezes on me.*

I thought that was might happen...was might happen? Nick laughed out loud as he hit the keyboard. *I's a good tipist, I is.*

Your icon was freezing my comp so I had to disable it.

Ahh. Sorry about that. Nick had put a new graphic intensive icon of a vampire on his profile. He'd have to switch back to the old one apparently. *So, hot body what you been up to? Police brutality? Beating the heads of pimps against the patrol car?*

Fucker! I don't drive bubblegum machines.

NO, Fuck-him, remember we had this discussion.

Try shithead, AH.

Nick clicked on the audibles and selected an animation of a blonde with big lips and slinky red dress. The canned voice echoed in the speakers. "They said you were a great asset... I told them they were off by two letters!"

A gothy little chick appeared in the chat window. She gave a computer-generated sigh and then "It must be really lonely being you" came back at him. Ah, it was taunting night, then. Taunting usually led to teasing. Teasing usually led to sexual innuendo and sometimes web cams. Brandon registered as typing a message. *Hey, I was thinking,* the line broke.

Nick jumped in with, *doesn't that hurt?*

A smiley face flipping him off came across. Where the hell had Brandon gotten the code for that? He was just about to ask when the rest of the thought came through. *I was thinking that maybe we could get together again.*

That stopped Nick mid-keystroke. He backed off what he'd been about to send. Brandon wanted to see him again. God, he really wanted to see those blue eyes again. He was so nervous that chills ran up his arms. *I'd like that. When were you thinking?*

I got a Thurs to Sunday off period coming up. I could haul out the bike and head out to Vegas. I know you have to work some weekends. Check the 9 to 12 and see if you're working.

Next month?

Yeah.

Nick dug for the schedule in the clutter on his desk. After some frantic searching he found it. *Weekend's free.* His heart was pounding. *I'm supposed to be off that Monday, too. I could try and switch it out with someone so we could have 3 days.*

Do it, baby. I'll be counting the days, hours, minutes. Got to bail. Helping one of the D's move his daughter. Talk later?

Later.

After that, the work week was pretty much a loss. Concentration was out the window. He'd start to run diagnostics or review error reports and find himself thinking about butt divots. Since they'd made their plans, Nick had been masturbating almost three times a day. It probably would have been more if he didn't have to work full time. A two-byte data deviation could hardly compete with memories of musky cologne and a tongue running across his balls.

Nick had a dozen or so EPROMS that had to be tested before the Frontier machines' field test. It looked like they'd sent a few extra…only six machine styles were slated for a floor trial. A little annoying, but good in the 'better safe than sorry' category. If a few of the chips were bad they could still go ahead and test the ones that passed inspection. He grabbed one out of the group and popped it in the Zero Insertion Force, ZIF for short, socket on the programmer. Before he could begin the diagnostics, the phone in the lab began to ring.

It was lunchtime. Pretty much everyone was either in the field or had bailed for food. After three rings, he realized he wasn't going to be able to ignore it. Nick grabbed the phone and jammed the receiver between his shoulder and ear. "Electronic Services, Agent O'Malley speaking. How may I be of assistance?"

"Dracula! You're stuck in the lab today." A familiar voice was backed by cell phone static. "They paying you double to play receptionist?"

"Hey Duke, how are you?" Mike Ducmagian was a former ESD lab rat. A while back he'd left the agency to take a job with Frontier. Programming specifications and compliance were the two hardest hurdles for anyone trying to break into the industry. Former ESD agents were courted by manufacturers large and small for that reason. If you knew how to tear it down, you should be able to make it work within the tolerances of the law. "The switch to the dark side going well? Frontier treating you okay?"

"You're a shit, O'Malley. Doing great. So when're you going to escape the prison of government life and come hang with people who have disposable income?"

"Right now I'm happy in my tax bracket. Besides you lost that whole little 'no state income tax' thing when you moved to Cali."

"Fuckhead," Duke laughed, "Then why don't you go work for one of the mega-resorts? You've got enough time and grade you could name your price with one of the big chains."

"Oh yeah, lovely work, changing out chips for casinos. Let's alter the percentages on the floor by point oh-two percent, 'cause we were just too loose on the slots last week. Blue-haired biddies spilling their Piña Coladas in the coin slots and shorting out the circuits. Drunken conventioneers mistaking their business cards for player's club cards and jamming machines. Pure Disneyland for EE's. Besides, could you see me going corporate? Interacting with the public? Fuck, they might make me cut my hair or something horrible."

"No shit, man. 'Excuse me, security, there's some scary guy all dressed in black breaking into the slot machines.'" They both laughed. When Nick did field checks, patrons always asked the other agents or the pit bosses or the change girls if he was "supposed" to be touching the machines. "Hey, much as I love shooting the shit with you, we sent you some EPROMS recently."

"Ah yes, work, I remember that. Got 'em here. Shouldn't be much of a problem on the approval end, I mean the basic source code is already a go with the board. You being the programmer and all, it ain't like you don't know the fucking rules. Was going to start running them today, probably chunk into the machines in a week or so, and get the games on the floor in a couple of months for the trial. You're doing it at one of the locals, Baron's or Boulder? How many machines you putting in for the test run? Seems like a lot."

"Yeah, Baron's with a dozen or so, some different variations to see which interface and program gets better play. Figured we might as well kill two birds with one stone so we're running a bigger test than normal. They're okay with it since they get a hundred percent of revenue off a trial. Well look, in that batch you got a couple of EPROMS that were meant for a cruise concession out of Ensenada. It's not Nevada stuff."

"I was wondering why we got so many chips. I mean, you only had to send us two of each variation, but my time, your dime." Nevada had solved GCB's funding issues by making the casinos and manufacturers pony up the cash for their required services. "You want a favor? Good ol' Nevada seal of approval on them? I mean we both know we're not supposed to work stuff that ain't for use in this state, but I could always say I didn't catch the oversight until it was done. Out of this batch, how many are there?"

"Not many, two or three maybe. Naw man, appreciate the offer, but let's play this one by the book, payout percentages are different anyhow. Shit, it ain't like we ever had enough people to work what we had to work." Most of the time, the lab was empty. Only eleven people worked ESD in Vegas, and that included the Division Chief and Lab Manager. Six agents were out in the field at any given time. Four more were permanently stationed in Carson City, but they did a combination of field checking and administrative computer work. Less than fifteen people to ride herd on a quarter of a million machines strung across the state of Nevada. Since one person couldn't check more than 100 chips in a day, it was a nightmare. Random checks were the best that could be done. "I don't want people saying that I get favors because I used to be ESD. I mean, we all know it's there, but let's not push it this go-round, especially since this gig is so green."

"Okay. Keep it all on the straight and narrow then. Wanna fax me over a set of serials and I'll pull them?"

"Naw, it ain't that many. They're all series starting 559A. Chuck 'em in FedEx and ship 'em back, you should have our charge number on file."

"Will do. You coming back for May's wedding?" One of the IT gals in the administrative division was finally tying the knot with her long time, on-again, off-again, boyfriend. The office pool gave it three months before they were divorced.

There was a pause. "Yeah. I'll see you there?"

"Yep. Okay, I'll get those EPROMS pulled and on their way back to you this afternoon."

"Thanks, O'Malley. Owe you a beer at the wedding."

"I'll hold you to it."

Nick found two EPROMS with a 559A code; all the others in the pile had a different number. Well, Duke had said two or three so that should be it. He scrounged a media box and dug out the company's FedEx number. Whistling as he dropped it in the pickup box that evening, he was in a good mood. The next few days he was in the field and then Brandon would be here.

CHAPTER FOUR

Thursday morning was spent at a quickie-mart with a small bank of slots. Toss an EPROM in the dock, run the diagnostics, check the readouts, and pop the next one in. The time-killer on these jobs wasn't the checking of the chips. That took mere minutes. Getting into the guts of the machines and then shutting them back up tight was a pain in the ass. The slot bank was dinky enough that all the machines could be done in less than a day. Probably the first and last time the place would see an inspection this century. Still, it was almost one before Nick could blow. He dropped the laptop and dock off at GCB, sneaking in as quickly and quietly as possible and avoiding everyone, before heading home.

Home was a tiny pseudo-Mexicana one-story east of the Strip. Everywhere in Vegas was calculated according to its relation to the Strip. A few blocks off Desert Inn Road, the neighborhood was rundown; a place where 50s and 60sera homes competed with shabby apartments for space. Quick and dirty ranch-style houses with gravel roofs spoke of a once hopeful past.

Nick's place was a little older, a little better kept up than his neighbors. Stucco-coated exterior and Mexican tile on the roof; it sported a wrought iron railing along a concrete porch and a long drive ending in a garage at the back of his property. Planters held drought-tolerant plants in dark shades of purple and red. Landscaping choices had been due less to any sense of conservation and more to Nick's realization that he'd never remember to water his yard with any regularity. Just to piss off the obnoxious woman across the street, he'd painted the house black. Served her right for complaining about a hearse in the drive.

After stashing his bike in the garage and ripping off his tie on the way through the kitchen door, Nick started the last minute cleaning to ready his place for Brandon's arrival. As he was doing the third once-over of his place, he grabbed the phone to make reservations for dinner. A tonal series of beeps announced messages waiting. First things first; he called in the reservation and then checked his voice mail.

The voice of Heather, one of the few female Electrical Engineers in ESD, came rapid fire. "Hey O'Malley, Mike Ducmagian has been calling all morning. Said he really, really, really needed to talk with you." God, the chick needed Ritalin. If she spoke any faster, her lips would fall off. "He wanted your home phone, but I wouldn't give it to him. Anyhoo…said I'd give you his number and you could call him back if you want to." She rattled off a string of numbers while Nick was still scrounging for a pen. It required two replays before he had it down correctly.

Three rings and a clipped "Duke," sounded in his ear. Cell static again, worse than the last time they'd spoken.

"Duke, it's Nick. What's up? Heather says you've been bugging the shit outta her all morning." Black cordless phone jammed against his ear, Nick wandered into the 50s-era kitchen and dropped a few stray coffee cups he'd corralled into the battered sink. Blue-green linoleum flooring, seafoam green tile back-splash and counter tops; he could remember his grandmother bending over the chipped, white stove to retrieve a loaf of bread and telling him how she always felt like she was underwater in this kitchen.

"Man, thank God! Nick!" Duke's voice was strained. "Listen, you only sent back two EPROMS."

Nick snagged a cookie from the vampire cookie jar he'd found at an after-Halloween sale at some discount chain, and dropped into one of the old wooden kitchen chairs. They were a legacy from his grandparents as well. Speaking through a mouthful of fudge-covered shortbread, Nick growled, "Okay, I'm off for the day and you're talking to me about work. Dost thou not remember the public service mantra…the State payeth me not for after hours." He stewed for a moment. "You said two or three, I found two, and I sent them back."

"Dude, look there were three, I need the other one."

If he had sent a fax with the serial numbers as requested, then Duke wouldn't be having this little problem, would he? "Well then, it's back at the lab somewhere. Probably just slid under something, you know how much crap is on those tables." The you-are-so-wasting-my-time sigh cultivated by all public servants slid up Nick's throat. He added a little emphasis so it would carry across the bad connection. "I'll look for it on Monday when I get in."

"No, I need it today. I'm on my way to Vegas, about State Line right now."

It burned Nick that some people just expected you to put out their fires. "You're coming in just for this?" Crap and more crap.

"No." Hesitation, or maybe Duke had hit a dead spot. "No, not just for the chip. I'm visiting friends this weekend."

"Okay, good, then I'll say it real slow then so you can understand… *Mon-day*. Shit, if it's so important drop by GCB. One of the other rats can get it for you."

"Heather was the only one in the lab and she's out to the field already; everyone's scheduled for field work Friday. The manager and the chief are at some meeting all day today and tomorrow. No one is there. I was going to head back to Cali Sunday afternoon."

"Well it just has to wait, 'cause I ain't going in." Nick looked down and brushed a few crumbs from his grey dress shirt. Black slacks and cheap, black dress shoes made up the remainder of his wage-slave attire. He tugged out the band holding his hair back. "I got a hot date showing up this afternoon, and I'm still freaking dressed like Clark Kent." There was no way he wanted Brandon to see him like this.

"Dracula, you could never dress like Clark Kent."

"Clark's evil twin brother then. I got shit to do."

"Hot date, huh?" Duke's tone eased. "That uppity investment banker? What's his name again?"

Duke and he had never been friendly, not unfriendly, just not pals. He was about to get hit with a come on and Nick knew it. Warily, he spoke, "Jake? No, Jake and I have been broken up for a few months. Someone new, from," he hesitated a moment, "California." It wasn't as if he'd said who was coming.

"Oh, so you're going to show them around, huh? Where're you two love birds headed?" God, it was so smarmy how Duke said it. It was one of the many reasons he didn't interact with most of the people at work. Show up, do your job, and head home. Nick wasn't unsociable, that wasn't in his nature. He just didn't go out of his way to make friends at the office.

"Dinner, and over to the club later."

"That dinky club in the strip mall off Flamingo you hang out at? Real suave, Dracula." Yeah, twice-divorced Duke would know suave. "You should at least take him someplace decent to eat."

"I was thinking Hugo's. Got reservations for eight."

"Now see, that's more like date material." Nick could almost see the slick smile. "Sure you can't just run by the lab?"

Duke was really pissing him off. Go corporate and you start to think the rest of the world has to run on your schedule. "No. Monday." A little bit of conscience crept up and slapped him. Duke wasn't just anyone; he used to be one of the *us* against the *them*. Even if he was a little 70s disco slimy, he'd never been a jerk to work with. "Fuck, meet me there. Shit, like sevenish Monday, and we'll find your fucking EPROM, okay?"

"Okay," Duke sounded less than pleased. "Seven in the a.m. Monday. I'll bring coffee."

"Make mine a double espresso, Americano." He hung up before Duke could say another word and headed for the shower.

Clean and shaved, on more places than just his face, Nick ravaged his closet for the better part of an hour. After discarding one outfit after another he was finally satisfied with the results. Black bondage pants, straps over straps with chrome D-rings, clips, buckles and zippers crisscrossing his legs, pooled over combat boots and sucked up against his ass. A charcoal T-shirt clung to his chest. Yet another cincher, this one zip front, PVC with three snap catches across the zipper, gripped his waist. He was obviously dressed up for Brandon's arrival, but not outrageously so. At least by Goth standards it wasn't outrageously dressed up.

God, he was already hard, and Brandon wasn't even here yet. Nick sprawled on his antique brass bed, picking at the black Ikea duvet cover and shifting himself where his pants pinched. It was about a four hour drive from Riverside to Vegas...it would have been less, but there was always construction dropping the four lane highway down to one in each direction. Cars backed up for miles. Even on a bike you'd get jammed since most stretches were shouldered by soft sand instead of blacktop. Brandon'd said he'd be heading out about noon. The red LED readout on the alarm clock said five to three. Brandon would be in Vegas in less than an hour.

The house was clean. The dishes were done and drying. Waiting was just so fucking hard. To distract himself, Nick tried playing Nintendo. Even Grand Theft Auto, with the hearse cheat up and running, couldn't keep his attention for long. Every fifteen minutes he would jump up and look out the front window.

The rumble of seventy-four cubic inches of thunder slowly crawled into his ears. Nothing in the world sounded quite like a Harley. Nick had the front door open before Brandon was even off the bike. "Inland Empire H.O.G.s" was emblazoned across the back of Brandon's black leather vest. The busy-body across the street was watering her dead grass. Nick smiled and waved from his porch. She bolted for her door. Old Mrs. Peterson, who had lived next door since his grandparents owned the place, said the bitch claimed Nick held satanic orgies. He was happy to let her believe that if it kept her out of his face.

After stripping off gloves, sunglasses and helmet, Brandon grabbed the small duffle jammed in the saddlebag and sauntered up the drive. He was so fucking sexy in his leathers. As Brandon slid past him into the house, Nick drew in his scent. He smelled like sun and sand and heat.

Swinging the door shut and stepping into Brandon's body, Nick drove his mouth onto Brandon's. The force of his assault sent them both tumbling over the arm of the couch. He nipped Brandon's jaw. He sucked on one ear. His tongue ran down the side of Brandon's neck as he ground his hips against black denim. Brandon's skin tasted faintly of salt. "I've missed you." Nick whispered against Brandon's lips before pillaging Brandon's mouth with his tongue.

Finally they both had to breathe. Nick pulled back, staring down into azure eyes. Brandon pushed a stray lock of hair behind Nick's ear. "Wow! I haven't had a welcome like that in… well hell, I've never had a welcome like that."

Brandon rolled his head and looked over the tiny living room. A worn oriental rug surged over the hardwood floor, underneath a chunky coffee table, and broke at the feet of a low, black entertainment center, where a flat panel TV squatted. Two chairs, upholstered in red velvet, sat at odd angles to the matching couch. Massive tassels were carved into the armrests and the backs were pitched higher on one side than the other. Brandon's finger ran along the ornate wood spine of the Victorian sofa. "Got your place done up real nice, Nicky." The walls were deep purple and the windows draped with black velvet and red sheers. "I should have you come over and do mine."

"Why, what's it like?"

"Mid-century California thrift store." Nick snorted at the image. "So, Nicky, what's the plan?"

He grinned. "I thought we could fool around some, then go to dinner downtown. The weekly club's tonight. Maybe we could go there if you're not too tired."

"Sounds like a blast. But if we're going to have a late night I'm going to need to crash. I was up 'til three booking johns. We ran a sting last night." Nick lit up at that, and Brandon added, "It ain't that exciting." He struggled to sit up. Reluctantly, Nick moved off his chest and slid to one side of the couch. "I spent six hours sitting in an unmarked, with no air, watching a female undercover lure stupid fucks back to her room. Jerks think they're going to get half-and-half and get bagged instead. The patrol officers in the room were bitching about how uncomfortable it was. At least they had a fucking bathroom." Laughing, he tugged at the clips on Nick's cincher. "And after the ride over here my balls have gone numb anyway. You okay with that, Nicky?"

"Yeah, I guess." Nick tried to keep the disappointment out of his voice. "I can wait a few more hours."

Brandon put his lips to Nick's ear. "Yeah, well, while you're waiting you can think about how I'm going to strip you down and fuck you like mad later tonight." Nick groaned. "Shower?"

"Yeah." It came out as a sigh.

"No, me, idgit." Brandon poked Nick's side, making him jump. "I need a shower to get the road out of my skin."

"Oh yeah, sure." As he stood, he snagged Brandon's bag from where it had fallen. "It's back here." Stepping through the arch into a short hall, he indicated the black and lavender tiled bathroom set between two identical linen closets. A door toward the front of the house led into a tiny bedroom Nick used for his computers, the one opposite to his own. "I'll toss your stuff in my room. You can crash there when you're done." The bedroom curtains were identical to those in the living room, but the walls were crimson. The drapes formed a false wall behind the bed offset in the far corner. To the left of the bed was a wrought-iron electric candelabrum. Nick tossed the bag on the bed. Red silk swags along the curtain tops wafted up in the slight breeze.

Brandon leaned in the doorway. "Where'd you find all this stuff?"

Nick shrugged. "Inherited a lot of the big furniture; Wal-Mart and Target for the drapes and stuff. Not the cool little things, those I picked up here and there." He fiddled with a statue of a demon doing a handstand on his dresser. The bedroom set was what his grandfather used to call tenement furniture: dark 30s deco. "Look, grab a shower, grab some Zs. I'm going to watch some TV. Let me know if the sound bugs you."

CHAPTER FIVE

Dim shadows crawled across the hardwood floors. Dusky shades of evening softened corners and blurred hard lines. Brandon woke to a set of blue eyes staring down at him. He laughed. Fuck, Nicky had a mirror on his ceiling. A big, ornate wood frame that must have come from some dresser was bolted above the bed. He was so tired when he lay down earlier he hadn't noticed it.

That boy had all sorts of secrets. It was going to be fun discovering them. He rolled out of bed and slid into a clean pair of jeans and a Harley T-shirt. Dust-covered boots would have to do, although he wiped them down with his discarded shirt from earlier. Hopefully Nicky didn't have anything too fancy planned. There just wasn't a whole lot of room to pack stuff on a bike.

Sounds of distant combat drifted in from the TV in the front room. The idiot box was tuned to the Hitler channel: WWII 24/7. Nicky was sprawled on the couch, asleep. God, the boy was sexy. Brandon hadn't been this turned on by anyone in a long time. Long hair had never really done it for him before. He liked his guys to look like guys. On Nicky the waist-length fall of black was anything but fem. Hard to look like a girl with the broad shoulders and narrow hips nature had endowed Nicky with. And the way Nicky dressed, the pseudo-bondage attire, vampire look; again, it wasn't what he'd normally be into, but Nicky was fucking hot in it. Large, dark eyes, sharp cheekbones, strong nose and chin, all of it packaged in light olive skin. Brandon couldn't help but think that there must be a little Native American lurking in Nick's genes.

Of course the hottest thing was his cock. Nicky was hung like a freaking porn star. It was like choking up on a baseball bat with both fists. Brandon knew he was on the upper end of average, years of locker rooms had proved that, but Nicky put his dick to shame. It was kinda strange how Nicky acted like he was almost embarrassed by it. That would change on his watch.

Brandon ran his hand along Nick's inner thigh and knelt down beside him. Nick sucked in his breath and slowly opened his sleep-fogged eyes. Jet, they looked like they were carved out of jet. "Hello there, sleeping beauty." There were women who would kill for those lashes. "Have a good nap?"

"Oh man." A smile played around Nick's lips. "Yeah, I guess I did. What time is it?"

Brandon looked back towards the VCR. "Seven ten."

Nick struggled to sit up. "Shit, I made dinner reservations downtown for eight. We need to book if we're going to make it."

"Let me fix my hair, and I guess I'm ready." Reservations…that sounded classy. Or at least it didn't sound like it was a jeans and T-shirt kind of place. "Although I didn't bring much more than this." Brandon tugged at the Harley logo on his shirt. "Will it be okay?"

"Yeah, this is Vegas." Nick ran his fingers through his hair. "You'll be better dressed than a lot of people there. Tourists have no taste."

The Freemont Street Experience was Las Vegas's attempt to revive the flagging downtown casino crowd. Except for a few vital cross streets, Freemont had been blocked off as a pedestrian corridor. Millions of dollars had been fed into a high-tech overhead canopy that stretched a length of more than five football fields. Larger-than-life animations, integrated live video feeds, and synchronized music crawled in endless pandemonium overhead. Slowly, the term Fleamont was dropping from the local vocabulary.

As they wandered down the center of Freemont, threading through stalls hawking tourist crap, Nicky fed him a running commentary. "It's in one of the older casinos downtown, but it's like a locals' thing. You hop in a cab and tell them you're coming here and they'll ask if you're going to Hugo's. Really good food, probably the best martinis in town." Stepping through the waterfall of air-conditioning that fell from a crown of cascading lights, Nicky led Brandon onto the casino floor. The ceilings were lower than those on the Strip and the carpets were worn, but the casino was packed. Around the flotilla of table games and down a set of stairs in the back wall, they entered a different era.

The small, dim tavern was wood panel and raw brick; old Las Vegas at its best. After checking in, they sat at the bar drinking and shooting the breeze with an older couple from Florida. They'd been a little hesitant when Nick had sat down next to them. Five minutes and his charm and warmth had won them over. By the time their table was ready, Nick knew what their kids did, the names of all their grandkids and had a snapshot of their lives. In exchange they had a list of what they must do, what they should think about doing, and what they should avoid at all costs.

The dining area was more of the same brick with dark wood, green velvet arm chairs, and waiters in tuxedos. Brandon couldn't remember the last time he'd been on an actual date. It was one of the hazards of not being out. Being here with Nicky just felt right. At the table, Oysters Florentine was followed by house salads and crab-stuffed steaks. Nicky was right, the food was pretty incredible. It was rumored that they had great desserts, but Nicky said he preferred the apricots, dates and strawberries dipped in chocolate that came complimentary, and Brandon couldn't have eaten another bite without exploding.

As they headed up the stairs back into the casino, he asked. "So, Nicky, we gonna clean up tonight?"

Nick laughed. His laugh was rich and deep, almost an octave lower than his voice. "You are 500,000 times more likely to die in an airplane crash than to win a big amount in casino. You know that, right?" When Brandon nodded, he continued, "You could play some blackjack or craps if you want. State regulations…I'm not allowed to gamble. Later, if you're up to it, we could head over to Purgatory. We don't have to if you don't want though. It's my friend Mirabella's birthday tonight. A lot of our friends are going to be there." He tugged at the straps on his pants in agitation. In a voice not meant to travel much beyond them in the din of the casino. "I mean, I guess what I'm trying to say is that most of them know I'm gay. If we show up together a lot of them will just assume you are. I don't want you to be uncomfortable. So, if you don't want to go, you know, that's okay with me."

"I don't want you to miss your friend's birthday party."

With a shrug Nick dismissed the concern. "If you hadn't come I would have missed it anyway…'cause I would have had to work tomorrow. Place doesn't even open up 'till eleven so I don't go if I have to work."

"Okay, dude, let's wander around, see the sights, and then we can blow about, what, ten forty-five or so for the club?" He popped Nick's shoulder with his fist and smiled. "It'll all be good."

CHAPTER SIX

After the happy birthdays and downing of the obligatory bites of cake, they'd pulled Miri out for one dance and stayed for three. Most of the remainder of the evening was spent out on the patio smoking and talking. Not that you couldn't smoke in the club, this was Vegas after all, it was just more comfortable outside.

In her black 50s style dress and purple petticoat, Miri'd bounced from group to group collecting cards and good wishes. Mirabella slid onto Nick's lap and gave him one of her Bettie Page pouts. "So, my birthday kiss?" She offered up her cheek. When he obliged, she whispered, "This one, he's cute, sorta looks like Chris Masters." Miri had a thing for comparing people to celebrities, usually the ones whose names you had to Google to figure out why they were famous. Sometimes Nick questioned her accuracy. He didn't think he looked at all like Raoul Trujillo. The only reason Miri resembled Bettie was she forced it, although Brandon did have a bit of Masters' look…not quite as buff. None of them would ever get asked to do celebrity impersonations on American Superstars. "You need to be careful dating cops though. My sister's ex was a cop and it just wasn't pretty. Some don't think the law applies to them." Brandon was on the other side of the table going over the finer points of Harley maintenance with another bike aficionado.

Nick kept his voice low as well. "It's not like that. He's just a friend, Miri." How was he going to handle this? "He's not even…"

Brandon leaned across the table. "Hey, I'm going to get something to drink. Want anything?"

"I'd love you forever if you got me a bottle of water." Batting her eyelashes, she looked at him. "Nick?"

His hand floated over the top of his glass. "I'm fine."

"Water it is." Brandon's fist bumped the table twice. "You two be good while I'm gone."

Both watched as he headed inside, sliding past a couple making out in the doorway. Miri's mouth tightened as she thought. "You lie. He is *so*."

"Trust me, Brandon is not gay." That didn't even sound halfway convincing.

With a flounce she quit his lap and sat on the table, scowling down on him. "Does he know you are?" Somehow Miri managed to look exactly like their high school English teacher, only prettier.

"Yeah, he's okay with it." He shrugged. "Look, you can have straight guy friends you don't sleep with. Why can't I?" Grabbing his smokes, he pulled one out and lit it. Usually he would have offered one to Miri, but his mind was on other things. "We both work in law enforcement, not the same, but there aren't a lot of dark-minded people in either of our jobs. We both like old bikes and classic cars. Brandon's pretty open-minded about shit, so, you know, we're just friends."

Belatedly he held out the pack to her. She fished a clove out with purple and black nails. Nick lit it for her.

After a few thoughtful puffs, she stood. "Okay, babe, if you say so." She sighed. "Don't get hurt, okay, 'cause I know you. I think you like him more than you want to admit." Miri took another puff and sighed again. "If he's really not, it could get very nasty if something happened."

"I love that you're worried about me, but don't be. It's all good." He pushed on her calf with his boot. "It's your birthday, go be a bitch to someone who cares."

She laughed and kissed his forehead. "Slut."

Nick bared his teeth in a wide grin. "Whore." His smile dropped as she turned away. God, he hated lying to his friends. The cig slowly burned to embers in his hand. People cycled through the patio area; some he talked with, some he didn't. Boredom was creeping up on him. Brandon hadn't come back yet; maybe Miri had yanked him onto the dance floor. She had a habit of doing that, with strangers even. But if he was dancing with Miri, then Nick could dance with him without it being obvious. God, you had to love group dancing.

The dance floor was just inside the entrance from the patio and small enough that Nick could tell with a glance that

Brandon wasn't there. Collide's cover of *White Rabbit* was throbbing. He scanned the room.

Knots of people were dotted throughout the tables shoved towards the walls. When it didn't play host to Purgatory, the venue was a fairly decent Mexican restaurant. Through the arches separating the dining room from the small bar Nick caught sight of Brandon standing at one of the tall tables. A girl, magenta hair streaked with blonde, was laughing at something he just said. His hand rested on her bare shoulder.

Brandon's hand dropped from the girl's shoulder to the center of her velvet-covered back. He leaned in and whispers passed between them. Lots of smiles, lots of sideways glances and dropped chins, and then his hand slid lower still. Fangs of jealousy bit into Nick's stomach and shot venom through his veins. It hardly registered that he'd walked back outside. His face was hot. His shoulders ached. Shaking, he lit another cigarette. Holy fuck!

"Hey, Nicky." Brandon's butt bumped up against the rail. He chugged the last of his water and tossed the bottle on the table. "What's up?"

Breathe, be calm. "I think I'm going to call it a night."

"Shit," Brandon glanced at his watch, "it's not even one yet." He leaned back, and Nick could tell Brandon was trying to get his attention. Black eyes slid from blue and stared at the parking lot. "Is something wrong?"

"No, nothing. I'm just not feeling real well."

"Probably the cake on top of that big meal. Let's head out then."

"No, you stay." If he clenched his jaw any harder it would snap. "I'll catch a cab and leave the key under the mat for you. You can crash on the couch when you get in."

"Nicky, what's wrong?"

His knuckles were turning white from their grip on the rail. "Nothing. Just let me leave."

"Bullshit." Brandon's voice had dropped to a tense whisper. "Don't pull drama on me here. Let's go back to your place and talk about whatever is eating you."

"Don't tell me not to pull shit." Now Nick glared at Brandon. "What the fuck's your problem? What were you trying to prove in there…with that bitch you were grabbing at?"

"Fuck, not here…"

Kuhk!

Kuhk, Kuhk!

Kuhk!

The sound echoed clean and crisp across the lot. Back-sound bangs built while ricocheting between the buildings. Both snapped their attention to the night, forgetting the burgeoning argument. Brandon was up and over the railing before most people even registered the noise. Nick vaulted it close on his heels. They pounded down the pavement towards the far end of the strip mall. At the end, a lone vehicle drifted in darkness. Wan light from the interior spilled out of an open door on the opposite side. The windows were too darkly tinted to see anything within.

The high-pitched squeal of rubber on asphalt jarred Nick's brain. A dark-colored compact shot through the intersection, running a red. It barely had time to gel when he was grabbed and thrown against the side of the building. Brandon's face was inches from his own. "Don't move from this spot." A cell phone was shoved in his hand. "Call 911. Don't let anyone come close, keep 'em back, Nicky. Those weren't backfires…mid-caliber handgun. I'm not getting too close, just gonna have a little look-see, understand?"

Nick swallowed and nodded.

As he watched Brandon inch along the side of the building, he flipped open the phone and punched the numbers. "911, what's your emergency?"

"Shots, there were shots fired." Nick realized that he was whispering. He upped his volume. "My friend is a cop from out of town, he's on the scene. He says it was gun shots."

"Okay, shots fired. Where are you?" The female voice was patient yet efficient.

"At Purgatory, a club up on Flamingo about six blocks above the Strip. There's a car at the end of the parking lot, interior lights are on and the door's hanging open."

Keyboard clicks sounded in the background. "What's your name sir?"

"Nicholas O'Malley."

"Okay, Nicholas, there is a vehicle with interior lights on and door open? Which door? Can you see? Do not approach if you can't see it from where you are."

"I ain't moving. Looks like the driver's side." Brandon slid up next to him and motioned for Nick to hand him the phone.

"I've notified Metro, they're on their way," the woman's voice faded as he passed it over.

People were starting to gather outside the club. A few braver souls were wandering towards them. "Nicky, we got to keep 'em back." As he walked back to the venue, Brandon turned his attention to the phone. "This is Brandon Carr of the Riverside, California P.D." With his head he motioned to Nick that he should go ahead. "There's an individual, possibly male, but I couldn't be sure, slumped over the steering column. No, I didn't get closer than about sixty feet..."

The scream of sirens cut the night. Within minutes the strip mall was swarming with police. Brandon looked like he wanted to jump in and help. He didn't. All either of them could do was stand to the side and watch and smoke. No one was allowed to leave until the police had spoken with them. Brandon and Nick gave their basic information to a uniformed officer—names, occupations, addresses—and then were told to wait.

Finally, two men approached them. Both wore dark suits with badges clipped to their belts. A lanky blonde was giving a run-down to an older Hispanic man with a graying handlebar mustache. The blonde was a good deal taller than his companion and had a habit of bending down when speaking to him. The tail end of the briefing reached them, "White male, possibly early thirties, slumped over the steering wheel with his hands in his mouth. A lot of blood coming out of his mouth." The detective scanned the patrons. "Clean-cut and definitely out of place." A jab of his chin indicated Nick and Brandon. "The two who called it in."

As his hand came out, the older man smiled. "Detective Emanuel Orozco, Metro P.D." His voice carried the faintest trace of an accent. A round, expressive face focused first on

Nick, then Brandon. The man's eyes were bright black marbles set back under bushy white brows. It gave the impression that he was slightly amused by life.

Brandon flicked a butt into a planter and stepped in to take the proffered hand. "Brandon Carr." Leaning against the rail, one arm across his chest and chain smoking, Nick watched the exchange. He was still shaken. This was as close to an actual crime as he'd ever gotten...he'd had a stereo boosted from his car once, but Jesus, this was major. How did Brandon live with this shit?

"You're the Detective with the Riverside P.D., California?" Wary eyes crawled over Brandon's pierced and tatted frame. There was a hint of disbelief in Orozco's voice. "You're...?"

A bright smile flashed and Brandon finished the sentence, "Vice." Brandon was obviously used to the reaction.

The blonde rolled his eyes, and Orozco nodded as though that had solved the riddle. "And you were the first on the scene."

"Yeah, but I didn't get closer than that shop there." Brandon indicated a storefront a good ways back from the car. "Just close enough to see there was someone in the vehicle. Didn't want to get too close, pollute your scene or risk getting capped myself. I was pretty sure by the blood and brains splattered over the windshield that CPR wasn't going to help."

The three laughed. Nick didn't get the joke. "You called it in?" Orozco was leafing through some notes. Lights from the club bled out onto the sidewalk. The owner had turned them on and passed around coffee when it became apparent that everyone would have to wait for the police. Various officers, in and out of uniform, were cycling through the patrons and taking down statements.

"I had Nick do it."

Orozco's attention went to Nick. "Nick...O'Malley?" He looked down at his notes and back at the long hair and bondage attire. "You're an Agent for Gaming Control?"

Chewing on his lower lip, Nick answered, "Yeah." His eyes kept wandering back toward the car, spotlighted and cordoned off with tape. Detectives and technicians swarmed over it.

Every few moments the light of a flash would burst. "Trust me, I don't dress like this for work. Not even on casual Fridays."

The mustache wiggled as if Orozco was thinking 'I should hope not.' "You're a regular? You come here often?" When Nick nodded in assent, he continued. "Would you recognize another regular even if he wasn't dressed up?"

"Yeah." Nick's eyes rolled; people just didn't get it. Dressed up was work. This was dressed normally for most of them. "It's not a big scene. There's Purgatory; a bunch of people get together for bowling every week. That's where you'll find the baby-bats, the under twenty-one crowd. There's a 24/7 punk place on Paradise. Once a month, there's a fetish venue. The people who like to hump legs show up there, I know some of them. Sometimes they come here, too."

The blonde handed Orozco a plastic card in a ziplock baggie. Gingerly Orozco held it out for Nick to see. It was an ID of some sort. "Recognize him?"

He had to lean in. "Holy shit, I think it's Duke." Nick reached out to take the bag, stopping just before he touched it. Orozco nodded in response to the query in Nick's eyes. Pulling it closer so he could be certain...there it was: Duke's new California driver's license.

"Duke?" The detective prompted. "He was a regular here? That's how you know him?"

"Mike Ducmagian." That was obvious; the name was on the ID. "No he wasn't Goth, rivet-head or part of the fetish crowd. Pretty mainstream as far as I know." Shaking his head, "Shit, no, I used to work with the guy before he went private sector and moved to California. I spoke with him this afternoon. I was supposed to meet him at work early on Monday. Fuck." Nick thought he might throw up.

"When did you talk to him?"

"I called him on his cell, maybe two or a little after." Man, he'd just talked to the guy and now Duke was dead. "He left a message for me at work this morning."

Orozco was taking notes. "What did you talk about? Did he tell you why he was in Vegas?"

"Yeah, he said he was coming into town to see some friends." Nick realized he was still holding the license and held it out for the other detective to take. "He called me because he needed to pick up an EPROM. He wanted to do it today, but I told him he had to wait until Monday, 'cause I was busy. My..." Nick hesitated for a moment. "Brandon was coming into town."

"EPROM?" With a quick flick of the eyes, Orozco read Nick's face.

"A slot chip. I work in Electronic Services. Duke used to, but now he's gone private sector. I was testing EPROMS for his company, and they sent some that weren't supposed to be in the test. He wanted to come get one that I forgot to send back with the others 'cause he said he'd be in town. Aw fuck, Duke! What the fuck did he come here for?"

Orozco mentally tracked back in his notes. "Did he mention which friends he was coming to see?"

"No." Nick mulled over the earlier conversation for a moment. "No, he didn't."

"Did he know you'd be here?"

"Yeah, he was pestering me to meet him at the lab today, and when I wouldn't because my friend was coming, he asked what I was doing tonight." Nick rubbed his temples. "I told him we were going to grab something to eat, and then head over here." Nick had never known anyone who'd been murdered. It was fucking creepy.

"Do you know why he would have come here?"

"No. This wasn't his kinda place." Boy was that an understatement.

CHAPTER SEVEN

The cops had kept them at the club until almost three, asking question after question. Nick hadn't been able to add anything more to what he'd already told them. The ride home, once they'd been allowed to leave, was strained. He shucked his clothes and slipped quickly into bed, avoiding interacting with Brandon as much as possible.

Kisses to his shoulder and touches on his hip were meant to gain his attention. Finally, he grabbed Brandon's wrist and whispered into the pillow that he was just too tired, too shaken. All he wanted to do was sleep. The one thing he couldn't do was sleep. Images of Brandon petting the girl fought with those of Duke's body slumped in his car. Sheer exhaustion finally shut his mind down as the first tendrils of the sun snaked over the horizon.

Sometime after noon he woke. As quietly as possible he slipped out of bed. Leaving Brandon sleeping, he grabbed a pair of army surplus BDUs and a Lock, Shock & Barrel T-shirt and dressed in the hall. His combat boots were still in the living room where he'd left them last night. Stopping in the kitchen to brush his teeth in the sink, he grabbed a diet soda and a handful of Red Vines and headed out the back door.

Light was in short supply in his garage. Barn-style doors protested as he pulled them open, letting in the early afternoon sun. It jeweled off the headlamps, spreading rainbows across the concrete drive. A 1968 Cadillac Miller-Meteor Endloader lurked inside. Faded-blue paint, long and lean and square in body; the leather top was cracked and the rear wheel covers were missing. The front grill was split. Nick grabbed a rag off the workbench and fussed at an imagined spot on the windshield. Along one wall, a waspy Kawasaki cowered from the presence of the massive hearse it was forced to room with.

Nick popped the hood. This was his Zen garden. A mass of steel components and rubber hoses slowly being resurrected from years of neglect. On his way home from an inspection in

Elko, he'd pulled to the side of the road and wandered into a weed-choked cemetery looking for interesting inscriptions to add to Miri's collection of grave rubbings. Miles between nowhere and next to nowhere Nick discovered the love of his life. She sat on blocks, hidden behind an old gravedigger's tool shed, her side peppered with bullet holes. Interior fabric hung in shreds. Every window was etched with dust and half were busted out. The Caddy was so filthy that at first Nick assumed she'd originally been painted brown.

He found a gas station, and then a ghost of a town, and then a house, and then an elderly woman whose husband had once been the local funeral director. Five-hundred dollars and a retelling of the lives of everyone the hearse had borne to their final rest while they searched the old files for the title, and the M-M was his. Two weeks later, he and six friends had cursed and shoved her onto the back of a rented flatbed tow and hauled her back to Vegas.

Parts were hard to come by. Time to work on her was harder still. The cab and chassis were fairly standard to any car of the same make. It was the rear of the hearse that made it, well, a hearse. Nick's plan was to take her back to her true glory and then trick her out a bit. Tenderness and dedication had brought the Cadillac this far. Soon it would be time to start the loads of body work she required to be top notch. He switched out the grimy air filter for a new one and spun the wing-nut down tight.

Nick looked up into a pair of crystal blue eyes. He started, thumping the back of his head on the hood of the Endloader.

Brandon leaned back against the driver side door, laughing. Black jeans rode low across his hips. His chest was bare except where the tattoos reached around his sides. A shower had softened the spikes and his black hair drifted in wisps across his forehead. For one brief moment Nick forgot just how mad he was and allowed himself to stare in awe at the muscles and the tats and the incredible smile. Then the memory of the previous night reared up. Hinges screeched as he slammed the hood down hard.

"So this is the hearse?" Brandon raised his eyebrows. "Are you sure it's a restoration project and not a junk yard?"

Nick offered up a thin smile. "Yeah, this is the rust bucket." As he pushed past Brandon and slid into the front seat, Nick twisted the key in the ignition. The hearse roared to life with a throbbing, primal growl.

"Whoa, she lives, I'm impressed." Brandon started to reach in and touch Nick's hair. Nick caught the movement in the rearview, slamming the door shut to stop him. "What the?"

The driver's window was down, semi-permanently. It had to be physically pulled into place. "Garage door's open." He slung his arm over the door and picked at the rotting weather strip. "Wouldn't want anyone to see us together."

"Nicky, what's up?"

"It's me, not you." His boot heel drew a red-brown line from the gas pedal back. "Don't worry about it." Probably time to order carpeting through Kanter. Probably should get floor panels first…or maybe fix the window and do weather stripping. Shit, there was still a lot to do. He'd hoped a certain someone could help him with that. That's what he got for letting his fantasies overstep reality.

Both hands on the door, Brandon leaned down to peer at Nick. "About what? Tell me."

"I'll get over it." Mouth set hard, his eyes slid toward Brandon. "Don't worry about it."

"Before I leave on Sunday? Come on tell me." Silence answered him. Brandon switched tactics. "I had a lot of fun last night, at least before everything went to hell."

"Yeah, you were having fun." Nick reverted to staring out the windshield.

"You weren't?"

"At first." Nick killed the engine. "When we first got to Purgatory and Miri's birthday that was fun."

"And…" Brandon prompted.

Nick tried not to let the pain show in his eyes. "Then you went to get a drink at the bar. And you stayed at the bar flirting with that girl. I mean, shit, we haven't seen each other in two months and you ditch me to chase tail…which, as far as I know, you're not going to do anything with anyway."

"Nick, I told you I'm not out."

"Okay. No!" Nick ran his nails across his scalp. "Not out is no public displays of affection. I can't tell anyone we're seeing each other. I get it. It's bad enough, but I understand why." His hand slammed the steering wheel. "It is not ignoring me for an hour while you grab some bitch's ass! You wanna cover...I'm seeing someone. Gee, you're cute, but I can't get involved now. I've really been looking forward to seeing you again, and that just fucking hurt."

"Listen, Nicky, I didn't do it to hurt you. I'm sorry. It's just habit."

More black flecks found their way to the floor. "You know what really hurt?"

"What?"

"That your first thought wasn't me...it was protecting your cover in the easiest way possible."

"I'm sorry, Nicky. I should have handled it better. All I can do is say I'm sorry."

"I know. I'll get over it. Like I said, it's my problem."

Hard silence broke between them for a time. "No, it's my problem. I really, really like you, Nicky. It's been a long time since I felt this way about anybody. Hell, I drove four hours across the desert, pulling bugs outta my teeth to see you." Nick snorted a laugh. "Let's not go out tonight. Stay home, just you and I. I'll give you all the attention you need. I want to. I want to be with you." Brandon leaned in through the window and turned Nick's chin with his fingers.

"The garage door's still open."

"I know." Brandon kissed him. Brandon hadn't shaved yet. Stubble tickled the edge of Nick's lips. "You broken it in yet?"

He pulled back. "Broken what in?"

"Big ol' back area..." Brandon's chin jerked towards the rear of the hearse. "Plenty of room." Nick's skin tingled under Brandon's feather-light touch as the other man reached in and pulled the T-shirt over Nick's head. The black material landed in a pile somewhere near the bike. Holy shit, Brandon was intense. A smile flashed, the latch clicked and the door eased open.

"You're fucking crazy, you know that?" Nick rolled his eyes, sliding back across the bench. "Jake would never have gone for that. He was always after me to sell it and use the money for a down payment on a Toyota."

It was almost feral how Brandon moved, crawling across the seat on all fours. "That's just tragic." The deep voice was mellow, soothing, sensual. Nick could get off just listening to Brandon talk.

Already things were beginning to tingle and tighten. "Well, this wasn't his lifestyle."

"How the hell did you meet him then?" Strong arms were on either side of Nick's hips as Brandon leaned in.

"He's part of the fetish crowd, dress up to party on weekends." Why the fuck was he talking about Jake? Especially with Brandon licking just behind his ear; damn it was really getting hot. "You know, club bleed-over and stuff. Otherwise he's pretty conservative." A strong hand stroked him through the camouflage. He began to swell in response to the touch. "He thought the hearse was weird. A sling in his bedroom, okay. A car that used to haul around dead people, gross."

Brandon's lips were working down the side of his neck. "I think it's wicked. What'd ya name her?" Fingers of frost danced under Nick's skin wherever the kisses landed.

Nick's skin clung to the vinyl against his back. "Querida." His own hands were tracing the ridges of Brandon's biceps, his hips grinding into the caress. "It means 'I desire you'…it's what Gomez called Morticia."

"I always wondered about that. Querida." The way Brandon said it, Nick knew he wasn't talking about the car. "Wanna climb in the back and fool around?" Brandon was just too damn sexy to stay mad at for long.

Nick's breathing was already heavy. The heat in the garage didn't help. "For a guy who's not out you certainly like to have sex in some risky places." Well, not that risky, they were almost sixty feet back from the street and in a garage. Still, if someone were standing at the end of the drive they'd get a show. "Besides, I didn't bring anything out with me."

Brandon chuckled. "Cops and Boy Scouts always come prepared." A thin foil package dropped between Nick's legs.

He twisted the packet in his fingers, sliding his gaze up to meet Brandon's eyes. "Make-up sex."

"Oh, hell yeah, baby." Burning hard kisses stole what little remained of Nick's resistance. "One of the best types around."

Through his sighs Nick whispered, "Fuck yeah."

Unlike newer hearses, there was no partition wall in an M-M. As Nick wriggled over the seat into the casket area, strong hands latched onto his hips. Miri had helped him with customizing the casket compartment. Rollers, lock-downs and skids had been sanded and re-chromed. Winter had seen all the interior panels recovered in black velvet with red trim. Red satin curtains, draped with gold fringe, hung in the windows.

His stomach tightened as Brandon's fingers popped the snap on his BDUs. Sliding forward and turning, the pants were pulled off his lean frame. Nick hadn't bothered to tie his boots. He caught one on the seat back and flipped it onto the floor. Brandon yanked the other off. With a tug, the pants were gone as well. "Damn, Nicky." One by one the buttons of Brandon's jeans were coming undone. "Look at you all pretty and nekkid and waiting for me."

Brandon lunged over the seat back and crawled forward. As he straddled Nick, the casket roller shifted. They banged against the rear gate. He drove his mouth down against Nick's skin, and his hand snaked between their legs to stroke Nick's throbbing dick. Nick's hips thrust into the tight grip. The sound of denim sliding off Brandon's body made him moan. Brandon was jerking him hard, sucking on his nipples and biting his chest.

He was still so pent up from yesterday's anticipation. "Fuck, I'm going to come if you don't stop!" Instead the pace increased. Fast and hard and determined, Brandon worked him. Lighting struck down his spine as he boiled over into Brandon's hand.

Pulling back, Brandon licked his lips and stared down at Nick. Slowly all the juice from Nick's body was pumped up with strong pulls. Brandon ripped the condom open with his teeth. Rolling it down with his free hand, the sheath covered his cock in a thin shield of latex. Then Brandon slid his come-slick fingers down across Nick's balls and up into his hole. Nick's back arched as he hissed with pleasure. Brandon would pull out, coat his fingers in more cream and slide them back in. Shudders crawled across his body as Brandon rubbed his cock against Nick's. Both were soon coated with come.

Brandon withdrew his fingers. The casket compartment was too low. There wasn't enough room for good ol' missionary. As he pushed Nick over on his side, Brandon slid down next to him, kissing his back and shoulders. Then, he drew himself down Nick's spine, teasing Nick's body with his own. "Come on, baby, I wanna watch you get fucked." He rolled them so that Nick was almost as much on top as he was beside him, and pulled one leg back over his hip. Slowly he pushed his cock, coated with Nick's own come, inside his tight hot ass. Both of them moaned as Nick was spread.

Brandon's hips began to rock them. Their bodies set the casket roller sliding on the skids. Each thrust was punctuated by the bang of the table against the gate. Nick twisted back and found Brandon's mouth. Their tongues fought as Brandon pounded from behind. The heat was intense. It soaked through both men, coating them with sweat. As he was biting Nick's cheek, Brandon pleaded, "Stroke your cock. I want to watch you come as I fuck you."

Nick was gasping as he grabbed himself and stroked. He was still so sensitive from when Brandon had jacked him off. Usually it would be hard for him to come again so soon, but he could already feel his thighs tighten. "I'm gonna fucking come again!"

His body was clamping down on Brandon's cock each time it thrust into Nick's hole. The frost of another orgasm was clawing from the inside out, crawling up his dick with ice. "Pretty, Nicky. Oh, God, hot pretty, Nicky!" Brandon chanted as he shuddered against Nick's body. As he was consumed, he kept thrusting hard.

Nick's head jerked against Brandon's shoulder. Brandon's whole body arched as Nick spasmed in his release. "Holy shit!" Brandon screamed. His fingers dug into Nick's skin as Brandon lost it again. Trembling, shaking, Brandon rocked against him.

"Oh man, that's never happened before." They lay trembling, surrounded by the scent of sex. As he sucked on Nick's neck, tasting the salt on his skin, Brandon put his arms around Nick's waist and pulled him in tight. "That was fucking intense. I'm never going to let you go, Nicky. You're mine from now on."

Nick reached back to run his fingers through close-cropped black hair. He snuggled into the strong body behind him. "I guess you like me then, huh?" His other arm wrapped over the ones encircling his middle.

"Fuck, babe." Brandon rubbed his head against Nick's fingers crawling along his scalp. "I'd give up the Harley for you."

Moments of sensual drifting swept by and first Nick, then Brandon began to laugh at the absurdity of Brandon ditching his bike. Now that the afterglow was fading, the inhospitable confines of the Endloader began to manifest. The casket area was a patchwork of recessed skids and tie downs meant to harness the dead, not the living. "Shit, there's something poking my side." Brandon twisted and crawled back. Yanking the handle, he pushed the rear gate open with his shoulder. He caught his body on his hands as he slid forward and pulled himself free, dropping the last few inches onto his knees.

Nick retrieved his pants from the front seat and wriggled his way simultaneously into them and out of the rear of the M-M. As they righted themselves and disposed of the evidence neither could resist a few more intense kisses. It slowed getting dressed down considerably. Finally, as Nick was hopping into his combat boots, Brandon moved to shut the rear door.

"No, wait." Nick slammed his heel into the boot and stepped up to the gate. "You have to shut it just right or it won't catch." With a practiced twist, Nick hefted the gate, lifted the lever and popped the latch in place. "The hinge is giving way…metal stress." They stepped out the doors and into the blinding afternoon sun.

Blinking as they walked back to the house, Nick asked, "So what do you want to do tonight?"

Brandon held his hands to shade his eyes until they found the relative darkness of the kitchen. "I vote for pizza with everything that is not good for us on it, any good horror flick so long as we don't have to go out to get it," his hand snaked around Nick's hips, cupping his ass and pulling him in close, "followed by lots of hot animal sex."

"I've got almost every version of Dracula there is." Nick's arms wound about Brandon's shoulders. "A lot of Hammer Horror, all three Blade movies… you name it." Sex still radiated off the tattooed skin. "Go look in the cases by the DVD player. I'll call in pizza." He couldn't resist the taste of Brandon. His lips slid along Brandon's jaw until he found Brandon's mouth. His fingers brushed through the fine pelt of close-shaved hair, and Nick ground his body into Brandon's.

The grip on his waist tightened and a hand ran up his bare back. "Change in plans. Screw the movie, sex now, pizza later."

"How about someplace actually comfortable this time?"

"You mean like normal people?" Backing up, his hands pulling Nick with him, Brandon teased. "In the bedroom or something?" They bumped into the kitchen door and set it swinging.

"Like you would know where normal people have sex." Nick ducked under a tattooed arm and shot into the dining room. Brandon followed close on his heels. Four steps in and both stopped dead.

Framed in the doorway was Detective Emanuel Orozco. His fist was raised to bang on the screen. When he caught sight of Nick and Brandon, he waved instead. "Good afternoon, gentlemen. I hope I wasn't interrupting anything."

"Ah, no." Nick stammered and stepped away from Brandon. Orozco couldn't have heard them in the kitchen, could he? "We were just, ah, going to order out for pizza." It struck him that they were both shirtless, not to mention sweaty and grimy from the back of the hearse. He waved toward the rear of the house, "Been working on the car most of the afternoon. Hot as hell out there."

Orozco's eyes went up toward the baking Vegas sun. "That it is. Might I come in and talk with you for a moment? I just have a little bit of follow-up." Nick looked to Brandon. "Nothing terribly important…I just thought you might remember something now that you're not so sleep-deprived." With a hint of laughter, Orozco continued, "Really, it won't take long. Just a few follow-up questions…for both of you."

Brandon shot a look back and gave a miniscule shrug. "Yeah sure." Nick stepped to the screen and popped it open. Brandon dropped into the farthest chair. Nick waited until the detective had taken the other and then settled uncomfortably on the couch.

A few forced pleasantries were exchanged before Orozco got down to business. "I wanted to go over some things we talked about last night…see if you remember anything more." Leaning in toward Nick, he asked, "What can you tell me about the phone call earlier yesterday between you and Mr. Ducmagian?"

"Not much more than I already did. Duke left a message with Heather at GCB that he wanted me to call him on his cell. I was out in the field yesterday morning, so she called here before she headed out. When I got home I rang his cell and he said he was heading into town to visit friends. He wanted me to meet him at GCB so he could pick up the EPROM and I told him he'd have to wait until Monday when I was back in. It kinda pissed Duke off."

"And this," Orozco nodded, chewing on his mustache, "was the first time you'd talked to him about the EPROM chip?"

"Actually, no. He'd called the lab at the beginning of the week and told me we'd gotten two or three chips we weren't supposed to have. We're testing a device for the company Duke works…worked for, Frontier Entertainment. They're trying to get their new slot machine licensed in Nevada, and we're working it up for a field test. I apparently missed one when I sent the others back."

"So Ducmagian was angry that you wouldn't get it for him before Monday since you were off yesterday and today?"

"More annoyed, I think, than angry. Actually I worked a half-day yesterday out in the field. I was scheduled to work today and have Monday off, but one of the guys and I switched our schedules so I could have today off. He gets a nice strip casino today and I have to hit a string of gas stations along the 15 on Monday."

"Why did you trade out days? Sounds like he got a better deal? What did you say his name was?"

"I didn't. It's Jack Alston. Well, Brandon was coming to hang out." Shit, he couldn't let that be the only reason. Nick swallowed. "I'm not a big fan of casino work anyway. They're too loud. And, ah, ya know, Miri's…Mirabella's birthday was last night at the club and I wouldn't have been able to go if I worked this morning. So I asked him to switch with me a couple of weeks ago."

As Nick spoke the detective took notes. He scribbled the end of a line. "Where'd you go for dinner last night?"

He answered without thinking. "Hugo's."

"Really?" Bushy eyebrows shot up. "That's an expensive place. Celebrating something?"

"Ah, not really." Shit! "Hugo's...it doesn't cost all that much."

"What, are you kidding? I can't get out of there for less than one-fifty, and that's if the wife and I are being good."

Nick chewed on his lip and slid his eyes toward his lover. Brandon shifted ever so slightly in his chair. Orozco said nothing, just sat with the pen between his teeth and notepad in his lap. Finally, Nick spoke, "It doesn't cost me that much." He swallowed.

"How so?"

"What's the joke with cops and donuts? It's 'cause they give you free coffee and stuff right?" Nick shrugged. "Same kinda thing at the casinos for me." Other than the drinks and cigarettes the casinos were willing to hand out to anyone to keep them at the tables, Nick had never taken a comp. Since he started with GCB he hadn't even done that. He knew of a couple of people who claimed they'd been offered them before. It was always from some low rent joint that didn't know the rules. "Maybe not everything made it to the bill." God, Brandon better appreciate this. A rumor alone could fucking get him canned if it ever got back to GCB. Every since the Harris debacle, the ESD was absolutely anal about ethics.

"You went there because you get freebees?"

"Maybe, I don't know." Picking at his cuticles, he added, "Yeah. I guess."

"Okay." Orozco kept scribbling. "When did you finish…and what did you do after dinner?"

"Probably finished around ten thirtyish." Nick loosened up a bit; he was back on familiar ground. "Wandered around downtown until eleven when we headed to the club."

"You went straight to the club?"

"Yep. We wanted to get there in time for my friend Miri's birthday, you know, so we all could surprise her."

Brandon chimed in. "We were there, dancing, drinking, hitting on chicks until the shit went down. Actually we were just about to cut out 'cause Nick was feeling sick."

"Yeah, German-chocolate cake just doesn't sit well on top of steak and Manhattans." Fuck, did straight guys drink Manhattans?

CHAPTER EIGHT

Monday was, well, a Monday. Nick was still wiped out from the weekend. Brandon hadn't hit the road until late Sunday afternoon. For the remainder of the day Nick had sprawled on his bed savoring the lingering smell of Brandon's cologne on his sheets. The quick call to let him know that Brandon had made Riverside safe and sound had turned into hours of murmurings and promises. He was falling hard, and he so didn't care.

However, the long, drawn-out phone call meant that Nick had forgotten to set his alarm. Now he was late by about an hour and a half. All the shit he'd get for being tardy was still worth it. "Hey, O'Malley." The lab manager caught him as he was heading towards the lab to pick up a laptop. Inwardly he cringed, waiting for the hammer to fall. "I heard Mike Ducmagian was killed Thursday night."

That was not the lecture he was expecting. "Yeah, did it make the news? I, uh, didn't watch much TV this weekend." Both of them were in Nevada civil service summer attire: slacks and short-sleeved dress shirts. Unlike Nick, his manager wore a tie.

"It might've, I don't know." The man shook his graying head and put his hand on Nick's shoulder. That was not good. He only touched someone if he had bad news to impart; empathic contact to make something awful go down easier. "There's a Detective Orozco waiting, says he just has a few follow up questions for you. He says you were a witness to Duke's murder?" It was said with the same intonation, as though he'd found out Nick had come down with some dreadful disease.

Fuck. "Yeah, sort of. It happened near a club I was at with some friends."

"Okay, well I stashed him in my office." His manager gave him another pat, the buck-up-and-be-brave type this time. "More private back there, go ahead and use it as long as you need." As Nick walked away, a last shot was aimed at his back, "And O'Malley, get a fucking tie!" A thumbs-up let the lab manager know Nick had heard.

Orozco was occupying himself in the manner of most people confined to offices that weren't their own; standing with his hands behind his back scanning the evidence of another person's life. Nick knocked on the jamb, and the detective turned. Orozco did a double take as Nick slid through the door. With his hair pulled back and the white shirt he hardly looked like himself.

"Morning, Agent O'Malley. Why don't you have a seat?" Nick eased into the lone guest chair while the older man shut the door then perched on the edge of the desk. "I'm really sorry to bother you at work, but I just wanted to make sure I got everything." He flipped open his ever-present notepad. Wetting his thumb, he leafed through a few pages. "I really hope my showing up here won't cause you any problems. Can we go over what you did Thursday night, from the top?"

His tone told Nick that what he wanted to do was make problems, put him on edge. He had succeeded. "Why? I already told you. Brandon arrived about four or so and we hung out for awhile. We went to dinner around seven-thirtyish, downtown. After that we wandered around Fleamont Street and then headed over to Purgatory about eleven."

"Yah, I know that's what you said." As if contemplating something weighty, Orozco rolled his eyes up and sucked on his mustache. "I went back and checked around. You were where you said you were, when you said you were there."

"Okay, great. So why do you want to go over it again?" Uncomfortable in his boss's office, Nick shifted in his seat. Almost apologetically, he added, "Look, I got shitloads of work to do. If I don't hit the road soon I'm going to be going until nine tonight."

The Detective nodded as though he had expected Nick to say that. "Ah yes, the drive down I-15; well, see, the problem is, you're not being straight with me."

"What do you mean?" Nick couldn't believe this guy. Irritated, he snapped, "What more do you want?"

"You could start by coming clean about you and your cop friend."

What the fuck did that matter? "I have no idea what you're talking about."

"Sure you do. See, I checked around. While I was waiting, I asked a couple of the other agents about you, whether you'd ever do anything shady." Orozco chewed on his mustache some more. "That nice gal in Investigations, the looker, she thought it was so funny she blew her pop out her nose. Of course, that doesn't mean much…other than you aren't so stupid as to take a comp like you said you did." He brought his black stare to bear on Nick. "That got me thinking what else would you have to hide, 'cause you were both hiding something. What could be so awful that you'd rather risk disciplinary action than tell me the truth?" After some thought, Orozco added, "And then, well there were some comments some of your co-workers made. One guy was especially nasty about it." His tone turned almost fatherly. "You probably ought to watch your back with him."

The detective settled back and crossed his arms in front of his chest. "Hugo's is a really nice place…I usually take my wife there on our anniversary. Had a look at the check. You dropped about two hundred bucks on dinner. Hell of a lot of money for just a friend. So, you want to tell me just how long you and your friend have been *an item*?"

Now it was Nick's turn to cross his arms. His came across as defensive rather than contemplative. "What the fuck does my personal life matter to your investigation?"

"You knew the deceased. You talked to him the day he was killed. You were, coincidentally, pretty much where he was when he died." Large, square-fingered hands went to Orozco's thighs as he leaned forward, bearing down on Nick. "You're not stupid; you tell me what that looks like. I need to know who might have reason to lie about what you were doing and you know it."

"I could tell you to get the fuck out of the lab."

"Yes, you could, you are free to end this interview at any time." Orozco growled. "But you're sworn to uphold the laws of the State of Nevada, just like I am. Lying to an investigating officer; refusing to cooperate during a murder investigation; that could land someone like you in a lot more hot water than you're prepared to be in."

Tense moments of silence ticked by. When it became evident that Nick was prepared to wait him out, Orozco softened.

"Listen, I don't have to work with the guy. I could really give a shit about what you two do for recreational activities as long as it ain't illegal in my state. You want to diddle each other's tail pipes until you're blue in the face, go right ahead. Understand though, right now this is just a friendly little follow-up interview. You can play it straight with me or we can escalate this situation. If that happens, a lot more people are going to know about it. Pick up the phone and call your buddy. Ask him what'll happen next."

Nick knew. He'd taken a few courses on evidence and investigation when he'd joined the GCB. Not that he did any enforcement, but on the off chance one of the agents discovered something criminal when they were inspecting a machine. No one wanted a case thrown out because ESD blew it at the starting line. "What do you want to know?"

"Good choice." Orozco nodded. The note pad went into his shirt pocket. "How long have you known each other?"

Defeated, he answered. "We met the end of April."

"You see a lot of each other since then?"

"No." Nick rested his cheek in the palm of his hand, massaging his forehead with his fingertips. This blew the basic rule...never out someone else. "We've talked a lot, over the internet, some phone calls. This was the first time we've been together since then."

"How'd you two meet?"

His hands dropped limp in his lap. "What the fuck does that matter?"

"Answer my questions, I'll decide."

"We hooked up at a Goth Con in San Diego."

For a moment Orozco just stared at him. "Goths have conventions?"

"Yeah, we have fucking conventions. Get to hear new bands. Merchants come from across the country. Party. Meet new people, see people you haven't seen in awhile, friends who've moved away or whatever. Typical convention crap. Think that's bizarre, there's a cruise that happens every January."

"Okay. What you're telling me is he doesn't know you that well."

Nick nodded. "Pretty much."

"What happened at the club that night?"

"You mean other than a guy I knew got his brains blown over the dashboard of his car?"

"Yeah, other than that."

"Got there around elevenish, a little after they opened." Nick looked anyplace except at the detective. "Normally, I wouldn't show up until about midnight, but it was Miri's birthday so we all wanted to be there before her, so we could surprise her with a cake and shit. And then Brandon and I started arguing out on the patio. And then we heard the shots."

"Why were you arguing?"

The memory still hurt. "Cause he was grabbing some chick's butt."

"Did you make any calls that night?"

"No, other than the 911."

"Not to anyone else?"

"No, what do you think is going on?" Christ this sucked. What was Orozco fishing for? Whatever it was, he'd gotten the worst there was to get. "Pull my fucking cell records, home phone, I don't care. You'll see."

"Maybe I'll do just that." Orozco stood. The interview was over. "I don't think anything is going on. I'm just looking at everything." As he opened the door, he turned back to Nick. "See, things are so much nicer when you're honest with me."

CHAPTER NINE

Brandon sauntered into the station about one o'clock. Today he was in black Dockers, a black bowling shirt with flames running down the front and lug-soled work shoes. It was his version of dressing up. His commanding officer made it clear that they were to dress better for court than what they could get away with if they were on the street. If he'd been at trial, he wouldn't have dared be in less than a suit and tie with all his jewelry somewhere other than on his person. For a routine evidentiary hearing he could keep the piercings.

"Hey, Carr!" Jeff Weaver called to him as he threaded his way through the sea of desks.

The Orange Street HQ had been built when Riverside was a hick burg. Now it was a major metropolis of close to three hundred thousand souls. Detectives, cops, and administrative staff were all jammed on top of each other, or cast off into one of the four other overflowing command centers throughout the city.

"What?" Brandon dropped into a chair and almost fell out of it when it lurched to the side. The problem with being the last one in was you got stuck with the shitty chair, if you were lucky enough to get a chair. Even if this one got replaced there'd be another within days to take its place. Good ol' city requisitions couldn't keep pace with the abuse the staff dished out.

Thick-necked, broad-shouldered, with a blonde buzz cut, Weaver looked like the aging high school athlete he was. "Man, first I ain't your fucking secretary." Weaver laughed and tossed a ball of paper at him. "Second, you got a couple of calls. One was from an Agent O'Malley at Nevada Gaming Control, said it was urgent and you'd know what it was about. The other was from a Detective Orozco in Vegas following up on an investigation. What the fuck were you doing out in Sin City my little baby D?" He'd been partnered with Weaver when he'd been brought into Vice. Routine practice—they put a newbie to shadow the steps of a veteran. Luck had caught him a good detective like Weaver.

He was going to kill Nicky. What was so fucking important that he'd call at work? "I told you, some guy got capped in the parking lot of a club I was at. Apparently the stiff used to be with the Gaming Control Board." Break down, tell a guy you're really starting to get stuck on him and he starts acting like he owns you. And calling him at the station, it was just fucking stupid. Since he was pissed, he decided to call Orozco back first.

As the number was ringing, Weaver looked up from his paperwork. "By the way dude, turn on your cell phone. Both said they tried to reach you there first."

Brandon yanked the cell off his hip. He'd set it to silent when he'd gone into court. Seven messages, six were from Nicky, two text. Orozco answered his line as Brandon flipped to the first text message. *911 DONT TT ANY1 B4 ME!!!!!* was the first; the second was just a string of 911s. Mechanically, he responded, "Detective Carr, returning your call." Oh, shit.

Orozco's voice sounded in his ear. "Detective, you someplace you can talk?"

"Why?" Brandon's elbows and knees had gone weak.

"I had a nice little chat with your boyfriend this morning." A cold, hard knot slid down Brandon's spine into his stomach. "I was afraid maybe he'd gotten to you first and that's why you hadn't returned my call earlier."

He spoke as evenly as he could manage, "I was in court on a suppression hearing this morning."

"Anything crucial get excluded from your case?"

"No." Brandon snuck a look at Weaver; still absorbed in making his reports come out right. "All pretty routine. I've got a good D.A. on this one." Mentally he tried to will his partner to go grab some coffee or something.

"Glad to hear it. You're at your desk aren't you?" When Brandon confirmed it, Orozco continued, "Why don't you take a walk someplace private. I'm going to take a drive. Call me back on my cell." He rattled off the number and Brandon jotted it down. "And, detective, you know better than to call your friend first, right?"

Brandon was shaking by the time he reached the roof of the municipal parking garage. People went there to smoke since you no longer could within twenty feet of a government building. Fucking health Nazis. He finished half a smoke while he waited for some secretaries to clear out. When they were gone, he dialed.

"Carr? Good boy. You didn't do anything I wouldn't approve of while I was waiting…wouldn't think so, hasn't been that long." Brandon took another drag and said nothing. "Okay, look you're thinking your career is about to go down the tubes. I'm going to tell you what I told your little vampire butt buddy. I don't give a shit. But I hate it when people aren't straight with me. And another cop, that really pisses me off, 'cause that means you think I'm stupid."

Brandon laughed. There was no humor in the sound. "What did you want me to say? This is Nicky, he can suck chrome off a fender? Get bent!"

"Fair enough." Orozco didn't seem to take offense. "He must like you a lot to be willing to claim he was taking comps rather than rat you out. GCB internal ethics investigations make Internal Affairs look like amateurs. If word ever got back to them that there was even a possibility of something like that they'd screw him six ways to Sunday."

"I guess." Brandon stared out over the brown-grey soup that made up Riverside's skyline. "Somehow I'm thinking you didn't want to talk to me just so you could stroke my choice in men."

"Okay then, I'll level with you on the expectation you're going to level with me. You gotta know your boy has got some problems."

The first forty-eight hours was blown, the detective was out of time and probably good leads. Brandon took another drag, paused again. "I know I'd be looking at him if it were my case; the phone call, he used to work with the guy, he was near the scene." Brandon didn't want to think like a cop when he thought about Nicky. The truth was he didn't really know the guy, no matter how much they'd connected. "It smells like set up. Opportunity, no motive, but that could come. He obviously didn't pop him, but it just feels like he was in on it."

"Glad to hear it. You're thinking straight. So let's talk about you two. What's the story there?"

"Met him a couple of months back in San Diego at this event." That was the last subject Brandon wanted to be talking about. "Did something I hadn't done in about a year and a half."

"What's that?"

He answered with deadpan delivery, "Got laid."

Orozco actually laughed. "How well do you know Agent Nicholas O'Malley?"

"Not well enough to know that Nick was short for Nicholas. Could have guessed it, but didn't know."

"Okay. Tell me about why you were in Vegas and what happened that day -- without the hedging."

"We'd been getting to know each other. My time off actually happened to correspond with a weekend so I pinged Nicky and asked if he wanted to get together." Brandon was starting to sweat. Not from the interrogation, but from the brutal heat that suffocated the senses of Riverside. There was no way to escape it. "He had a Monday off, but he switched it with someone for that Friday so we could hang out. I got to Vegas maybe three-thirty, four o'clock, grabbed a shower. Nicky and I both crashed at his place for a little bit; planning for a late night. We went for a real swank dinner, his treat, hung around downtown, and then hit the club for his friend's birthday party."

"Did he make any phone calls? Do anything out of character? You know what I want to know."

"I don't know him well enough to know what's out of character for Nicky." God, wasn't that the truth. "We weren't together the entire night...I mean I hit the can a couple of times. He could have done just about anything while I was asleep. And at Purgatory I was at the bar for a bit and danced with some of his friends. He had his cell phone with him. He could have made a phone call and I wouldn't have known."

"He said you two had a fight." Ah, great, so it all came out.

"Yeah, we argued, don't know if you'd call it a fight." He thought for a moment. "Nicky went a little passive-aggressive possessive on me; thought I was getting too cozy with some of the girls."

"I guess you two managed to make up."

Brandon flicked the spent butt over the wall. "I was buttoning my pants as you were banging on Nicky's door."

"That, detective, was actually more information than I needed to know."

CHAPTER TEN

Brandon hadn't called since Monday. And that was less of a call and more of a scream fest. Nick had tried to apologize. God, had he tried. E-mails drifted in cyberspace. Messages weren't returned. Nick knew he'd fucked the relationship big time. Why did he have to open his big mouth? There was something he could have done to keep Orozco off of it. Lots of coulda-shouldas kept him from sleep that week.

He moped through his assignments Tuesday and Wednesday. Now he was at the lab again. Thank God nobody was ever in the lab. He wouldn't have to be nice to anyone, be expected to carry on a conversation. He sat down at the workbench and turned on the computer. What was in the dock caught his eye. No one had touched the station for a week. There it was, an EPROM. And dollars to donuts, Nick knew if he pulled it out the serial number would start 559A. He could almost see himself drawing it out of the pile last Thursday. Because of Brandon's arrival and Duke's pissing him off, he'd been distracted. If he hadn't been distracted, Nick would have looked at the chip in the dock when searching for the EPROMs Duke wanted. Fuck and fuck again.

Duke had wanted that chip bad. Why? He had wanted it so bad he'd driven out to Vegas to get it. The "friends" story just rang of bullshit. First he'd tried to give Nick the holier than thou come on. When that hadn't succeeded he'd gotten more buddy-buddy than they'd ever been at work. Why hadn't he just come by HQ and gotten it? Nobody would have been in the lab, but hell most of the agents and employees in the other divisions knew Duke. If he'd just explained the situation to any one of them they probably would have gotten it for him. But then he would have had to *explain* it to them and it would be notable. Meeting Nick at GCB could be passed off as dropping by the lab to say hi to someone Duke used to work with.

Maybe he had shown up at Purgatory to pressure Nick into getting it for him. There was no other logical reason for Duke to be in that parking lot. Purgatory had been the only open business; there wasn't even a gas station nearby. And he had pumped Nick for his plans for the evening. Downtown would have been too crowded. But Purgatory, sometimes maybe less than fifteen people showed up, including the DJ and owner. It was also not 24/7. Everybody got kicked out when the guy decided he needed to go to bed, usually two-thirty or so. Nick had bitched about all of it at work.

Show up, catch Nick in the parking lot, or worse follow him home. God knew how Duke thought he might pressure Nick, but he must have been desperate. And it didn't really matter because now Duke was dead. Somehow, someway this chip was connected to the murder. It had to be. It was too much of a coincidence to be just coincidence.

What was up with the EPROM? Whatever it was, Duke thought it worth risking his neck over. Something maybe someone else was willing to kill Duke over. Well, there was one way to find out; time to start looking at the code.

Most of the checking was done by the computer; comparing where the chip code deviated from the source code through a program called DEPROM. What it was telling him didn't make sense. He'd run and re-run the program. Then he'd gone old school: printed reports and a highlighter. It was a gaff, to be sure, but it wasn't a cheat…or maybe it was, but it just didn't make sense why it would be where it was. Habit dictated. He logged everything he found. After an hour Nick's eyes started to cross. There was only so much programming language his mind could comprehend at a time.

He stretched. Curiosity was biting at him. He'd perused the Frontier files when he first been assigned the project. Taking another peek might spark something. Not that the company hadn't been given the third degree during the background investigations. But then again, maybe not. All the key players of Frontier had gone through the wringer before, when they worked for other outfits. Shit, Duke passed the GCB background check. One of the guys in Enforcement, with only a little bit of exaggeration, claimed it was easier to get a secret clearance out of the government.

GCB was a multi-layered defensive shield against the kinds of crooks who had once overrun the Vegas casino industry. The Investigations Division was the part of GCB that scrutinized all gaming applicants for viability, integrity, and suitability for licensure. Paper junkies, they thrived on minutely detailed reports which they fed to the Board and Commission. While Nick's department determined whether a particular game could come in, Investigations determined whether the company would ever be allowed to do business in Nevada. Audit, Securities and Enforcement divisions all ensured that existing companies kept their noses clean. Tax & License, if you were a cynic, was the IRS of the gaming world. They wore more hats than their name would imply…including oversight of Indian Casinos in the state. Admin made it all hum.

Time to go visit the bean counters in Investigations. That was as unfair as others calling ESD a group of hackers. There were experts in white-collar crime, drug trafficking, and banking scams within its ranks.

When Nick sauntered up to her desk, Ada Lopez looked up. She'd been a SEC auditor before taking a position with GCB. Anxiety turned to relief when she realized who it was. "Hola, Dracula, how's business?" She flashed a rare smile as she gave her attention to him. Ada was built like a Penthouse Pet but dressed like Mother Teresa. Even with that defense tactic, all the straight guys were hot for her. No matter how they tried to hide it, lust oozed out of their pores. They all knew it was futile. Ada was devoted to her family and her church. Unlike many who professed faith, Ada lived it. That made Nick's interactions with her tense in the opposite direction.

"Same ol', same ol.'" His hip went against her desk. Nick was about the only male she'd tolerate getting that close to her. Not that she'd ever said anything, but her attitude carried messages loud and clear. "I need the Frontier Entertainment file."

They got along fine, very professional. She had no hesitation in calling him if there was something that her department needed from his. But Nick knew, even if Ada never said it, that she firmly believed he was going to hell because he was gay. It just oozed from her pores. "Any particular reason?"

"You haven't heard?" God, he couldn't believe that rumor wasn't running rampant. Then again Ada didn't believe in gossiping. It was un-Christian. "Mike Ducmagian died."

"I did; terrible news, so sad for his...oh my!" Only Ada could say that without sounding like a character from a 50s sitcom. "I totally forgot. He was with Frontier wasn't he? A programmer there?"

"Yeah, and a key player. I've got to pull some info so I can see if I can reach one of the other principles." It wasn't a complete lie. ESD would need that information. "We need to know who's going to take over for Duke. We're in the middle of testing and we have to have a contact for that."

A delicately manicured, but unpolished, hand drifted towards the direction of the files. "Well, you know where it is."

"I'm going to copy the face pages so I don't have to keep bugging you if I can't get a hold of them. Is that okay?"

"Oh, sure, go ahead." She turned back to her computer and the project she'd been working on. Talking into the screen, she added, "Just put the file back when you're done. Can you do me a favor when you talk with them? Let them know we're going to need a new sheet if they're bringing in someone new as a key. Or we'll need an update on ownership distribution if they're just going to split his portion between them. It's probably going to hang them up for a while if they bring in someone new."

"You got it, Ada." As he spoke he backed toward the door. If he was quick he could blow before she realized he was leaving. "Happy to be of help. I'll run it to the copier and be right back."

"Yeah, just drop an out-card in the cab for me, okay?"

"Will do."

"And Nick," Ada's voice caught him as he was darting through the door. Damn, not quick enough. He turned and smiled, waiting for it. "God can forgive anything if you just ask him with your heart."

"Thanks for reminding me."

CHAPTER ELEVEN

North of downtown, on Las Vegas Boulevard, caramel brick and turquoise wall-tile baked in the heavy heat of the Nevada summer. The oddly rounded bulk of the funeral chapel seemed indecisive as to which faith it should copy and thus had chosen the least inspiring portions of all. Its roof peaked like the vault of a cathedral, but the flat front was broken only by three undersized lozenge-shaped windows. Before reaching the ground, the pitch of the roof slumped, melting into the walls as though it had lost the will to continue.

Centered perfectly at the base was a set of glass double doors which would have been more at home in a supermarket. Like a broken dove, one low wing of the funeral home swept left. An afterthought of a veranda, supported by square concrete pillars, started at the chapel entrance and continued unabated across the front. All the charm of a high-school cafeteria radiated from the building. Its odd mixture of points and curves promised a bland, efficient, and non-confrontational mass service. Sanitizing death with box hedges and dyed green lawns. Nick shuddered as he rolled the bike to a stop.

This was not what he wanted to be doing with his Thursday afternoon. Funerals sucked. Death didn't bother him. Dealing with the grief of the living did. Everyone in the department just figured that he should attend Mike's funeral on behalf of all…some tenuous link between being there when he was shot and being there when he was buried. He'd have blown off everyone else. When the chief had caught him as he returned the Frontier file and told him the time off was already approved, it didn't seem he had much option.

This was not going to be a small funeral, judging by the number of cars in the lot. Duke was a born and bred local. High school had been at Green Valley. His electrical engineering degree had come from the Vegas branch of the University of Nevada. Damn, it was scary that he could remember these types of things about people. One of Duke's exes lived in Henderson.

There'd been a barbeque at the house of the other out in Red Rock. Nick had vague recollections of being introduced to brothers, cousins and aging parents while there. And Duke, in one of his less than charming habits, tended to bring them up in conversations just to show how much better off he was than the rest of his clan. If he thought about it he could probably bring to mind where they all lived; he just didn't care enough about it right now. It would be enough to be able to put names to faces if he ran into them here.

The heat lay thick on his shoulders and seeped into his lungs. Nick fidgeted with his suit as he trudged across the parking lot. His coat was cut more like a frock than the traditional jacket, although the fabric was a conservative black blend. A purple silk vest and tie flashed when he moved, and his hair spilled loosely down his back.

A reedy bottle-blonde stood adrift before the chapel entrance, greeting a flock of mourners. Large, red peonies on a background of black bloomed across the sheath dress. Sleepless nights were hidden under a thin veneer of foundation. Tired, drained, her movements were counterpoint to her grief. Catching sight of Nick, she waited as the group trouped through the doors.

He didn't even have to think to put the name to the face. "Hey, Carol." Nick leaned in and kissed her cheek. "How you holding up?" Of the two ex-Mrs. Ducmagians, Nick preferred Carol. Mike had still been married to her when he first started with the ESD. Of course he didn't have much to compare. He'd only ever met Sheila once and that was by accident. The woman had seemed brittle. Nick'd run into Mike at a taco stand when he and his first ex were swapping out kids from a day with daddy. Aw, fuck, Mike had kids. He'd pretty much put that out of his mind. This was going to really suck rocks.

"What can I say, hon. I'm holding up, that's about it." She wound a hand under Nick's arm, and yanked hard on the door. A rush of chilled air drove goose bumps under his skin. "She's inside." The pronoun was drawn out and harsh. "I couldn't stand being in there with her a second longer than I had to. Everything's a problem. The flowers aren't right. I brought the wrong suit. Like that's going to matter. It's a closed casket."

The heel of her palm went up to smudge her eyeliner. "I shouldn't be like that. Sheila has to deal with Kyle and Josh, and they're torn up. She's just coping the best way she knows how: by fighting."

If anything, the interior was even more insipid than the exterior. Magnolia walls and pseudo-Victoriana came off as a half-assed attempt at comfortable country home decor. Instead of homey, it was barren. Alcoves were cut here and there, and furnished as mini-living rooms. Sheila was holding court in one. A little thinner, a little more bleached than her replacement, a dress of navy pinstripes caught on all the angles of her body. She sat beneath a swag of dried flowers, stroking the hair of a boy with hollow eyes. Carol dragged Nick towards the vignette, her fingers digging into his arm.

"Sheila, I think you've met Nick before?" As he mumbled something vaguely sympathetic, Carol pushed him into a chair. Then she commandeered another, sliding it next to his. "He used to work with Mike." Crap, as much as he didn't want to be at Mike's funeral, he really didn't want to be at Mike's funeral talking to his ex-wives. Slip in the back pew, do some Catholic calisthenics and genuflect the hell out of there before they dropped the casket. "Nick was the one at that place where Mike was killed."

Both former spouses swung hungry stares towards him. "Finally the fucker is making enough money that I can give the kids what they deserve and the idiot goes and gets himself carjacked." Okay, well, that sentence pretty much confirmed his vague memory of Sheila. "You were there? Did he suffer much? Say anything? What were his last minutes like? I need to know what it was like for him. What the fuck was going through his mind." With each question her voice became more strident. Orozco's interrogations were preferable to this.

Nick shrugged. "I don't know. I mean I didn't see him get shot. It just happened in the parking lot of a club I was at." Somehow Nick doubted Mike had suffered once he'd been shot... there was too much brain splattered on the windshield. His stomach rolled. Why did he have to remember that?

"Isn't that just like Mike?" Having gotten nothing from Nick, Sheila turned on Carol. "Finally starts earning decent money and does something stupid like this. I mean good fucking money. He just bought Josh a Civic for his sixteenth birthday, brand new. He couldn't do that when he was working for the state. He was going to pay for Kyle to go to band camp." She swept a stray lock of brown hair out of the boy's eyes. It came off as fastidious rather than motherly. "Couldn't keep anything good going."

"He bought Josh a Honda? He just bought me a Saturn." Carol's hand went to her mouth. From behind her fingers, she added, "He said it was the car he kept promising to buy me when we were married." She sniffed and Nick offered her a Kleenex from a box on the coffee table. "I'd rather have him back than the damn car."

Shit, Frontier must have been paying Duke good if he bought two cars recently. He hadn't been with them a year yet. Mentally thumbing back through what he knew of the company, Nick couldn't imagine they'd be that lucrative. They were a start-up, trying to break into a pretty tight industry. Both those cars would have run about sixteen thousand. Without thinking, Nick blurted, "What kind of payments did he get?" It was one of those questions he wished he could take back the moment it slipped past his teeth.

Mistaking his inquiry for concern over her welfare, Carole answered, "Don't worry hon, I'm not stuck on the line. Mike said he didn't want me to have to worry about the payments. It was all paid for up front." She turned to Shelia. "You know how he was never good with money, paying bills on time."

"Never was. Always late with child support." Shelia's eyes drifted unfocused. "With his first paycheck from Frontier he made good on all his arrears."

Once Carol had latched onto him she wasn't about to let him go. Front row instead of back, dragging him from group to group; she could just thrust Nick forward and say, "He was there." It absolved her from any need to confess her grief to well-meaning inquirers. It got so bad that she'd pulled him into the funeral home's Town Car for the trip to the burial site. And then she told the startled driver, "He was there," as though it magically made Nick a member of the family.

As they wound their way downtown, bound by the hopscotch escort of off-duty cops, Carol had finally fallen apart. What she couldn't allow herself to show to family and friends came gushing forward before a virtual stranger. Nick could only thank God that the trip was relatively brief. A short distance separated memorial park from memorial chapel. Woodlawn was one of the oldest cemeteries in the state. It was a mix of monumental markers and simple stones. Old growth trees were sprinkled randomly about the green spaces.

Duke was to be buried in one of the more modern areas. Flat concrete markers lay flush with the ground. It lacked the charm of an old-fashioned cemetery. Cars lined the serpentine drive. What comforting words he could think of, he offered to Carol as he tried to mop away her mascara. She looked like shit. Hell, it was a funeral and she'd just lost her ex-husband…who was apparently trying to get back with her before he died. Why shouldn't she look like shit? Nick had the feeling that if you looked past the puffing, life just hadn't dealt many aces to Duke. Once out of the car, he shifted her death grip to the arm of Duke's younger brother and slipped away for a cigarette.

Cutting across the lawn into one of the older sections, he figured he'd have twenty minutes or so before he could catch a lift back to his ride. The tail end of the funeral procession was parked along the curb a few feet ahead. Two Hispanic men in chauffeurs' uniforms were leaning against a Town Car sharing a smoke. One was facing completely away from Nick, the other offered half a profile. It was unremarkable except for the palm-sized, intertwined MM backed by a bleeding rose tattooed on his neck just below his ear. Nick ducked behind a tree before they could see him. He really didn't know why; other than maybe he was sick of having to retell the same story about Mike Ducmagian's death for the thousandth time that afternoon.

Their conversation drifted back to him. A voice that sounded like it was poured over crushed glass asked, "Why the fuck was Duke-man in that parking lot?" That seemed to be the question of the day. At least this time it wasn't directed at him. Sliding unnoticed behind an old tomb, using it as a backrest, he fished out his lighter and lit a clove.

"Don't know, man." The other guy sounded younger then either of them looked, like fourteen. "But did you see the little Dracula his ex-wife was hanging on? She told someone the boy was at the club where the dude got whacked. My bet, Duke was ticked that that boy was getting the nice piece of ass he used to have. Was probably going to smack him around a bit…Chingado kept saying he was going to try and win the ex back when he got enough." Whoa, way off base there. Nick almost laughed. Then it struck him. These guys knew Duke. "Stupid fuck," that was also a consensus among attendees, "Reg tells him he's got to get that chip thingy back and he's driving around chasing some guy who's screwing his puta like it's nada." They both laughed and it wasn't a good kind of laugh. "Teach those other gringos when Reg says jump, you jump."

Nick crushed the cig out in the dust as his breath went cold in his chest. Teach who not to mess with Reg? Crap, who were these guys? Who was Reg?

"Stupid fucking pig sending them here." Someone hacked and spat. "When they going to be done back there. It's fucking hot, man. Driving the idiots around so they don't go outta sight. What a stupid, fucking shit job. And then what, we gots to find it? How we gonna do that?"

"Yeah, crap job. But Tio says we do it 'cause Reg wants it done. You gonna mess with Reg?" Nick missed the answer his heart was beating so loud. "He said Duke was trying to sweet talk it back from an Agent O'Malley 'cause he couldn't just walk into the place and pick it up. Tio says we just find this O'Malley guy and ask him real nice to give it back." Somehow real nice didn't sound real nice.

"What's this O'Malley hombre look like?"

"I don't know, Irish maybe? Like Darby O'Gill and the Little People." Holy Christ. For the first time ever, Nick thanked God that his dad had been adopted off the reservation at a time when people thought it was a good thing not to admit you were anything other than white. Dad grew up thinking he was "black" Irish. At least until Grandma had died and the whole truth came out. Gramps O'Malley had actually looked a lot like a leprechaun. "You've watched the Travel Channel right? They have gaming agents on the Vegas shows sometimes. They all look like tight-assed feds. Ese's probably something between Bill Gates and FBI."

"You finished?" The other man grunted a positive response. "Okay, let's go baby-sit these Cabrones." Nick could hear their heels on the asphalt. He peeked over the stone confirming they were walking down the road. Damn near sprinting, he cut back across the grounds to play Carol's boyfriend for their benefit. *And shit*, he thought as he merged with the far edge of the crowd, *don't let anyone call me by my last name.*

CHAPTER TWELVE

"Hi-ya, toy-boy." A trim redhead was leaning against his little blue Miata at the end of the drive. Mirrored sunglasses hid poison-green eyes Nick knew all too well. Oh, so very clean-cut and professional, at least on the outside. Slacks pressed just right, loafers polished, and shirt perfectly coordinated to match his tie; Jake's co-workers would never guess at the latex and leather Dom that lurked beneath. When he wasn't playing, he looked like an ad for Hugo Boss. Even when he was, he looked like an ad for the Hugo Boss bondage collection.

Nick glared as he fished his mail out of the box. "I told you not to call me that, Jake." First the funeral and now this; some days weren't worth getting out of bed for.

"Well, yeah." A gold pinky ring flashed as Jake ran his fingers through his hair. It was always clean-cropped, as though he'd just had a haircut, with feathered bangs that blew across his forehead. "Hey, club's tomorrow night, I thought I might give you another chance." It was scary how well Jake could pull off the transition. No matter how conservatively Nick dressed for work, everyone just knew he was weird. After the first few months with the State he'd given up and started wearing ties with Hollywood movie monsters on them. Strangely, he'd gotten less flack about his appearance after the reversion to his darker self.

"I walked out on you, Jake." Nick shuffled the envelopes, hardly reading them. Ninety percent were credit card offers anyway, some from cards he already had. All were destined for the cross-cut. "Still ain't found anyone to fuck yet? What happened to the piece of ass I caught you with? Wasn't he a waiter at the Olive Garden or something?"

"He decided he wasn't into the whole scene." Jake shrugged. "Ya know how some people can't handle it."

"My guess," Nick slammed the box shut, "it was your lying he couldn't handle, Jake."

Jake leisurely draped his manicured hands across the top of the box. "What did I ever lie to you about?" Jake never seemed to rush. Every movement was slow, calculated. It was probably why he did so well in the financial markets. When everyone else was frantic over some upswing or downturn in the market, Jake would purse his paintbrush-thin lips, think a moment and then take deliberate and decisive action.

Turning, Nick headed back up the drive to the house. This was really not a fight he wanted to have in the front yard. Still, he couldn't leave it be. "Bullshit, Jake," he shot over his shoulder, "you're a slut and you know it."

"Hey...I was your slut, man." Jake's strides brought him even with Nick. His voice was low and seductive. "Dude, we had some great times. Don't you remember? You loved the chains. You loved the riding crop. You loved the blowjobs!" Oh man, there was always an edgy charm about Jake, as though he wasn't quite safe. When he wasn't being a selfish bastard, Jake could be an exquisite lover. "Have you completely forgotten about me already? All I ever thought about was you. You know that, babe. I only wanted to give you everything."

One hand on the door, Nick stopped. "That's complete bullshit, and you know it." He was sick of Jake's excuses, his lies, fed up with being treated as somehow lesser than Jake. The whole Dom/sub thing was fine for sex. It just didn't translate well into actually having a relationship...at least not for Nick. "All you ever thought about was getting on top, and it didn't matter with who."

Jake's fingers wrapped about Nick's arm as he came up the steps. Leaning against the side of the house, deep green eyes searched Nick's face. The mirrored shades had gone into Jake's pocket. "I've missed you, man." Yeah, he missed using Nick. Jake was a selfish, self-righteous jerk.

But that jerk had access to all sorts of financial data sites. Maybe it was time for Nick to use him. There were things in Frontier's file which had to be taken at face value: net worth and that sort of stuff. Background checks were looking for bogus investors, shell companies and straw men fronting for those permanently banned from the industry. Whether they were actually solvent wasn't as much a concern to the GCB.

Not when it was a manufacturer. Not so long as the company could pony up the deposits and costs for the machine trials. If you were going to run a casino, you'd better damn well have the funds to keep it solvent or at least plans to take it into Chapter 13 when your creditors came knocking.

Some financials he could pull up on the web, but Jake could get the Dunn & Bradstreet's, Standard & Poor's and a lot more arcane things as well. One stop shopping, all laid out on neat and tidy reports. Nick could get it all, too, maybe, eventually. GCB had done the basic shake down before Frontier could even get their games tested. They'd be less than happy if he asked for another so close on its heels. A full financial audit, assuming he could convince Investigations to pull one, could take months. He blew out his breath. As he opened the front door, Nick asked, "Do you wanna come in for a drink?"

Jake's smile said he'd won.

After grabbing a bottle of wine they settled onto the living room couch. Taking opposite ends, a gulf of red velvet kept Jake safely at bay. Strained small talk passed between them. When Jake finally asked him how work had been lately, Nick seized on the opening. "I'm looking at going private sector."

Nick was actually not that bad at lying when he wanted to. Something about Detective Orozco always caught him off guard and made it hard for him to not give away clues. Maybe it was the whole authority thing. The guy came across like his grandfather, real strict, but loving underneath. You wanted to tell him the truth. Plus, he'd been out for so long, Nick couldn't remember what it was like not to be. It meant he was always second guessing himself when talking about Brandon. Smooth and sincere, he lied, "I've been thinking that maybe it's time to leave the GCB."

"About fucking time." Jake laughed, pleased with himself. It was as though he had somehow brought the decision about. "Where?"

"You hear about the carjacking over by Purgatory?" Nick rested his arms on his knees and leaned over and in, like he was involving Jake in a conspiracy. "The guy was a programmer for Frontier Entertainment Services. Now they're stuck halfway through a project and I've been doing their workups and know basically everything about how their machines work." He let his smile light up his black eyes. "But, they're real new in the industry. I wouldn't want to jump ship and find myself out of a job in six months."

"So you want a little help from the Jakester." God, Nick hated it when Jake talked about himself in third person. "Planning ahead? Want to know what kind of backing they have."

"Yeah." Nick took a swallow of wine, scanning Jake's face over the rim of his glass. "And well, I thought, maybe, you might be able to, ya know, check into them for me."

A wolf's grin spread across Jake's face. Smooth jaw line meshed into sharp and prominent cheekbones, a narrow roman nose; that face used to make Nick melt. "It'll cost you." Jake was not talking about money. With Nick and Jake it was never about money, or love, or even sex...only about power. Who had it and who didn't.

He wasn't sure he was prepared to give Jake what he was asking for. "Look, I've been seeing someone else for awhile."

"Wow." Jake slid across the couch. His touch drew fire down Nick's arm. "New boyfriend already?"

Brandon's last phone call still stung in his mind. There were all the unanswered e-mails and ignored IMs. Really, what had they had? A few hot nights, an online flirtation; relationships weren't built on one-night stands. "Not really." God, it hurt to admit that.

"If it's not really, then what's the problem?" Jake slid closer. Sandalwood—his cologne smelled of sandalwood and spices. Memories of what he could do to Nick's body slithered into Nick's brain with the scent. Knees and hips touching, Jake coaxed, "You want to know. I want to fuck. Just for old time's sake."

Oh God, Nick couldn't believe he was about to do this, give in like this. "For old time's sake." He couldn't believe how much he wanted it. It was exciting and revolting at the same time.

"On the floor," Jake hissed just behind his ear, "On your knees for me."

He slid off the couch. "Yes, Jake." Never master, never sir…Jake wanted his name to be what caused fear and respect.

"Take off your clothes." There would be no foreplay, no passionate kisses, no excited touches, only obedience.

Slowly, like he'd been taught, Nick slid the jacket off his frame. "Yes, Jake." Folding it he placed it on the floor by his knees. Vest and tie came next. Nick's fingers worked down the front of his shirt. As he undressed himself the echo of Jake's shoes on the hardwood floor retreated. Nick knew better than to ask, although he was pretty certain what Jake was after. Jake returned as he started on his slacks. Everything went neatly into the pile. Jake hated disorder.

"We're going to play a little game, toy-boy." Eyes kept straight forward and cast slightly down, Nick could hear Jake moving behind him. "I'm going to let you stroke yourself. What you're going to do is hold your mouth open real wide." They'd played this game many times. "I'm going to put my cock in your mouth. And you can't touch it. If I feel your tongue, lips or any part of your mouth on me, this ends and you don't get to get off at all." Leaning in, staring into Nick's eyes, Jake asked, "Are we clear?"

It was a challenge. A perverse game of "Operation" and Jake's cock was the buzzer. "Yes, Jake."

Nick opened his mouth, stretching his jaw wide, lips curling back over his teeth. Jake stepped up. Unbuttoning his fly in front of Nick's face, Jake smiled. He pulled his cock free and placed the very tip of it in Nick's mouth. The u-bend piercing dangled just above his tongue. Nick had watched Jake get pierced, back behind the head of his cock, watched it cut into that sensitive skin. It was always so hard not to set the little piece of metal swinging.

Touching himself lightly, Jake ordered, "Play with your cock, toy-boy. Jack yourself off."

Nick could taste come as it leaked from the head of Jake's cock and dripped on his tongue. His own hand slid along his cock. Working the frost under his skin, he wanted to close down and suck so bad. But he could do this. His brain fell into the old patterns. He wouldn't fail. He'd please Jake, whatever it took. If he pleased Jake, Jake would do wonderful things. God, it was so hard not to give in. "Come on, toy-boy. Speed it up. At this rate you're never going to get off. If I'm ready before you've finished, you ain't getting off."

As his hand ran up his own chest, Nick pulled on himself. Twisting his cock in his hand, alternatively rubbing his balls and nipples with the other, he fueled himself with memories. He couldn't see the one he was with. Thoughts of Jake had always done it before. Tonight they gave him nothing. Recalling his first time with Brandon, the patio, the salt air, being kissed and touched, that made him tremble. And the hearse, in the back of Querida with that low, rumbling voice in his ear urging him on as he was pounded...chills tightened his stomach. Brandon's tongue ravaged his mouth in his mind. Ghosts of Brandon's hands explored his body. His shoulders jerked as he hissed. Fighting the primal desire to close down on Jake's dick, or pull off and scream, Nick's brain imploded.

He'd done it. Nick was good at this game. His black eyes drifted up to Jake's. "Damn, you got jizz all over my Braganos. That's three-hundred-seventy-bucks worth of shoe, toy-boy." A red tongue wandered across those thin lips. They both knew what was coming next. "Lick it off."

Lowering himself to the floor, Nick did as he was told. His tongue ran across mahogany-colored calfskin. As he licked he imagined it was Brandon's cock. Brandon said he loved the way Nick gave head. Lapping at his head and shaft, Nick would make his dark biker moan. He'd whimper and sigh as Nick toyed with his cock. When he sucked, he sucked hard and Brandon would lose control, his whole body spasming with ecstasy as he came. Why did he have to fuck that up? Bitter leather and dust mixed with the musky taste of his own come.

Jake's hand was under Nick's chin, fingers digging into his neck, dragging him back to now. "What a good toy-boy you are." Snake's eyes came level with his own. "Grab your ankles. Put your ass in the air." Nick assumed the position as bid.

The silk of Jake's pink Forzieri tie sang as he pulled it off his neck. Shaking his head, he moved behind Nick. "Good thing I wore one of the cheap ones today." Jake twisted the silk in figure eights, binding Nick's left arm to his left ankle. Digging out the purple tie from the pile of Nick's clothes, he taunted,

"Where'd you get this piece of shit, some discount chain?" Right to right was tied in purple. "I guess it serves its purpose."

The nap of the carpet dug into his cheek. "Yes, Jake." Nick whispered, imagining, wishing it were someone else's name. Heat radiated across Nick's ass as Jake struck him with the flat of his hand. "Ah, God!" Nick writhed fighting the restraints. Another slap landed hot and hard. Jake's fingertips curled, catching the swell of ass cheek. The grip tormented his abused skin. It felt so good. It was almost good enough to stifle the memories of Brandon.

Nick could hear leather sliding through belt loops. "We're going to take this up a notch." Jake popped the belt between his hands, and the crack thrummed anticipation under Nick's skin. The crocodile-embossed Raffaello belt burned across his cheeks. Jake's thumb traced the welt. "Man, your ass is sweet, toy-boy. I love that hot ass. So, so sweet."

The leather snapped and bit into Nick's skin again. "I've missed fucking this ass." A third strike cut across the first two. It stung. It burned. It was so intense. The belt lashed across Nick's ass, back and thighs; his body writhed, pulling against ties binding his arms and legs. Pain crawled across his skin, down his balls and into his cock. "Look at you, getting hard again. You always liked it rough."

Nick's frame went limp as Jake's hands explored the criss-cross pattern. "Yes, Jake." Re-awakening the sting, Jake's fingers admired where Nick's skin bore his marks. Moans came as the pain slowly wound into pleasure.

Jake slid his knee between Nick's thighs, pushing his legs apart. Cold drops of lube caused Nick to hiss and jump. Jake's slick cock slid along his ass as Jake coated himself. The little U-bend snagged Nick's skin. Oh yeah, Nick knew what was coming, wanted what was coming. Impaled by a single thrust, Nick could feel the walls of his body being pushed aside. It felt like hot oil as Jake slid to the core. Shaved balls collided with Nick's sac. All the years they were together were driven home in that thrust. All the nights of playing came welling back. All the hopes he'd had for them shoved their way into his brain. All the hurt when Nick had walked in on Jake and watched as that blonde little piece of trash, hands cuffed behind his back, had taken it in the ass. Jake had looked up, "Hey, toy-boy," he'd hissed, "take off your clothes and suck this pretty thing off."

Nick lunged against the restraints. "Wait, **no**! Jake…" Oh Christ, it had been months. He'd caught Jake fucking someone else. "Stop, you need, you need…"

"I don't need shit, toy-boy." The laughter bit hard into Nick, even harder than the fingers digging into his skin. Harder than the belt that had cut into his flesh.

He begged, pleading, "Please, Jake, stop! Red! Goddamn it, Red!"

"Oh, yeah, my little toy-boy, struggle for me." He slammed into Nick again, his hips slapping against Nick's ass, nails digging into his hips. He pushed into Nick with long deep strokes. "Try and get away. It ain't gonna happen. You're all mine and there's not a damn thing you can do about it."

The carpet ground into Nick's face and knees. Musty fibers clawed into Nick's nose and mouth. Jake pulled back, teasing his entrance with the thick head, then shoved it in deeply, relishing Nick's protests. He suffocated on the smell of the rug as Jake taunted him, grew rigid, exploded inside Nick's ass.

Jake withdrew, settling back on his knees. His hand traced the welts he'd marked on Nick's skin.

Cringing under the touch, Nick shouted, "Fuck, Jake, I said stop!"

"So?" Jake snagged the belt off the floor where he'd dropped it. He slid the leather through the loops "You've said stop before. You never meant it." Shirttails were tucked into pants as Jake spoke.

Nick spat out a hank of hair that had found its way into his mouth. "Yes I did." Nick's chest heaved. The next sentence came out as a sob. "And our safe word, I used our safe word."

Jake buttoned his khakis. "Oh crap, that's why you were screaming out 'red.' I forgot all about that." He laughed. "Is that what you're all upset about? Get over it, you're not hurt."

"How do you know? You slut, fucking that trash I found you with raw. How dare you put me at risk now?" It was hard to sound righteous when he was tied up on the floor naked. "You bastard, I can't believe I didn't walk out on you sooner!"

For a moment everything was quiet. Then came Jake's voice, low and menacing, "Thanks for reminding me." Jake knelt next to Nick's head. He toyed with the long black hair spilling around Nick's body. "You know what? You're just a whiny little toy-boy. What a pain in the ass you are. Dumping me like that, I'll have to teach you a lesson." Standing, he fumbled for his keys in his pocket. "Sleep tight."

He was leaving? "Jake! Jake! Where the fuck are you going?" There was no answer, just the sound of expensive shoes across hardwood floor. No, this wasn't happening. Jake wouldn't be that stupid. "You're joking, right?"

The latch clicked. Rolling his head, Nick blinked from the stream of light from the door. Sunglasses on, keys out, Jake blew him a kiss as he stepped through.

"Don't leave me tied up, Jake!" Nick screamed as the door slammed shut. It was a joke, a really bad joke, but a joke. It had to be a joke. When he heard the Miata's engine rev, he knew it was anything but.

Everything was sore. Oh God, he was alone. This was so wrong. Nick twisted onto his side scraping his back against the coffee table on the way down. His hands were on the outside of his legs, the ties knotted between wrist and ankle. Grunting and pulling he managed to wriggle one of the bindings to the front of his leg. More effort rewarded him with the same position on the other. Now that his hands were relatively close to each other, he drew his knees up to his chest and began to work the knots. The slick fabric slipped through his fingers time and time again. With each tug the bindings gave a little more. Finally, when his hands were cramping, his legs falling asleep, the first came loose. With one hand free the other soon followed.

Time meant nothing to him as he lay on the carpet. All he could smell was old wool. All he could feel was the scratch of the fibers on his back. His face and knees burned from the abrasions. Pain danced through his joints as he stretched. Invisible bees stung his veins as the blood rushed back in. Nausea finally drove him into the bathroom where he retched. Once the convulsions had died down to dry heaves, Nick threw himself into the shower. Sitting on the floor of the tub, with his arms crushed about his knees, the scalding stream loosed his joints and tears. He stayed there until the hot water tank ran dry.

CHAPTER THIRTEEN

With a practiced flip, Brandon's keys sailed across the room and landed on the kitchen counter. Home was above a garage out in the boonies of the boonies. Narrow living room, efficiency kitchen, tiny bedroom, and even tinier bath...the kind of place only college kids and single cops would rent. Nothing matched, although it wasn't quite cinderblocks and 2x4s for bookshelves. Cast-offs from other people's lives furnished Brandon's. A black leather couch had a few thin spots now. The same went for the tubular steel and grey leather recliner. Faux ebony laminate on the entertainment center screamed cheap, but functional.

The place was a sauna. It always was during summer. Protesting, the window unit wheezed to life as Brandon ruthlessly cranked it down. He stripped his shirt and tossed it on the couch. Shoved into one corner of the living room was a black metal student desk. Brandon slid into a patched office chair and flipped on the laptop. The only new-bought items were the electronics. Shit, even those were Fry's close-outs. One message flashed on his machine. Shayna needed new clothes, could he send some extra money with the support payment this time? Sighing, he snagged his checkbook and pen from the drawer; might as well do it sooner than later.

On every spare inch of bookshelf, every exposed bit of refrigerator, were pictures of a little girl. An infant rolled on the floor or slept in her swing or snuggled in a woman's arms. She toddled off to chase the cat, or sat with a wicked grin and a bowl of cheerios over her head. Swinging in the park in one, first day of school was captured in another. The only time he really ever got to see his Shayna grow up was in other peoples' pictures. Photos were all he had to fill the gaps between infrequent treks up north.

At least she got to see her grandparents a lot. Both pieces of his former family lived a few hours north of Los Angeles. Edith, his step-mom, helped Shayna's mother with babysitting and summers when school was out. Both he and Dian realized their mistake the morning after they'd eloped to Vegas. But then Dian was pregnant, and he'd just started on the force, and hell, life just got complicated sometimes. It had taken them more than a year to disentangle themselves. Dian had been happy enough to see him go.

There was no way in hell he'd ever tell Edith why he had to leave. She, unlike his ex-wife, had never forgiven him for walking out on his marriage. So he left her believing her husband's son was just a class-A jerk. Maybe she was right. The pictures were not meant for comfort, but as reminders of what he was missing by not being there. Edith sent thick packets of them at regular intervals. Brandon would take what he could get.

Only one picture did not feature the blue-eyed pixie. Crammed between the monitor and speakers was a small plastic frame. Hugo's, both over- and under-exposed; Nick and Brandon sat at the bar with goofy grins. A quick snapped pic off Nicky's phone. He'd e-mailed it to Brandon that same night. Damn, he wished he had better software or printer. Grainy and off-color; again, he'd take what he could get.

What the fuck was he going to do about Nicky? God, he was still so pissed. And it was unfair, he knew it, he just couldn't help it. Late Monday he'd finally returned Nicky's frantic calls. He'd slipped back to his place, allegedly to catch a little sleep…four days on meant on-call, not that he had to be at the station the entire time, although sometimes it worked out that way. Over and over Brandon had screamed out, "Why?"

There was no answer that Nicky could give that would have satisfied him. Nick could have said it would have saved ten thousand lives, and Brandon still would have shot back, "But why the fuck did you tell him?" Nicky had been reduced to chanting a crushed mantra of contrition. The parting shot, just before he'd cut off the call, had been particularly hateful. "You queer little piece of shit, how dare you ruin my life?" If there were a way to turn back the clock and take it back, Brandon would. He knew he had no right to ask Nicky to risk his own neck that way. Shit, the guy was the closest thing to a suspect that Vegas Metro had. They had to be leaning on him hard. It was unfair. And it just hadn't mattered at that moment.

Orozco was a good detective, tenacious. He'd hounded Brandon into pulling up Mike Ducmagian in the system as a "favor." That, itself, could land him in hot water with the department. California required reasons to pull someone on the system. Nasties selling movie stars' warrant/conviction records and a few cops caught using the system to stalk former girlfriends had occasioned that. Certain records, like O.J. or the Govenator, would flag if you ran them. You actually had to choose from a list of options before the result would display. Ongoing investigation wasn't exactly a lie in this case. It wasn't his investigation though. Cooperation between jurisdictions was considered a good thing, but there were channels it was supposed to go through. Most likely a reprimand and a slap on the wrist would be the result if it ever came up. Still, he was working through his probation as a detective and something like that could derail him.

He'd wanted this so bad. All his life he'd wanted to be a cop. And all his life as a cop he'd wanted to be a detective. He'd busted his ass, showing up to classes still in uniform and on two hours sleep, just so he could have the BA that might push him over the top on candidates. Vice was shit work to most Ds. You ran through your tour as fast as possible and moved on to something more prestigious. Popping prostitutes, staking out men's bathrooms and investigating underage cigarette sales just didn't have the glamour of a good homicide. Brandon didn't care. He still loved it. Being sent back down on the beat wasn't an option.

He grabbed the phone off the charger and sat staring at it. Twenty times in the last three days he'd picked up the phone to say he was sorry. Twenty times he'd hung it up. Not because he didn't want to tell Nicky, but because he was just too embarrassed by what an ass he'd been. Brandon didn't want to hear what Nicky's first words might be. His own imagination had conjured enough versions. The problem was, he deserved whatever Nicky wanted to throw at him. He deserved it even if it was 'I never want to see you again.' That was the one possibility that Brandon didn't want to face. Once again the phone went back into the dock.

Outside, the groan of decrepit stairs told him he had a visitor. He opened the door in time to catch a meaty guy in a custom suit raising his hand to knock. Two men were jammed onto the tiny landing. The suit was balding and had shaved his hair down to fuzz to hide it. His companion was about the same age, somewhere toward middle, taller and probably Asian decent. Both could stand to lose a few pounds. The taller one held a plate of cookies. Brandon would give odds that they were chocolate chip and baked this afternoon. "Can I help you?"

A badge came up. "Detective Bryant, LAPD. This is Detective Chin. Do you have a moment?"

God, he was winding up on the wrong side of these interviews way too often these days. "Why, you make a wrong turn on the two-ten and wind up at Mrs. Fields?" What the hell was up now? These guys were two entire counties outside their jurisdiction. "Need directions on how to find your way back to civilization?" As he was teasing, he held open the screen and motioned them in.

Chin set the plate on the counter and swept thick black hair from his eyes with the back of his hand. "Well, we, ah, went to the front house first. Your landlady said we should bring them up as long as we were coming this way." They had to walk through the tiny galley kitchen to get to the living space. It was a lousy set up, but the rent was dirt cheap. And fringe benefits, like cookies or an occasional meal, made up for some of the hassles.

Bryant filched one as he passed. "She insisted we share."

"Yeah, Deputy Ferris would have liked it that way." Mrs. Ferris only rented to cops. Just after Brandon'd walked out on his wife, he'd found the listing tacked to the department bulletin board. Back then the rent had been a stretch. It was better now, but not by a whole lot. When his pay went up so did the support payments. Maturity had brought better money management skills, though.

Once, having come to pester him about being late, Mrs. Ferris had picked up a picture of Shayna. After that she'd never mentioned he had sometimes paid the rent a little tardy. Again, he was better at that now. Occasionally, a bag with a girly-girl outfit would show up on the stoop with a note that she'd bought the wrong size for her granddaughters. Hardly...they were all in their late teens now.

"Deputy?" Bryant chose the arm of the couch, leaving his partner to fend somewhere in the middle.

"San Bernardino Sheriff, retired. Stroked out just after retirement. Died a few years ago." Folding himself into the recliner, Brandon asked, "So what the fuck are you city slickers doing out here?"

"Well, we tried to catch you at the station, but there was an overturned rig on the 10. That slowed us down by about two and a half hours." Bryant caught one half of the cookie as it dropped. Little rivers of sweat trickled down from the buzz cut. "And this place isn't the easiest to find." There were some nice areas on the border between Riverside and San Bernardino counties. This wasn't exactly one of them. Weed-choked yards, junker cars, dirt instead of sidewalks; half the houses didn't even have numbers.

"And if someone had remembered to charge his phone, we would have called the station and had you wait." Bryant flipped his partner off.

Enough with the niceties, this wasn't a social call. "Okay, do I need to play twenty questions or are you going to tell me what's so important that it was worth that drive?"

"You were looking into a guy named Mike Ducmagian." Chin leaned forward, arms on his knees. "You ran him on the system."

Fuck, "Yeah, why?" Ducmagian was flagged?

"We're with OCID... Organized Crime Intelligence Division. Anyways, this guy Ducmagian you were checking up on, we're kinda interested in him."

Cold fingers worked across the inside of his chest. Holy crap, OCID was like Hoover's FBI; a sucking black hole of information. The current incarnation was a result of the merger of Organized Crime and Administrative Vice Divisions. Word on the LA beat was that the wedding had combined the worst of both and left nothing good behind. Some of that might just be cop paranoia, but then again some of it might not. There were lots of rumors about how they did or did not use the information they hoarded and how they got it. Some of their activities might not be strictly legal. Again maybe true, maybe not. The only ones who knew for sure were OCID themselves. They didn't talk about it.

Nervously he asked, "Why?" Internal Affairs divisions throughout California had wet dreams about the contents of OCID files. Spying on other officers, looking for skeletons in the closet, was allegedly a hobby of the division. They dug in departmental sandboxes across the state. The last place any cop wanted was to be on the wrong side of OCID. The last place Brandon wanted to be was on the wrong side of OCID.

The two detectives traded glances. Bryant nodded, and then turned his attention to Brandon. "Why don't you show us yours and we'll show you ours."

It wasn't as if he had much choice. If he didn't come clean they'd start asking around and realize there was no investigation. That could end up as a report for unauthorized access. Even something as minor as a call to his captain, coming from OCID, would be enough to bust him down. They wouldn't even have to say why they had issues with him. A mention about some possibly-not-kosher activity discovered in connection with one of their investigations could ruin him.

There was a small upside. Crime was not solved by science. Science just capped what you already knew. And you knew things because people talked. The trick of it was figuring out who was talking to whom. If you offered up a sacrifice of information you could get in tight with OCID. They used other officers in much the same way Brandon used his small stable of whores and junkies: information. And they believed in a somewhat warped form of reciprocity. If you were tight with OCID they could be an unending, if sporadic, fountain of knowledge.

Unlike the Fed's info spiders, OCID didn't make their own busts. They didn't want the publicity. They were so good at avoiding the spotlight that most of the residents of Los Angeles didn't even know they existed. If something was going down they doled it to one of their stable; walking quietly away while some other cop took credit for the collar.

And if you wanted something done outside your jurisdiction, OCID often knew who could do it for you. Unlike "regular" cops they didn't often worry about little things like city boundaries. Because, well, organized crime didn't worry about little things like jurisdiction. Exchanges were always on a quid pro quo basis...a lot more of your quid than their quo, but what the hell. "One of my primo contacts at Nevada Gaming Control is a person of interest in a homicide in Vegas. I was giving Metro a little help so they won't ride my boy too hard."

Two sets of eyebrows went up. "Who got capped?" Partners were like married couples; the longer they were together the more they seemed like one person.

They didn't know. It wasn't often a lowly probationary D could trump OCID on info. "Mike Ducmagian."

"No fucking shit! When did that go down?"

"Last Thursday. Vegas Metro is crawling up my guy's ass 'cause he spoke to Ducmagian about some slot chips before he got whacked."

"Fuck!" Chin was seriously pissed.

Now it was time to see if they'd live up to their end of the bargain. "So why is OCID all hot and bothered over the late Mr. Ducmagain?"

Again a look and a nod from Bryant, probably the senior of the two. Chin answered, "He's been keeping some not so nice company these last couple of months. We've logged him with Reggie Mendoza aka Renaldo Mendoza aka about half a dozen other aliases. Anyway, we suspect our dear Reggie of being in with the Mexican Mafia." Straight-up guys they were. Most were. Only the cops on TV got overtly territorial. Criminals didn't give a rat's ass where one beat began and another ended. "We're keeping an eye on who he's been associating with. Our boy's been getting active lately."

Brandon tended to think better on his feet. He stood and wandered around the room. "Wow." Well that would make some sense...at least as far as why the pair drove all the way out to Riverside for a chat. Drifting to the fridge, Brandon popped it open and held a cold can towards Chin. "So then you got all wet when Vice in Riverside made an inquiry?"

The detective held out his hand. Brandon tossed him the beer, which Chin promptly passed to Bryant. Another followed. "Yep, all dressed up and apparently no place to go."

"Wow, la Eme, that's heavy duty shit."

Over an hour, and a couple of beers later, Brandon had given them everything he knew about Ducmagian and his murder. It wasn't all that much really. That he'd used to work for the GCB was news to them. He hadn't been the main focus of their investigations...just a person that they thought they should keep an eye on. They'd been planning on getting around to him when they had time. Now he was dead in what was looking, at least to Brandon's eye, like a hit. In exchange for what he knew, and an implicit promise to feed them more if he found it, Bryant had agreed to call Orozco first thing. Some of the heat should fall off Nicky if he followed through.

At one point Chin had picked up one of Shayna's photos. "Cute kid. Lives with her mom?" Brandon grunted in assent. The blue highway, in any incarnation, was a matrimonial demolition derby. Only the strongest survived intact. "Almost lost mine this month; took the kids and headed up to Frisco to her mom's. Finally had to jump Southwest and get down on my hands and knees to beg her to come back." He shook his head as he set the picture back on the shelf. "No matter what anybody says, it was worth it. I can't imagine living without her...being alone all the time."

A weak smile was meant as apology. It was pretty obvious he'd just summed up Brandon's life.

CHAPTER FOURTEEN

Work was a blur. Nick hardly knew where he'd been on Friday. Stumbling out the door in a rumpled shirt and faded black dockers, it took all Nick's concentration just to make it through his assignments. Every machine he touched had to be logged; time in and out, place, floor location and serial number. Nick's records were a shambles. When he'd turned in his reports that afternoon, they were in such a shoddy shape that his manager couldn't believe they were his. Nick's attention to detail was renowned in the department. New personnel were shown his log sheets as examples of how they should be kept. Other than mumbling that maybe he was coming down with something, he had no reasonable response to offer when asked why. That, combined with his scruffy appearance, earned him a tirade and a verbal warning. He just stared over the lab manager's shoulder, responding "okay," whenever it seemed appropriate. Disgusted, the man had thrown him out of his office telling him to quit partying so late.

Saturday, Nick crawled out of bed around ten. The previous night's sandwich was still uneaten on the table. He wouldn't have bothered to get dressed except his friend Sean was helping him install a new sound system in the hearse. They'd arranged the appointment days ago. Most of the work on Querida Nick preferred to do himself. Electrical was just one of those things he didn't like messing with...not on a car. Disk changer, extra battery, sub-woofer and premium speakers; the works were going in. Sean was beyond excited that the parts had finally arrived. It had been hard to find an aftermarket system that would fit in the Caddie's dash without extensive modification. Or at least it had been hard finding one meeting Nick's particular tastes. He'd refused to let Nick back out of their meeting.

On the way to the garage, Nick dropped off the living room rug at Goodwill. He told himself that it was time to get a new one anyway, something better, nicer. Every time he walked through the room the dusty, musty scent of the carpet had almost suffocated him. The redecorating mood had struck about midnight during a bout of insomnia. Nick had rearranged the living room half a dozen times, dragging the couch and chairs about the room. By three a.m. the furniture was all back in the same place it always had been. Now the floor was bare.

A slew of off-the-shelf speakers were already installed. That part was easy. Nick had cut the panels when he re-did the interior. The space behind them was adequate for low profile speakers. A new set of really high-quality ones and the sub-woofer would go just behind the seat. The one thing a hearse didn't lack was room in the back. In preparation for the install, Sean had worked out the placement and support structure. Nick looked at the schematic, but never saw it.

As much as he liked working on his car, his heart wasn't in it today. Sean and his partner crawled through the hearse connecting wires and tweaking settings. Nick sat on the battered truck bench that served as seating and flipped through the latest PC Magazine. Nothing held his attention for long. Every time Sean pestered him about did he want this or that, Nick would mumble "whatever works," and leave it at that. Finally his friend quit asking.

Just before lunch the phone on his hip rang. A real ring, polyphonic re-master of a 30s-era phone. Hope died when he saw the number wasn't Brandon's. Hope died a second time when he realized he knew the number—Jake's work.

System installed and Sean paid, Nick slid the hearse into a shopping center not far from Jake's office. He knew the place well. They'd often met for coffee at the overpriced chain store. Mainstream America cramming its buying habits down the throat of the western world. Give him a greasy spoon where the waitresses called you "honey" over a place with forced ambiance.

He saw Jake's car long before he saw Jake. Parking was always an issue with a vehicle as big as Querida. Easing her into a slot at the far end of the lot where there weren't many cars, he noted the Miata ahead of him. Jake had found his favorite place at the end of an aisle. A small planter, two spaces and then the drive; if he took both no one could park next to him and ding a door. The spots on the other side of the driving lane ran perpendicular to where the Miata was parked. For a while Nick just sat and stared over the hood at the little blue car.

Jake had refused to just drop the stuff off at his house. It was out of his way. The reports might get wet because it was supposed to rain. What if somebody stole them? There were dogs and kids in the neighborhood that might rip it up. Nick had finally agreed to the coffee shop just to end the conversation. Now he regretted it. He really didn't want to see Jake. But, if he didn't get the stuff now, Jake would keep calling. That wouldn't be good either. He sighed, forcing himself from the sanctuary of his hearse.

Singles and couples swarmed on the patio enjoying the afternoon. The temperature was dropping to something more balmy than hellish with the advent of rain. Jake sat at one of the tables, two white paper cups with brown sleeves on the table in front of him. He was dressed for a Saturday at the office; khaki shorts, blue polo shirt and loafers without socks. Jake smiled when he saw Nick approach. "I bought you a latte."

Nick shoved his hands into the pockets of his oil stained jeans. "I don't like lattes, Jake." Battered T-shirt and skull-patterned Vans, also without socks, made up Nick's attire. Jake had probably studied his outfit to achieve the correct air of casual indifference. Nick had just been indifferent.

"Sure you do." Jake slid a vacant seat out for Nick. Metal legs grated harsh across the concrete. The sound made Nick's shoulders tighten. "That's what you always have when we got coffee."

Nick ignored the proffered chair. "That's because it was what you always ordered for me." He looked out across Sahara Road. More traffic was heading in toward the Strip than away from it. People flocked to buy a faint chance of what might happen in exchange for what they had in their hands. An entire city built upon separating fools from their money.

"Okay, then what do you want? I'll get it for you." As Jake raised his own cup, the pinky ring caught the sun. Its twin lived in the bottom of Nick's jewelry case, an ivory-inlayed box that had belonged to his gramps. The ring had never been worn; gold and his skin didn't get along. Probably could get fifty, sixty bucks for it at a pawn shop. That sounded like an acceptable plan for the evening.

"Nothing, I'm good." This was bullshit. Why was he acting all nice with Jake? He owed Jake nothing. "Just give me my fucking reports." He snapped loud enough that the people at the next table looked up.

Jake hated public scenes. He flashed a smile to the couple, and then glared at Nick. "You look like shit, toy-boy. You've got to get yourself some B-12 if you're going to be pulling all-nighters at the computer." It sounded like he was trying to be soothing. "Come on, sit down. Coffee will do you good."

Nick didn't lower his voice. "My name is not toy-boy. It's Nick." He'd give Jake a scene the man would never forget. "Give me my reports, Jake. You said you had them. I want them now."

"What the fuck is your issue today?" The redhead hissed.

"My issue...my issue?!" Nick slammed his hands down on the table. Twin waves of coffee washed across its surface. Jake jumped up, barely avoiding the caramel-colored waterfall. His chair clattered to the ground, nicking the table behind him. A trio of coeds grabbed their coffee to avoid the same fate suffered by Jake's. "You fuckhead!" As Nick came around the table Jake retreated until they had exchanged places. "You know the rules!"

Stumbling back as he stepped off the sidewalk, Jake shot back, "You know what I never liked? Your fucking rules." Nick followed. "So many rules, it ruined all my fun." Voice taunting, Jake kept talking. "The one I really hated, that stupid fucking 'no glove, no love' rule. You and I, we moved past that, remember?" Several people were staring now. A few were pretending nothing was happening.

Nick glared at the other patrons. Some, but not all, shied away. Oh, yeah, look hard folks, a gay catfight—not every day that your four-dollar cup of joe got you this kind of entertainment. Keep watching, it's about to get better. He punctuated his accusations with his arms. "You fucking left! You left and I was still tied up, asshole...tied up face down on the floor. Christ, I could have gotten hurt and no one would have been there."

"Aw boo-hoo, I'm devastated." Sarcasm thrummed in Jake's tone. "I took your spare key. I came back in the morning on my way to work. You'd already gotten yourself undone and gone. Put it back under the rock for you." Retreating again, putting patio furniture between himself and Nick, he spat, "Besides you and fucking Houdini...I've seen you do your trick where you get someone to tie you up and then you get free."

By now the manager was out to see what was happening. "What if something had happened?" The other patrons were giving them a wide birth, vacating tables left and right. "People have died from shit like that! I ought to turn you in for it you son-of-a-bitch."

When Jake was pressed, he got mean. "Oh yeah, go to the police. Officer I asked my big, bad, gay boyfriend to tie me up, spank my ass, fuck me like mad, but then he didn't use a condom and left me all by my wittle wonesome, so I'm all violated now. You're just a whiny pirate! You always were! I don't know why I even bothered to put up with your shit for all those years. I only asked you to move in with me so I wouldn't have to hear you whine about 'it's a work day, I can't stay up.' You're such a goddamn baby! Drove me fucking nuts with your pissing and moaning about everything. It certainly wasn't worth getting head first thing in the morning!" Jake grabbed a manila envelope from the ground near his feet. He pitched it at Nick. "Here's your fucking reports." Nick grunted as they slammed into his chest. "Get out of my sight!"

As Nick stalked past the manager, he shot out, "Don't bother, I'm leaving." Portable phone in hand, the girl was obviously debating whether to call the cops. She watched him until he got into the hearse. Then she turned her attention to Jake who was trying to mop up the earlier spill. Nick bet he'd get all her sympathy and probably a cup on the house, regular customer and all that. What a shit Jake was. How could he have ever thought they had something together? Jake had never treated him any better than he had Thursday night. Always thinking of himself, always putting everybody else at risk. Nick was so much better off without him.

Of course, now he had no one. That hurt. Alone was not something Nick handled well. And knowing, just the knowing, that he'd never meant more than a convenient lay to Jake was devastating. If you cared for someone, you looked out for them. It was painfully obvious Jake had never cared.

Twisting the key in the ignition, Nick glanced up. That little blue piece of shit was still straddling two spaces. Mouth tightening, he remembered when Jake purchased it. Wandering from lot to lot, haggling. An entire weekend blown on car shopping because that's what Jake had wanted. Jake had gone prepared with an Edmund's Report. He knew what his Acura was worth in trade. He knew what the car he wanted was worth. He knew what he was willing to pay. When Nick had pointed out the Miata with the jeweled blue paint, Jake had damn near drooled. After that it wasn't so much which car as it was what toys he could load onto it.

While Nick counted ceiling tiles, Jake had negotiated a Bose six-speaker sound system, parchment leather trimmed seats, leather-wrapped steering wheel and the appearance package with large sills, dam and guards. Custom rims had gone on not a month after purchase. Every Thursday the Miata went to the car wash. Every third week it got waxed. A micro scratch on the door from one of Nick's rings had sent her into the shop for a touchup. He wasn't allowed to wear his combat boots in the Miata for fear they'd snag the carpet.

The clutch went soft under his foot. He palmed the column shift, sliding it deftly into first gear. Nick released the parking brake. It gave with a pop and a jolt. He blew out the breath he was holding. Looking back at the coffee shop, he could see Jake was absorbed in fussing over his coffee-spattered shorts. Not for long. Nick floored the gas pedal. Querida lunged forward. Just before he hit, he jammed the clutch and brake down. Tons of steel went screeching into molded side panels. His chest thumped against the steering wheel. The Miata bounced off the front end of the hearse. The impact shot it up into the planter, ripping the undercarriage.

It was probably the most satisfying crunch Nick had ever heard.

People poured out of the various businesses. Nick looked up to find Jake standing next to his window. "My fucking car! You fucking hit my car!" Distraught did not even begin to cover

Jake's state. Nick hadn't just hit it; he'd damn near totaled it. The Miata's profile was no wider than the front end of the Cadillac. The right side looked like a giant set of wolf's teeth had sunk into the body. Its muffler hung up on the foot-high planter, rear driver's side tire wrapped around a decorative boulder; there was no way Jake was driving the car home. His face was purple as he swung towards Nick. He screamed, "You better have fucking insurance that's going to cover this!"

Nick rubbed his chest. Damn, he'd bruised himself and it hurt. "You would know, Jake." He shrugged. "It's what you told me to buy."

CHAPTER FIFTEEN

A graphite wall of water bisected the purple-blue sky. The scent of old tin crawled from the dust as it begged for release. Sunset licked gold into the boiling clouds. Where sand touched air the horizon frothed red, black and orange. Low-voiced seductions rumbled through the evening. They bounced off the hills and the canyons and the buildings. The world waited in metal-sharp relief for the promised touch of rain.

Dark-thirty fell in the desert as Nick turned into the drive. The thick volume of financials rested on the bench seat by his hip. Loose metal sounds emanated from the front end of the hearse. It was going to be a bitch figuring out what he'd damaged. A security guard from the adjacent Bank of Nevada had intervened between Jake and Nick, getting Nick's insurance for both Jake and the owners of the mall. Nick had managed to convince the guy that he'd been so upset over the fight that he just hadn't realized the hearse was in drive. That had forestalled the police being called. Good thing, or he'd still be in that damn parking lot.

Now he'd have to choose which would consume his Sunday: Frontier or Querida. Reports first, and then survey the hearse when his eyes started crossing...it sounded like a reasonable plan. Slamming on the brakes for the second time that day, Nick nearly ran over the black Harley blocking his garage. Brandon. Brandon was in Vegas? The tickle of invisible spider's legs ran across his skin. He was shaking so hard he almost fell out of the Cadillac as he opened the door.

The dark haired biker was sprawled in one of the mismatched, wrought-iron chairs residing on the broken stone patio. A six-pack, minus one, sat at his feet. He took a swig from the missing bottle then gestured with the butt-end across the small yard. "You need to mow." There was little grass hardy enough to survive the inattention it received. Most of the backyard was taken up by the patio. Nick had spent a good portion of one summer cobbling together an ersatz mosaic of cast-off concrete, brick and stones. A twisted mesquite tree threw a bit of feeble shade at midday; when darkness fell it was full of shadow. The empty slid into its vacant slot. Brandon snagged two more bottles, holding one out for Nick. "Sit, I need to talk to you."

"Look, Brandon, its okay..." A cold nothingness dropped into his belly as the desert teased lightning from the sky. Seven breaths to count before the thunder spoke low.

"Nicky, sit." Using the beer to indicate the seat, Brandon continued, "I said some really hurtful things to you. I should have apologized sooner. I just kept thinking about what an ass I'd been and that you have every right to tell me to just go to hell. I had no right to expect you to not say anything to Detective Orozco." As the true sun moved behind the horizon, the false sunrise of the Strip polluted the sky. Fence lizards scrambled near the back wall. Their scurrying was the only sound for a time. "I thought you deserved to hear it from me in person. I'm sorry it took me almost a week to do it."

"It's okay, it doesn't matter. I should have just kept my mouth shut." The bottle was still outstretched. Nick took it and dropped into another chair. Sighing, he twisted off the cap and tossed it towards the wall. After a long pull, he added, "I should have just told him to get lost." Nick wasn't sure who he was talking about.

"Are you nuts, Nicky?" Brandon's voice came out of shadow. "Fuck, the guy was thinking you were in on it. You were the last guy who talked to the vic and he was in a parking lot of a club where you were at. Nobody knows why, but he was there."

Blue white light tore the air. "He was looking for me." Five breaths this time until a rumble.

"How do you know that?" Brandon's voice was low, wary.

"The EPROM." Nick took another swallow. "He was there so I could get the EPROM from HQ."

Brandon's shoulders tensed. Voice still cautious, Brandon probed, "That's what he said in his call?" Brandon leaned forward, bottle dangling between his knees. "You told him to be there?"

Implications woven under Brandon's tone snapped Nick upright in his chair. "No!" Oh shit, what did Brandon think was going on? "No, I didn't know he was going to be there." Backtracking, he explained, "It hit me just before Duke's funeral why he would have been at Purgatory—'cause he knew I was there. And he was so pissed that I wouldn't get the chip before then. There had to be something to do with that EPROM, something he had to make sure no one found. I still have it. I ran it the other day. It's gaffed."

"Gaffed?" Now Brandon just sounded confused.

"Fucked with, programmed as a cheat. All slots are electronic these days. The EPROM tells the machine when to stop the reels and the payouts based on the money played and the specifics of the program." He was being technical because he wasn't sure he could handle anything more. "The gaff in the chip is the place where they fucked with the programming."

Suspicion had vanished from Brandon's voice. "You can mess with the programming inside slot machines?"

"Oh, hell, yeah." Relieved, Nick sagged back down. "One of the biggest slot cheats was an ESD agent. He reprogrammed a series of EPROMS. You'd put the coins in the machine in a certain sequence; say one, two, three, two, two, three and it would trigger the machine to pay out big."

"How did he get caught, someone else pull one of those chips and test it?"

"No actually, he changed his MO and it screwed him. He probably could have gotten away with the slot scam for a long time, but he wrote an algorithm to predict Keno numbers and that's where he was busted. It was a real embarrassment to the agency. One of our own agents going bad; I mean that publicly. There's always scuttlebutt about which chiefs are getting payola for easy approvals and that stuff. But this was major press. Anyway, something big is up, I just know it. I went to Duke's funeral and his exes were talking about all this money he's been throwing around before he died. It just didn't make sense. Duke never had money. So I've been looking into things. I had full financials pulled on Frontier."

"The GCB has the resources to do that? Every department I know of is strapped." Brandon shook his head and relaxed back into his seat. "I wish Riverside did. Half the time we're just operating on a hunch. You just go with your gut and let the D.A. work up the financial details."

"Yes and no. The auditing department can, but I couldn't take it through them. They're concerned with what's happening in Nevada. If I had some harder proof, I could take it to them and they'd start a fiscal shakedown since it could impact Nevada. But I have one EPROM and a hunch."

Brandon tipped his beer towards Nick. "So where'd you get it done? E.F. Hutton?"

"Well, kind of." God, this was going to be hard to explain. He swallowed, "Jake showed up the other day. He's an investment banker. I had him do it for me. Told him I was thinking about taking a job with Frontier and wanted to make sure they were solvent. I, ah, just picked it up."

"What the fuck were you doing talking to him?" Suddenly everything was very cold.

That was the million dollar question. "I just…I needed the information. It was the only way I knew how to get it."

"There had to be someone else. I don't want you fucking talking to your ex-boyfriend. Hanging out with him, any of it, no! Don't go there. 'Cause, if you start just asking for a favor here or there, then you'll go get coffee and maybe lunch, and then you're fucking back together! Don't do that to me, Nicky. If you want to hang out with him, I'll just fucking leave, 'cause I don't need to deal with that shit. It's either just you and me, or it's not at all."

"Well it's done, okay, don't worry about it. It was nothing. Forget I mentioned it."

Nothing was said for a time. The storm moved closer. The lizards scrambled for cover. Finally, Brandon asked, "You guys go out and have dinner, just for old time's sake?"

"No." Nick stood and downed the last of the beer. Heading towards the back stair and garbage cans, he added, "We didn't go out anywhere." The bottle shattered on impact.

"Oh, so you stayed at home," Brandon's face was cloaked in the blue-black light of evening, "with him?"

Nick shrugged. "Yeah, he came inside, we had a drink, and we talked. Drop it."

"You're the one who brought it up." Now Brandon stood. Thumbs in his pockets, bottle dangling from his left hand, he prodded, "Drinks huh? What one, two... twenty?" His voice was snide.

"We had a couple of drinks. Nothing big. And we talked about getting the reports."

"Really, that's it. No catching up. He didn't try and get to you? I mean, how long were you together?"

"Three years. Yeah we talked a little about the past." Nick started for the stairs. "Drop it!"

Brandon's arm shot out, blocking his path. He shoved his face in front of Nick's, staring into his eyes. "A little chit-chat about the past, a few drinks, talking about the future, asking for favors; sounds like more than nothing to me."

Nick couldn't meet Brandon's gaze. Ducking under Brandon's arm he headed for the house. He was sick of fighting. "It was nothing, okay. Drop it!"

"No! You're lying." Brandon's accusations stung his back. "I can tell. What'd you do? Get all romantic? Make out? Oh, baby I've missed you so much..."

A hand landed on Nick's shoulder and spun him around. The adrenalin from the fight with Jake hadn't wormed out of his veins yet. "I fucking slept with him okay!" Nick spat. "Is that what you wanted to fucking hear?"

Nick was as stunned as Brandon looked. "What?"

Fuck what had he said? Why did he say it? "I'm so sorry. Oh, God, I'm sorry." Retreating up the steps, he tried to explain, "I was weak, and I was lonely and I'd just gotten back from Duke's funeral Thursday, and I left you all those messages and you never called back and there he was."

"You fucking slept with him?" Brandon hadn't moved. "You fucking little slut! We have one little fight and you just can't wait to fucking go hop in the sack with your old boyfriend!"

"What do you mean one little fight?" Nick dug his keys from his jeans and jammed the one for the back door in the lock. "Christ, I thought you dumped me!"

"What the fuck gave you that idea?"

Nick stopped and dropped back down the steps. "I don't know, maybe being called a queer little piece of shit and then told that I've completely fucked up your life." He threw his hands up in exasperation. "What's that supposed to make me think? You won't return my phone calls. You ignore my IMs and e-mails. What the fuck would you think?" That was it, Nick was going inside. Turning to the house, he started back up the stairs. Jake was out of his life, this was going to put Brandon out of his life. Time to drown the evening in a bottle of Jack Daniels.

"Maybe that we were having a fight." Brandon stood at the foot of the stairs. "Three goddamn days, Nicky, it had only been three goddamn days!" Brandon set his hands on Nick's back and shoved him towards the door. "Come on then, you want to fuck let's go."

Moving away, he went up another step. "Stop it, Brandon!" The air was getting heavier with the storm.

"No! You want sex, come on then." Brandon yanked his arm, pitching him against the railing. "I drove four fucking hours to say I'm sorry and find out you've been screwing around... might as well get fucking laid for it!"

Nick swung around and pushed back. "I said stop it! You arrogant bastard! Why is this about you? Always about you? You decide when we're going to be together. You decide if we're a couple. You give me your phone number, but I'm not supposed to use it. You think you can just smile your way back into bed with me. The first time, you hurt me, but I'm not allowed to be pissed off at you." He yelled out his frustration. "You can go walk all over me and it's supposed to be okay! What you said, I don't care if you are gay, how you said it, it was fucking hateful! This whole fucking relationship is running on your goddamn time table. I don't want that! Not with you! Not with anybody else! So don't go be all wounded on me, 'cause you've fucked things up, too."

"Fucking hell," Brandon shoved again. Nick stumbled back on the stairs. "You couldn't have at least waited a while before you decided it was over?"

Struggling to maintain his balance, he fumbled the keys in the lock. "How long was I supposed to wait while you decided if you were ever going to forgive me? A week, a month, a year? Bite me!" He charged through the door. The kitchen was dim and cold. "You tell me I'm shit and I'm just supposed to hang around feeling like no one in the world gives a shit about me while you get yourself straight?" The empty room echoed with his anger. "It's not like we had a relationship anyway...I can't even tell anyone I'm seeing you."

Everything was boiling to the surface, all the disappointment, all the pain, all the hope Nick had kept inside. Two fingers jabbed toward Brandon's chest. "Twice we've been together, twice. And one of those times you're acting like you play for the other fucking team! Whenever I'm with you I feel like we're sneaking around behind my parents' backs. I'm fucking twenty-eight years old; I don't need that high school shit! It's hard being with you, Brandon. If we're alone in bed, everything's great. The moment we step out the door, it's like I don't really exist. We're just buds, hanging out, so it's okay if I ignore Nick, he's a cool guy, he'll understand. I'm not and it's not! I want a boyfriend, not a fuck buddy! I may not be the best looking guy in the world, but if all I wanted was to fuck around I could find someone for that!"

Brandon followed him, yelling. "I've never thought of you as just a fuck buddy! Shit, if that was the case, I wouldn't give a shit who you goddamn slept with. I sure as hell wouldn't be driving to Nevada for it. That's not how I feel, and I'm pissed off as all hell at you!" Brandon slammed the door shut. The kitchen windows rattled from the impact. "How the hell do you expect me to act? You expect me to act like some flame on Queer Eye? Get all kissy with you in the park? The first time I met you I told you, I ain't out! We don't get to play cute little couple!"

Their shouting was drowning out the sound of the approaching thunder. "And the first time I met you I told you I was re-bounding! Fucking three years I was with that asshole, I lived with him for Christ-sakes. And he shows up at my door when I'm about as low as I can get and all the old feelings came back. I thought you dumped me and it hurt, it hurt bad." His voice cracked. "Hurt worse than I ever thought it could. You can't hate me anymore than I hate myself for it." The volume but not the tone of his voice dropped. "I walked out on him because he used me and treated me like shit. And I let him back in for one moment and he uses me and treats me like shit again. I feel like such a fucking moron." His face was hot and flushed. Nick kept telling himself he was not going to cry in front of another guy.

Brandon dragged one of the chairs out from the table. Twirling it on one leg, before straddling it the wrong way, he laced his arms across the back. Distant thunder ticked off the time on the clock. Finally, Brandon broke the silence, "You are a moron, Nicky. A cute one...but a fucking moron." Almost in a whisper, he added "I told you I really liked you, didn't you get it?"

Butt against the tile counter, Nick slid his arms across his chest. "And I really like pizza, but that doesn't mean I have a goddamn relationship with it. Especially not with the way you act. You really like me when we're about to fuck, but the rest of the time you act like I'm barely tolerable. We go out together and you talk to everyone else but me. You can touch me, but if I touch you in public, you freak. What do you expect me to think?" The bitter edge was meant to cut deep. It felt more effective than the screaming and yelling had been.

"It's so hard, Nicky. It's so fucking hard. I wanted to be with you... only you. But I can't do that if I think you're going to be off cheating on me." He could see Brandon struggling to get himself under control; lowering his voice, releasing the white-knuckle grip on the back of the chair. "Okay, so you didn't understand, and I didn't understand and everything has gotten all fucked up here. I'm sorry I said what I did. I was mad and I was venting, and I shouldn't have. It doesn't make what you did right. And it ain't comparable, but I'm gonna give you another chance. I'm going to be real clear this time. You fuck it up again and I'm gone. It's going to be really hard for me getting past this. I don't know if I can but I'm going to try. But when I say I like you, I mean I really like you. I want exclusivity. No seeing someone else, no calling your ex-boyfriend for favors. Just you and me from now on; and I'm not saying it's going to work, but I'll try. Okay?"

"I want that with you." Nick couldn't stand seeing Brandon look so hurt. Nick couldn't stand that he was the one that hurt Brandon so much. "But just because you don't want anyone to know we're dating doesn't mean you can't treat me like I'm your friend. If we go somewhere, don't ignore me. No one's going to think you're gay just because we're horsing around or something. Straight guys do it all the time. I won't talk to Jake any more, I promise. But, don't treat me like I don't exist. I can't be with you like that."

"I don't know if I can ever forgive you for this." Brandon chewed on his bottom lip. "All I'm promising is I'll try."

How could he have almost fucked this up? "I'll try, too." He couldn't believe how much he wanted to make this work.

Blue eyes rolled. "You'll try not to have sex with your ex-boyfriend? Gee thanks."

"Fuck you, you jerk." A towel from the sink sailed across the room and landed with a squelch on the floor at Brandon's feet. Shit, he'd missed. "You're such an ass sometimes, Brandon." Nick stalked across the kitchen to retrieve it.

With a grunt Brandon leaned down and grabbed the wayward missile. "I'm a cop." He held the towel out to Nick. "It's in my job description."

Tossing the towel on the counter without looking, Nick ran his damp hand across tattoos. He stroked Brandon's neck and shoulders. "Can I show you how sorry I am?" For long moments his fingers worked at loosing tight muscles. Thumbs riding either side of Brandon's neck, he pushed up along Brandon's spine and back down again. His strong hands eased out tension. When he felt the shoulders relax, Nick bent down and licked behind Brandon's ear.

With a moan, Brandon pulled Nick to him, pressing his mouth against a T-shirt-covered stomach. "Make-up sex?" A damp stain seeped into the gray cotton beneath Brandon's lips. His hand went between Nick's legs. His fingers felt good through the fabric. All tight and hard, Nick pushed his denim-covered hips against Brandon's palm.

"Yeah." Nick popped the button on his jeans. "Well, someone once told me it's the best type around."

"Sex doesn't solve things, Nicky." Sucking on the denim as Nick tried to unzip his pants, Brandon's mouth kept getting in the way of Nick's fingers.

It felt so incredible. "It's pretty much all I've got to offer."

Brandon stopped. "That's not true and you know it." As the sky finally cut loose with drum beats on the roof, Brandon stood, pushing his long black hair out of his eyes. "You're smart, you're sexy, you're stable...more or less." Brandon's arms looped across Nick's waist. "There're some freaky things going on when you get hissy. You make some *stupid* decisions. All in all you're pretty well pulled together." Brandon's hands cupped Nick's butt cheeks as he pulled Nick in. "I, on the other hand, on top of the usual levels of cop paranoia, am pushing thirty and still living in the closet. I don't know what the fuck you see in me, Nicky, but I'm glad you saw something. Life was starting to get real lonely. I've never been so thrown by someone; wanted to be with them so much."

He'd never had anyone this hot before; never had anyone this interested in *him* before. Jake had wanted someone to worship him. Nick had done it at first because it was a game, and later because, well, that's just how they were together. But Brandon was wanting, and offering, something a lot more satisfying. "Like right now?" Nick slid out of his jeans and shoes and onto the table. "Right here?"

"Shit, Nicky." Brandon yanked his wallet from his back pocket. Tossing it on the table, it fell open, the gold shield flashing as more lightning broke. "Fuck, I'm going to have to start investing in Trojan with you around." His hands worked his own belt loose as Nick dug the condom from beneath a wad of ones and fives. "Oh hell, I don't have any lube."

"There's oil in the cupboard." Nick laughed as Brandon lunged for the cabinet. "Of course I'll smell like salad, but hey." He tore open the condom pack. "Or there's butter in the fridge, then I'd smell like cookies."

The bottle thumped on the table as counterpoint to more thunder. "I love cookies." Brandon drove his mouth onto Nick's, pushing his tongue down between willing lips. His hand snaked up under the T-shirt, teasing Nick's nipples as they kissed. Low-throated moans rewarded his touches. "God, you're so hot," Brandon whispered in Nick's ear as he traced it with his tongue.

Nick's fingers pulled him free and rolled the condom down his shaft. Brandon fumbled the cap off the oil. As he tried to get just a little, the container upended and oil gurgled across the table and onto the floor. He swept his hand through and wrapped his fingers over the ones sheathing his dick. Brandon's mouth was working its way down the back of Nick's neck. "Probably not the best stuff to be using, huh?"

Nick managed to breathe between moans, "It's okay." Oil was pooling around his butt and thighs. "Don't stop now."

Brandon was driving him wild with his kisses. There would be one hell of a hicky left where he was sucking on Nick's neck. And how Brandon was touching him -- it gave him chills. He leaned back on the table, pulling Brandon down with him, tugging the shirt from his lover's jeans and pushing it up his chest. With the table so slick he slid, only saved from falling off the edge by slamming into Brandon's hips. Brandon rubbed their cocks together as he moved to sucking on Nick's nipples. God, he was in heaven. "Fuck me, baby, fuck me now." He laced his legs around Brandon's hips.

Brandon was sliding his dick down along Nick's balls, teasing Nick's hole with his head. "Right now?" Shifting his weight on one hand, using the other to guide his cock, Brandon slid into Nick's body. Nick hissed, his back arching as Brandon impaled him. For a moment the pleasure froze them in place. Oil glistening on Nick's light copper body; Brandon's forehead pressed into Nick's chest; pure ecstasy written on both their faces in the lightning flash. Slowly Brandon began to move. Nick's hips rose to meet him as Brandon caught one leg up over his arm. He bent down to ravage Nick's mouth again. As Brandon fucked his ass and screwed his mouth, Nick shook beneath Brandon. "Did it feel this good when Jake fucked you?"

Moaning, "Fuck no!" as Brandon drove into his body, Nick drew his other leg up and over his lover's shoulder. Brandon shifted again pinning Nick's hand under his own. "Not even half." Fingers twined together, the weight of Brandon's arm pressed his hand into the wood. He locked his ankles around Brandon's neck. His other hand gripped the side of the table as he was pounded. "Oh, deep, go deep." Brandon stroked him as the big cock slammed his hole. "It's so good." Icy rivers ran through his veins. "So fucking good!"

Nick wasn't sure who was driving them harder. He was ramming himself onto Brandon's cock like he'd lost his mind. Brandon was pounding him deep. It was brutal and hard and felt so goddamn good.

"Fuck me," Brandon panted. "I'm fucking coming!" The heat poured inside Nick. Brandon kept pounding and pulling at Nick's cock. "Come for me, come on, baby!"

Nick's body was jumping like it was shot through with a thousand live wires. His fingers were digging into the wood, going white with the pressure. An unintelligible mixture of Brandon's name and half a dozen swear words boiled out of his mouth just before his mind let go. Ecstasy exploded through his cock and spattered his stomach.

Brandon dropped, exhausted, against his chest. They both gasped for breath as the rain thrummed in the night. As the world came back into focus, Brandon pushed back and helped Nick slide his legs down to a more natural angle. Pulling him to a sitting position Brandon wrapped his arm around the back of Nick's neck, kissing him again and again, driving his fingers under the thick mane. "You are incredible." Brandon's palm skidded in the come/oil mix covering the table. His other hand was coated from the liquid soaked into his lover's long, black hair. "I think we made a mess, Nicky."

Lightening sparkled in Nick's black eyes. "Yeah, but we can have so much fun cleaning up."

CHAPTER SIXTEEN

Monday dawned clean and clear, like only the desert after a thunderstorm can. A sky as vivid blue as Brandon's eyes graced the morning. Memories of a rainy Sunday spent more in bed than out of it tickled Brandon's thighs as he pulled on his jeans. Cross-legged on the bed, Nicky had pored over his reports. Brandon had watched ESPN, one arm wrapped around Nicky's middle. Both had distracted the hell out of each other all day; not that either wasn't willing to be distracted. Now warm coffee smells called him into the kitchen. Nicky was leaning over the counter eating cheerios and reading the morning paper.

"Morning sexy," He dropped a kiss on the back of Nicky's neck. A mug had been set out by the pot for him. Pouring himself a cup of wake up juice, he devoured the sight of his lover. "Fuck, Nicky, look at you. You've gone all corporate on me."

Nick did a once-over to double check what he was wearing. Today it was black slacks, black dress shoes, maroon dress shirt with a black tie and hair pulled back into a ponytail. The seven-pointed star of a sheriff-style badge, the state seal of Nevada centered with Gaming Control Board etched on the circumference, hung on his belt. Emblazoned on the ribbon spanning the top two points was one word: AGENT. "What did you expect me to wear to work? BDU's?"

"It's kinda sexy in a repressed, geeky kinda way." Brandon's arms slid about his waist. "How you feeling? Doing okay?"

"I'm fine, especially with you here." Nick tossed the paper on the counter. As he smiled at Brandon, hints of the slick shine on the kitchen table sparked memories of previous evenings. That table was going to be in Brandon's memories for a long time. "It's going to be hard when you go home, but I'll be okay. You feeling better about us?"

"Starting to, although it's not going to be easy." It was anything but easy. Every time he thought about it anger began to bubble inside; anger at himself and at Nicky and at that fuckhead ex-boyfriend of Nicky's. Anyone else and Brandon would have walked out so fast the door wouldn't even have had time to hit him in the ass. Something about Nicky made him want to work past the hurt. Breathing through it, he added, "The moment I'm done with my shift I'm going to come back up. Gas for the bike is cheap enough. I like the ride, gives me an excuse to let her go full throttle." That would help clear his head some. Long rides always helped. "I figure I'm just gonna make you so exhausted you can't possibly be tempted."

"Oh, promise?" Nicky rubbed his hips against Brandon's. "Damn, maybe I should just call in sick or something," He laughed. Nicky had a wonderful laugh. "So should I tell the Chief that I can't take any weekend assignments because my boyfriend won't let me out of bed?"

He was Nicky's boyfriend. God, it had been so long since Brandon had been anybody's anything. Chuckling, he nuzzled under the collar of Nicky's shirt. "How do you handle working with a bunch of gaming cops and being gay?"

"I don't work with a bunch of cops. I work with a bunch of computer nerds. And I'm a computer nerd and Goth at that, so everyone assumes I just don't get laid. I get more shit about having long hair, or the music I play on my iPod, than my sexuality."

"You know, sometimes I think it would be so much easier if I just walked into roll call and yelled it out: 'I'm a fucking cop and I'm gay!' If I was a dyke no one would give a shit." One hand traced the line of Nicky's hip as he tried to put it into words. "Anything, anything that makes you different and they're gonna screw you. I've seen cops leave guys hanging on calls where they really needed backup. Or everyone shows but hangs back and watches some poor jerk get the shit kicked out of him 'cause they think he's not playing by the blue code." For a while he just savored the feel of Nicky pressed against him. Then he drew back. "Speaking of the boys in blue, I'm going to have to hit the road in a bit, see if I can sleep some this afternoon. Shift starts early Tuesday, like midnight early."

"There goes calling in sick." Nick toyed with the rings in Brandon's ear. It tickled. Brandon swatted his hand away. "So if you're on four days that means you're off Saturday, Sunday, Monday, Tuesday right?"

Coffee, he needed coffee. One hand resting on Nicky's hip, leaning against the counter he brought the mug to his lips. "Yeah, why?" The first swallow always tasted the best.

"Why don't we do something fun?" Nicky's voice went seductive, persuasive. "I was looking into some stuff. We could do a cruise."

Brandon almost choked. "You're fucking kidding me, right? A cruise, like with old people and stuff?"

"Like one with gambling. It's a small outfit called Windward Cruise Lines. They do three and four day cruises to Ensenada." Brandon'd woken Sunday morning to find Nick sitting nude in front of his computer looking into the Cruise concession Frontier was locked into. All the reports indicated that wads of cash rolled in from the line. From their web site neither could fathom why. "We catch it Friday night and get back Tuesday morning. They run out into international waters so that they can operate casinos. Basically they're junkets."

"Why the fuck do you want to cruise to Ensenada?" When he was fifteen, Edith had roped his dad into a cruise to Alaska. All Brandon could remember of the voyage was being supremely bored and slightly seasick. "If you really want to go to Mexico we can drive down in half a day. You can gamble in Vegas while you're at the fucking 7-11 if you want to. Half of them have slots."

"Well, no I can't; its part of my employment with the GCB. I don't gamble anyway, it makes me too nervous." Nick dumped the cereal bowl in the sink and the paper in the trash underneath. "Windward was the line Frontier had the concession on. It's the only cruise concession they have. Duke said the chips were for their cruise concession. The money trail keeps leading back there."

"How'd you figure that out?"

Nicky shrugged, "They had to tell us when they applied for their license. As part of routine background investigations all the gaming connections have to be listed. That way we can see if they've been banned in another state or if they're affiliated with someone who we have suspicions about. If Duke started hanging around someone new that wouldn't have gotten picked up, at least not for a while. Plus it's all over the reports I pulled, industry announcements and crap. All the other tie-in business looked legit; this is the one that gives me the willies."

"What do you think you'll find, Nicky?"

Focusing somewhere within himself, Nick thought for a bit. "I don't know that I'll find anything." With a shrug he returned his attention to Brandon. "I mean, it's a cruise ship with hundreds of people on it. But I just have to see it. Maybe it'll make sense if I do."

"You know what, Nicky?" It was finally starting to make sense, him and Nicky. The thing that was missing in all the other guys he'd known; his boyfriend had it strong. "You're a fucking cop. Ya just got to dog it 'til you find it, just like a cop."

CHAPTER SEVENTEEN

Brandon's last comment kept him smiling all morning. Even as he endured the pointed questions of the lab manager, he smiled. Between Friday's depression and Monday's elation the man was muttering 'manic-depressive' and 'drug tests' as he cut Nick loose on his assignments. Baron's casino was set for inspection. Serendipity; Nick got to do his job and dig a little at the same time. That alone would have kept him from actually calling in sick. It was all good.

Baron's was an older casino, a locals' place...probably the first true locals' place. Off the Strip on the wrong side of the freeway, she offered good odds and penny slots. The casino ceiling was slightly domed and the decor Victorian with polished brass, marble, and wood trim dominating. Soft amber glass chandeliers dangled from insets tiled in warm tin and trimmed in mahogany. Dizzying patterns of navy, gold and red swirled across the carpet. It was meant to recreate the ambience of the turn of the century cattle baron's estate. Nick guessed they succeeded, although he had no clue what a cattle baron's estate would have looked like.

It was far from their humble beginnings in the 70s as a crummy hotel with a few slots and four table games. Throughout the decades they'd expanded the casino, added rooms and brought in high-class dining. Their habit of developing and marketing their own innovative games spawned trends in the industry that quickly became Vegas staples of play. Baron's was the cornerstone of a gambling empire spreading across the US. Hell, one of their casinos had its own reality show.

The makeup of casino floors had gone through a rapid-fire evolution in the space of twenty years. One of the biggest changes was the domination of slots. In the old days, most of the casino's revenues came from blackjack, craps and roulette. In a modern casino more than seventy percent of revenue was generated by electronic games. That held true at Baron's. Their floor held almost two thousand five hundred slot machines, a small island of table games, and an enormous bingo room. Banks of slots and video poker, four deep, were lined up airline style: stacked row after row after row along the walls. Ringing bells, electronic muzak, the rain of coins into trays; Baron's casino virtually crackled with excitement. Nick's nerves were jangling two minutes after he walked thorough the doors.

The movies had it right, except for one thing. In a casino the dealers kept their eyes on the table. Players kept their eyes on the dealer. The floormen monitored the dealer and players, and the shift boss scrutinized the floormen, the dealers, and the players. Security guards studied everyone and their kid brother. Surveillance, through the eye in the sky, observed the dealers and players and the floormen and the shift bosses and security, as well as the maintenance men, change girls, and any one else who might wander onto the floor.

Gaming Control watched them all. At any time a sting could be in progress against the card counter or slot cheat. But it might be the lax dealer, pit boss and floorman who were stung by an enforcement card team cheating the hell out of the table.

Nick had been on board during an investigation into the actions of one of Baron's slot service personnel. Allegedly, the man embezzled over a quarter million, taking coins meant for refilling slot machines and converting them into cash for his own use by forging fill slips. GCB's audit had discovered hundreds of improper fill transactions each month for almost a year. Review of the slots themselves had fallen on Nick. Pulling chips and code, he had shown that, by their internal records, the money had never reached the machines. Enforcement succeeded in getting a confession, and restitution of less than ten percent of the money. From that point the District Attorney took over prosecution, and a civil suit followed on its heels.

GCB had wrapped up their part of it a little less than two years ago. That gave him an in with the host and security. Not that he really needed one. Nick's badge opened any door in a casino. As an agent of ESD, Nick had the right to gain entry, without notice, to any premises where electronic games of chance were located. Given that Vegas was a 24/7 town that translated to anytime, anywhere. But having been involved in the hunt for a common enemy, he'd bonded with a few people who were still around. One was Director of Ops Rosemarie Listrom.

Nick walked into Baron's, twirling the roll of yellow police tape on his right arm. The computer equipment was slung over his left shoulder. His badge was prominently displayed. Fun inspections were where they pulled the whole floor. A dozen agents, a Friday night; close down the roulette wheel, pull cards and dice from tables, rope off banks of slots and watch the floor manager piss himself while they tore the place apart. Most inspections were like today's; a single GCB tech quietly testing a few machines. Still, he didn't even need to say anything to the first security guy he met. The man was on his mike calling for the shift boss. Waves of panic rolled through the casino employees. What a great way to start a week.

Agents generally tested between three and a dozen slot machines per inspection. Each one was checked to insure the meters properly recorded money inserted and paid out, the casino's computer system properly recorded when someone opened the case, the machine's internal computer was not physically compromised, the computer program was the correct one, and the prize payout percentage was within the legal limits. There was always someone on hand at a casino to smooth the process. They opened the case and locked it back up tight. All Nick had to do was pull the chip, put it in the ZIF and run the software.

While Nick entered the third machine's identification into the computer, Rosemarie caught up with him. A slight twang in her voice identified her as a non-native. "So when are y'all going to stop issuing all those industry letters and do something useful with your time?" Generally very professional in appearance, she did sport the over-teased and badly dyed-hairstyle of many a Vegas housewife.

Nick settled onto one of the barstool-style chairs and let the computer put the EPROM through its paces. "Well, the chief has to justify his existence somehow."

"Oh, honey, ain't that the truth." They both laughed. "So whatcha up to besides ruining my revenue stream?" Spinning another stool to face Nick, she dropped heavily into the chair.

"Like you've got full seats on a Monday morning," he teased. "Got time to talk about Frontier? They were going to hold their trial here."

Rosemarie was suddenly defensive. "Why, is something wrong?" The Baron's empire had taken some major hits lately. Since 9/11, Suspicious Activity Reports, SARs, were required on all large cash transactions. There were questions about whether they'd been keeping up on the records.

Until recently Nevada's gaming industry was exempt from SARs. They'd always reported under Nevada Gaming Commission Regulation 6A, but unlike other states, they didn't have to report identifying information on payouts over $10,000 in verified winnings. Unlike the Feds, Nevada state requirements prevented certain cash-for-cash transactions. GCB believed their regulations were far more effective. Hell, it took the Feds damn near three years to figure out one of the Mega-Strip-Resorts stopped filing its SARs. Nevada was down the throat of any Casino missing 6As in the space of months.

Nick rolled his eyes. "You know I can't talk about that kind of thing." What Nick had never figured out was why criminals insisted on posing as Whales, the fat cat gamblers who got comps for everything. It was like wandering about with a big sign screaming *bust me!* GCB had fingered a Yakuza boss that way – and after years of trying to get the Feds' and Tokyo Police's attention they finally nailed the guy. "But I have some questions I could use answers to."

"There is a problem." Dead serious and a little scared, the director searched Nick's face for any clue.

He stayed relaxed. "I'm not going to say one way or the other." Nothing about his demeanor gave anything away. Casually, somewhat indifferently, he glanced over at the D-EPROM program and fiddled with things that didn't need fiddling with.

"Frontier, huh." After a deep breath, she went on. "I only dealt with Mike Ducmagian and their marketing guy...Tom Ukropina. Actually, I think his title was president. Tom's a typical used car salesman kinda guy. Mike could be a real ass sometimes. Real pushy, but he was former GCB so I figured that was normal." She gave a nervous twitter. "Ya know we're under scrutiny. There's no lie there. We've got the SARs issue. One of our Midwest casinos had six employees hit for smurfing. Is there something we should be worried about?"

At casinos, smurfs purchased large quantities of chips, gambled for a few hours with small bets, and then exchanged the chips for "clean" cash at the cage. Sometimes, like the incident Rosemarie was relating, employees got a cut for not filling out SARs. Enough little problems, and Baron's currently had more than its share of little problems, could equal a big problem with the GCB. "Well, Duke's dead. Can't run the machine trials without a technical contact, so until he's replaced I wouldn't say there's anything you need to worry about." He paused, sliding his eyes up from the screen to meet hers. "Not right now."

"Holy shit."

Now it was time to act like the big-shot GCB Agent. "I want to see everything they've given you. The marketing materials, contracts, technical specifications, e-mails, memos; give me all of it."

"Don't do this to me."

"Well, we can do it now, nice, quiet and easy." Orozco wasn't the only one who could play those cards. "Or I can call audit, and we'll just dig until we find something. Your choice; just the shit that has to do with Frontier, or a detailed review of the entire casino's books." He went for his cell phone figuring he'd just leave a message on his home machine. "That would take what, five or six months?"

"Okay, I'll get someone on it. You'll have most of it before you leave. I won't be able to get all of it today. Can you give me at least a couple of days to pull the rest?" Nick gave a noncommittal nod. It wasn't like he had the power to push the issue. Rosemarie stood, massaging the bridge of her nose with her fingers. She sighed deeply. "You know Mike Ducmagian wasn't so bad. A jerk, but not awful." Something was coming, something big. Nick just felt it in his bones. "But this guy he was hanging out with, brought him with the last couple of site visits. Guy gave me the willies. A friend, Reggie, I think was his name. I'll have the host pull the bills for the rooms Frontier used. His name will be there."

Reg equaled Reggie maybe? That was big enough to justify his gut. "What did he do?"

"Nothing. Just something about him tripped my bells. He played a little black jack, some slots. Never did a big chip exchange so he wasn't a smurf. But he and his cousin, they gave me that feel."

"Cousin?" Two for one, what more could he ask? "What do you remember about them?"

"Not much." She toyed with her hair as she thought. "Reggie, yeah I think that's what Mike called him, pretty much a regular guy. Dressed like most people who are trying to sell us stuff, business casual. Good looking Mexican guy. Knew a lot about computers and electronic games; he and Mike would have conversations way over my head. What weirded me out about him was how he looked at people, real predator's eyes. It was like a cougar sizing you up, wondering how you'd taste. His cousin, if I had to guess, was straight banger. Only brought him with them once." She thought a bit more. "He called him Chino. The guy had this huge rose tattooed on his neck, with these two M's over it, never seen one like it. Got into a fight with another guy in the bar. Nothing big, just words, but Mike had to put the guy's bill on Frontier just to calm things down. Then the casino host had to ask Mike to not bring the guy back. You could tell Reggie was not happy about any of it." Double M's over a rose, it had to be the guy from the funeral. And his name was Chino.

CHAPTER EIGHTEEN

The phone yelped, dragging Brandon from sleep. He fumbled it off the dock. As he pressed the offending machine to his ear he glanced at the clock. 4:15 a.m., not a human time of the morning at all, especially on two hours sleep. He managed to mumble out some form of his name as an acknowledgment.

"You naked?" whispered a sultry male voice.

"Hey captain." Brandon shut his eyes against the world. "Got ten strippers in bed with me right now...wait, no, that was my fucking dream you woke me from." Of course he wasn't about to tell his captain he'd been dreaming about male strippers, all of them looking like Nicky.

The captain dropped the seductive tone. "You worked Narc before I got stuck with your sorry ass, right Carr?"

Narcotics was always on the look out for officers who "fit" a particular profile. It was one of the few chances for an officer to work out of uniform without being a detective. "Yeah, did some plain clothes buys for them." They needed people they could rotate in and rotate back out when it became obvious anyone who bought from or sold to the "new" guy was getting popped. One of the Narcotics dicks watched him go from his blues to the tatted guy on the Harley. A few days later she'd pulled him in. White supremacist biker was his tag; kind of funny for a Jewish kid out of Grover Beach. He learned more about Bo Grietz, Ruby Ridge and the Turner Diaries than he ever wanted to remember during that stint. Palming his face, Brandon yawned through his fingers. "What's up?"

"Get down to Orange Street. They busted a super-factory. We got to pull in people to process. You get it, princess, 'cause you know about cooking meth. The lead dick wants you in, says she trusts you." 'I don't understand why' was carried across the line with the captain's snort. "See ya in fifteen."

The receiver was lost in the tangle of sheets as Brandon crawled off the bed in search of last night's clothes.

"You're late, Carr." Elaine Schuster was already chugging a latte from Legal Grounds, best coffee in downtown Riverside. A high octane blonde in a Jones New York pant suit, she'd been his backup when he'd done street time. She was the one who'd put in a high sign for him when he went for D. Every move Schuster ever made, she explained to him. Every fuckup on his part, she'd debriefed him on...not ass-chewings, but "here's what you need to learn, kid." Elaine walked on water as far as Brandon was concerned.

Brandon was sputtering. "Fucking Highway Patrol gave me a ticket." Heading down the I-15 and some idiot on a cop-cycle flipped the lights. At first Brandon hadn't pulled over. It couldn't have been him. Then he'd flashed the badge with his license and the fucker still wrote him up.

A uniform shot in passing, "Goddamn those bastages, that's the fifth cop they popped this week!"

"Fucking amen, brother!" Shoving the citation in his pocket, he jogged towards Schuster. "Last time they had to get the unions in on it, right? Reps and everything to calm it all down?" Brandon shook his head in disgust. "How'd this war get started?" Normally that would be a rhetorical question, but Schuster and Weaver had friends in the Highway Patrol. One of the guys they went through the academy with was now a chippy sergeant. Elaine had suggested Weaver take Brandon in hand. It was one more reason he owed her big.

She shrugged. "Scuttlebutt is, rookie CHP ticketed an off-duty patrol officer for reckless. Not even a wet reckless, speed testing. So then he and his buds decided to get back and cited like fifteen chippies in one day. So now there's a war on. They're looking for excuses to ticket."

"Fuck me raw!"

"Yep, you got caught." Schuster wiped the foam off her lip with her tongue. "So what did you get a ticket for?" If he'd been straight, all that blonde hair and overflowing bosom would have set him rocking. As it was, she still demanded attention.

"Not much, doing 90 in a 65 zone. That's just going to fuck the points on my license."

She handed him a sheaf of papers with the basics on the warrants and busts. As they headed down the hall towards the interview rooms, she cut to the chase. "It's a Nazi lab – lithium batteries, psuedophed, Draino...the works. Only this is a big time production factory model. On a bad day they'll churn twenty-five doses. On a good one they could do fifty." Your average lab could only crank about ten hits a day; anything above that was a super lab. Nazi referred to WWII production methods, not politics.

A flash caught in the fluorescents. Brandon picked up on the new rock gracing Schuster's finger. He'd have to razz her about the engagement. She was dating an arson investigator with Rancho Cucamonga's Fire Department last time he'd worked with her. Cops tended to date among other emergency services personnel. No one else understood what you saw, heard, and felt on the beat. Things must be going well for her if she'd made a commitment.

"With the limits on buying cold pills now they're bringing up the shit from Mexico. We used to bust mules loaded with coke and pot, now we're popping guys hauling 20 lbs of pseudoephedrine. Tweakers are going outside their circles for the shit." Working class whites traditionally cooked their own ice or bought from within their cadre of contacts.

Good old American work ethic; faster, cheaper, better. In prison, white guys mixed with Hispanic workers recruited by La Eme. White and Hispanic gangs banded together against black. Racial equality didn't work for shit when you were doing time. Everybody came out buddy-buddy, setting up full-time factories. "Mom, dad and gramps can only buy two bottles at a time...not quite enough to keep a habit going. When we popped these assholes they had about twelve box labs packed up as well. Cook their own lith, but have a side industry going. Pack everything you need for you own home cooking inside a Styrofoam cooler; Mr. Science all the way."

While they walked she gave him the bust run down. "We pulled five kids out of the trailer. Had to strip them at the hospital; the staff and dicks had to chip in their undershirts...hospital ran out of kid's clothes days ago. Five kids living at the factory, one of the 'hoes is preggers and cooking glass; what a family life. The four-year-old can't even talk; don't know if it's meth-related or just a classic case of no attention."

Tweakers often forgot they had children. They'd get so fixated on the next score that the yard-apes were left to fend for themselves. "We're also down two officers who had to go to the beauty parlor. The kids were crawling so bad that the nurses told 'em the only way they could ensure the buggies didn't spread was to shave everything off. A third is getting stitches; little shit bit him...all she does is scream and bite."

"So, Carr," Schuster swept a manicured hand about the room. A bargain-basement assortment of lowlife was stashed in various corners. They had to try and keep the suspects separated until they could be interviewed and processed. Pull in this many perps and there just wasn't any room left. "You want a 'hoe or one of the cookers? Three of the mules don't speak any English, so they're waiting on bilingual officers, but there's two more who do. We hit them on delivery day. Lucky us. Take your pick of what's left sweety-peety-pumkin-pie..."

Casting a glance over the motley collection of suspects, he chose. "I'll take the pregnant girl."

Shuster's eyebrows went up. "You sure about that?"

"Yep, let me have a go at her." He stopped by the water-cooler and yanked a cup from the dispenser.

"What, you're going to charm her with your underwear-model good looks?" As the cup filled, Shuster fanned herself with a file. "Okay, bitch's all yours then." Two steps and then she turned. "I'm giving you an opportunity here, Carr, don't fuck it for you or me...got it?"

"Yeah, I know. Thanks for asking for me. I owe you, a lot."

Now she walked off. "Ah yes, sweety-peety, you surely do."

Brandon dropped to one knee in front of the woman. Tipping his head so that he was looking up, into her face, he smiled. "Hi." He held out the paper cup of lukewarm water. Using his Barry White voice for maximum effect, he asked, "How are you feeling?" The muddled cologne of unwashed body, Draino, paint thinner and corroding metal crawled up his nose. "Can I get you anything? Need the bathroom?"

A snake-like tongue darted over chapped lips. She just glared at him with her red-rimmed eyes. Tweakers, methamphetamine users, often looked like they had permanent colds. A nasty side effect of shooting the shit: permanent post-nasal drip. Plus, almost all the chemicals used in the Nazi labs, besides being volatile and unstable, were irritants if inhaled. The cookers would wear goggles, masks and gloves when working directly with the stuff, but take the protective gear off if they walked a few feet away. Labs became time bombs of fumes. Hazardous material contamination wasn't covered in Druggy 101. Keeping with the times, it was now covered at the academy.

Moving onto the seat next to her, draping his hands between his legs, he tried again. "Ya know, my ex-wife had to piss like every fifteen minutes when she was pregnant." It earned him a shift of sharp-bladed shoulders and another glare. This one was less hateful than the first. There were barriers to break down. The woman had already been stripped and cavity searched. With tweakers you had to make sure they weren't hiding anything they shouldn't be...anywhere. The process was as invasive as it sounded.

For a while they just sat. Then in a chemical-stripped voice, she asked, "Can I have the water?"

"Sure." Only one of her hands was free; the other was handcuffed to the chair. She had to reach across her own body to take the cup. A rose was tattooed on her inner arm. "Nice tat. Who inked you?" He'd have preferred to interview her in a room where he could have made her more relaxed, taken off the cuffs. There weren't any left. Making do; it was the mantra of the police force.

After she swallowed, she said, "A friend." It hadn't helped her voice. "He says I shouldn't talk to the cops."

"They all say that. And you know it because you watch TV and the officers read you that little card when they put you in the car, right?" In a mock-u-mentary voice, he continued, "You don't have to talk to us, anything you say could be used against you, you can have a lawyer if you want one..." Brandon dropped the comedy. "We'll get you a P.D. if you want" Both of them snorted in derision.

She looked up and smiled; half of one front tooth was missing. "I don't have much use for the public defender."

"Neither do I, but we'll call them if you want."

She shook her head. Her hair hadn't been washed in days. "Naw. They're useless anyhow."

"Your call on that." He was still hunched over, trying to be the least threatening thing in her immediate surroundings. "So do you want to tell me what's what?"

"Doesn't matter. Don't got much to say anyhow." Somehow, Brandon doubted that.

He let some time weigh on her while she finished the water. When she passed him the empty cup, he balled it up and threw it toward a detective's trashcan. Purposefully he missed and nailed the desk's occupant between his shoulder blades. Pissed, the guy turned and started to stand. She giggled as Brandon spread his hands, denying malice. Confrontation avoided. Talking to her like they were at a bus stop or in line at the store, not like she was handcuffed to a chair in the police station, he asked, "Is this your first?"

"No, got three others."

"Were they at the house when it got busted?" Brandon figured they were.

"Yep."

"Want me to see if I can find out where they're going?" Promising without promising. "Let me know and I'll see what I can do."

"I shouldn't be talking to you."

She was almost there, he could feel it. "Your choice, but it helps."

"Helps what?"

"When you're ready to get your kids back, it helps." It was one of those hard calls to make. Tomorrow, if someone asked him, Brandon would say there was no way in hell this woman should ever get her kids back...not unless she got clean. Maybe not even then. Today, he put it aside. "The social workers and stuff, they like to see you've been cooperating." Attitudes didn't generate empathy. Without empathy you didn't get confessions. Beating suspect's heads against the wall had gone the way of the dinosaur long before Brandon hit the force. Now it was all about psychology. There were guys in sex crimes that would get down on the perp's level, get the confession, and spend the rest of the afternoon puking their guts up in the can. You did it because you had to. That was your job.

"Ya think?" It was a primal thing. Let the babies starve, sit in their own filth, while you found your fix, but they're your kids, damn it. Have the state take them away—and it was hard enough to get that to happen when it was needed—and the tweakers would fight like wet cats to get them back.

"Maybe; it would mean something to me if I was looking at your case." He studied his fingernails for a time. Sitting up, sliding down, he ended up slouched in the plastic chair so that his head was level with her shoulder. "It's hell not having your kids."

Her tone wasn't hateful, just curious. "How would you know?" It was a good sign.

"My ex has my daughter. Full custody...I don't even get joint." He sighed. Tough as it was letting them in your skin, sometimes you had to do it if you wanted the suspect to think you were a stand-up guy. "Don't get any holidays, never seen her open a birthday present." Delicate dancing was called for. Like as not this 'hoe couldn't remember the last time she fed the kids. Somewhere inside he was betting there were a few trips to the park or Barbie dolls that lit her up as a child. "It's the holidays that are the worst. All these commercials with these cute kids running around, happy as hell. I remember what it was like when I was a kid with my folks and it was great. And I'll never even get the chance to try to make that happen." Most people wanted to think of themselves as good parents. Even as down as she was, giving her an up that she might be able to do it, give that feeling to her own kids, brought them a little closer.

"Why don't you try for joint custody?"

Inside he winced. The pain of thinking about it jarred with the elation over reeling her in. "What would be the use? Shit, I'm a single male cop...I work fucking vice which is late nights and long hours. Before that I did this gig," he waved his arm towards the general chaos of the Narcotics division. "Great fucking father material there. And shit, she hardly knows me from Adam. Probably hates my guts."

"Naw, kids always love their folks. Even if they're assholes." She paused, probably thinking about her own parents. Brandon didn't even want to imagine what her home life had been like. "You always still love them." Probably a lot like every other suspect's; a lot of drinking, a lot of fighting, a lot of getting smacked around. It was rare to hear any other story.

"What's the use? I mean the courts are just stacked against dads."

"So you're not going to fight it?" She was incensed, almost righteous. It garnered them a few stares from others in the room. "I wouldn't just lay down and take it. Anything I got, I'd use to get my kids back. Fucking tear down the courthouse if I had to."

"Ya think I could?"

"Sure, why not." Now she was important, telling a cop what he should do. "Do it." Her life was completely fucked, but she could fix his.

"Maybe I will. Yeah, I think so." He stared across the room for a bit, then turned and lit up one of his brilliant smiles. "Thanks for caring."

A mumbled, "No problem," drifted between them. More silence, more waiting. Brandon was used to waiting for what he wanted. "So, can you help me?"

"Help?" She had to ask for it now.

Preoccupied, she picked at the scabs on her arms. "Get my babies back?"

"I'll do what I can..." Now he had her. "But you got to tell me what you know so I have something. I got to give that blonde bitch over there," his chin jerked, pointing out Schuster, "more than just 'yeah we're cooking ice.' 'Cause if she doesn't think you're straight with us, not a damn thing I do will matter."

Ruby specks of blood dotted her lower lip as she chewed off the flaking skin. "Okay."

While the rest of the world was waking up, reading the news, getting the kids off to school, Brandon was learning about new levels of meth production: taking notes, writing it down, showing it to his suspect, and getting corrections. She wanted him to get it right. If he didn't have it right, she wouldn't have a hope in hell of getting what she wanted.

The guys they worked for—she said with, but Brandon knew better—used to bring up glass from Mexico. That carried stiff sentences. Illegally bringing in cold pills got a mule time served and a bus back across the border. While they cooked their own—almost all cookers were addicts—they'd been upgraded by the partners her old man had met in county. Once a month they'd get a shipment of pills and materials brought up from the border. She didn't know where. They'd pack the money they made and send it back down. She didn't know where for that either. She and her crew were paid in ice and a little bit of cash.

They always ended up with extra materials. One of the cookers, Jose, and she, while getting high, had dreamed up the idea of selling the to-go kits. Markup was good and they could bring in the people who didn't want to buy ice from someone else. Drug snobbery among tweakers; some just felt it didn't hit right if you didn't cook it yourself.

There were names and nicknames: Tio and Franky, Loco, Chino, Niño, Bob and Hank. Chino she had down pat; he was their main source, the guy who picked up the cash. Scrawny guy with a buzz cut and a voice that would make dogs howl, his neck bore the entwined M's of full membership in the Mexican Mafia backed by a blood-red rose. His cousin Niño got his nickname because of his voice; high pitched and squeaky, like a kid. If one cousin was around, the other wouldn't be far behind. Aside from Chino, probably none of them were big fish. But Brandon had descriptions of about twenty people revolving around the enterprise. As tweakers went, it was a fucking convention.

CHAPTER NINETEEN

Three raps on the door caught Nick's attention. He pushed aside the blinds and peered out onto the porch. Detective Orozco was framed in the wan yellow light from the fixture. What the hell did he want now?

Nick had ditched his tie the moment he'd hit the house. Sitting in front of the computer, shirt open to his waist, hair loose; he'd been reading through the correspondence files on the Baron's-Frontier deal. Brandon had sent him an e-mail saying he'd been up since four and wouldn't be online tonight. Disappointment was tempered by the virtual licks Brandon'd sent.

Whether to actually button his shirt was decided in the negative as he walked through the dark house. The detective could take him as he was. Nick opened the door to find Orozco poised for another knock. "Fancy meeting you here. Selling tickets to the police ball?"

"Evening, Agent O'Malley." A quick once over didn't even get Nick a raised eyebrow. "Mind if I come in and chat with you a bit?" Hell, Orozco had probably seen everything under the sun. A half-dressed, Goth, gay gaming agent must not rate high on the detective's weird-o-meter any more.

He shrugged. "Yeah, I mind, but come in anyway." Threading his way through the furniture, he flipped the switch on the floor lamp. Nick preferred the ambiance of occasional lighting. A good thing since there was no ceiling fixture in his living room.

As Orozco followed, his gaze dropped to the floor. After a pause, where he just stared and wiggled his mustache, his eyes flicked up to Nick's face. "Where's your rug? Wasn't there a large rug there?"

"Just got tired of it." Wilfred Brimley, it finally clicked. Detective Orozco reminded him of a Hispanic Wilfred Brimley; especially when he messed with his 'tache. Damn, Miri's celebrity fixation was becoming contagious. "Thing was pretty ratty. I dropped it off at Goodwill on Saturday."

"Ah yes, Saturday." Orozco took a chair, even though Nick hadn't offered one. Settling in, the detective continued, "That is what I'm actually here about. It came to my attention that one of my witnesses was involved in a little to-do in a parking lot. Jake Railin, blue Miata? Ring any bells? Apparently you ran your big, nasty hearse into his pretty little car."

Fuck, how did things like that get around? "Yeah, you know, column shift." Nick shrugged. "I thought it was in reverse and it was still in drive. I pretty much totaled his car actually. Gave him my insurance stuff; I've got good insurance, it'll be covered."

"The problem is he says you did it intentionally." There was that fatherly tone again. "Wants to press charges. I just happened to be at the desk when he came in screaming about this psycho Nick O'Malley who screwed up his car. I told him I'd come talk to you, just to get his ass out of the station. So..."

Cigarettes were kept in a small coffin box on the mantle. Nick fished out a clove and dug the lighter from his pocket. "So?" The flame cast an Anton LeVey shadow across his features as he inhaled.

"So," the single word was followed by a sigh, "why did you toast his penis substitute?"

Shit, he was just no good at lying to this man. "Because if I actually cut off his cock and shoved it down his throat, you'd arrest me for assault." If you couldn't lie, be a smart-ass; either one was good at deflecting attention.

Orozco didn't take the bait. "I take it then you weren't happy with him?" That was the king of all understatements.

Lies were out. Smart-mouthing was out. Guess he'd have to play this one straight. "We were fighting." Nick took another drag and cocked his hip against the hearth. "Or not really fighting, he was gloating and I was pissed off. I asked him to get some information for me and the terms were a little more than I expected."

"And that, of course, is an excuse to wreck his car?"

"No it's not an excuse." God, why was this so complicated? "Listen, okay, we used to be involved. He showed up Thursday and well...old habits die hard. We ended up, you know, together and everything kinda went to hell."

After a few minutes, Orozco asked, "And the sex was so bad it was worth jacking your insurance rates?" Everything about how he crossed his arms over his expansive gut, how his shoulders sagged under the weight of his job, how his voice suddenly went so gentle, said Orozco had heard this story before. Not Nick's story...but *this* story.

"No." Sharp and loud, some anger at Jake and some embarrassment at the situation coloring his voice. "Look, if I let him fuck me he'd get me some information I needed." He took another deep drag and stared over the detective's head. "And then I was pissed because well, look, I have rules about what I will and won't do. I don't do anything that's going to put me at risk and Jake is just a fucking slut. So safe sex, always, no exceptions..." Nick's tone softened. Now he was mad at himself, how stupid he'd been. "Except we'd been together for almost three years and I thought we were really committed to each other so, you know, that rule kind of went by the wayside. Then, a few months before I met Brandon, I walked in on Jake fucking some cabana boy. Pulled my shit outta his closet, threw his key in the garbage and walked out."

Silence hovered over the room for a time. Finally Nick stepped to the coffee table and ground out the butt in the ashtray. "Three goddamn tests in six months. And now I'm going to have to fucking start all over again."

"You're talking about AIDS tests?"

"HIV; once you've got AIDS, baby, it's too fucking late for tests." Nick shuddered. "Syphilis, gonorrhea, all sorts of other crap. Who knows where that dick has been?"

"What about Detective Carr? Where does he fit into this?" Why did Orozco care what was up with him and Brandon? It was nice that he seemed concerned, but it was way outside his job.

"He dumped me, or I thought he had, Monday after your phone call. After you talked to him he was majorly pissed. So, I was feeling real low all week. Then I had to go to Duke's funeral, which just didn't help. When I got home, Jake was here, and things just happened."

"I'm sorry if I threw things off for you." The detective actually sounded as if he meant it.

"What? That you're doing your job? It sucks, but nothing can be done about it now. We made up this weekend." Now that he was talking about it, Nick couldn't seem to hold back the words. "Of course I was stupid enough to tell Brandon I slept with Jake...that just about ruined everything permanently. Anyway, so I'm just miserable and Jake starts coming on to me, and I needed a favor out of him so I gave in. Jake and I had always been into bondage and he tied me up and then he decided that he wasn't going to play it safe. I started screaming that I didn't want to anymore and he...he just didn't care, kept going while I'm screaming stop. He thought it was funny."

The room filled with stillness, the kind that pressed up against the walls and suffocated the senses. Unable to stomach such quiet, Nick broke it, trying to keep the tremble out of his voice, "When I went to get my papers Saturday he starts laughing at me—poor little Nick all worried that he's going to get hurt. Fucking shithead. And then there's his little blue piece of shit in the space in front of me, so instead of backing up, I put it in drive and floored it. Little foreign jobby just didn't stand much chance against a good ol' American-made steel chassis."

"You know that's rape." Orozco's voice was very soft; it was the word that screamed. After letting it sink in the detective continued, "If you said no, and he didn't stop, that's rape."

"Okay, yeah...so maybe it is. What do you want me to do about it?"

"Well, you could do something impetuous, like file a police report."

Nick almost choked. "Great, and then *maybe* Jake'd be arrested and then we'd go to court and the high-priced defense attorney he'd get would put me on the stand." Mocking a Jimmy Stuart trial attorney style, he played it out. "*Agent* O'Malley, let me get this straight. It was okay with you that my client, Jake Railin, smacked you hard enough that he left welts on your ass. Now he tied your wrists to your ankles and fucked you up the ass...*that* was alright with you? You get off on that kind of thing, don't you? And you'd been in a relationship with

Mr. Railin for three years previous where you'd moved past the whole condom thing...and let's talk about that relationship. You two were really into the whole S&M thing; whips, chains, the whole nine yards, right? Isn't it all part of the game for someone to say no and you just keep going?" Nick threw himself into the couch, arms hugging his sides. "Just what I fucking need! On top of worrying what I could catch from that bastard is to have my sexual preferences shredded in public."

Orozco sat in silence for a while. Finally, he asked, "Was it worth it?"

"What?"

"The information you got, was it worth it?" Orozco leaned forward, elbows resting on his thighs.

"Yeah, sure." Nick pulled his knees up under his chin. "Fuck no, nothing's worth that. I can't go back and change time. But I've gone over some of it and things just aren't adding up. Especially when I compare it with the GCB's file."

"On who?"

"Frontier Entertainment."

"Isn't that the company..."

"Yeah, it's who Duke was working for."

"Look, I know you're concerned." This time the detective's tone was anything but fatherly. "I know you want to help. What you see on TV and all, it seems really glamorous and fun to play PI. Bottom line, Nicholas, I don't want you dicking around in my murder investigation. You've gotten yourself hurt once."

"I ain't fucking with your murder investigation! I'm doing my fucking job! I mean I'm not in audit or enforcement, but I've been assigned the approval of Frontier's systems, to clear them to put their machines in Nevada. Duke's murder just flagged that something ain't right. When I've got more than just a hunch I'll take it to my chief and he'll take it to the other divisions."

"What do you have?"

"Why?"

"Because maybe it might help find who killed Ducmagian."

"What, you've finally decided it wasn't me...that I wasn't involved?"

"Actually, no. You are still, officially, a person of interest. You're going to tell me what you've got or I'm going to toss your butt for interfering. But because I'm not a bad guy, and I think you're being reasonably honest with me that you're just doing your job, if, and I mean if, I find out something that might affect your investigation, I'll pass it on to your chief."

"Not me, huh? Don't trust me that much?"

"Not until I completely rule you out."

"Okay," he jerked himself upright. Motioning for Orozco to follow, Nick headed to the extra bedroom at the front of the house. Originally it had been his dad's room; the 60s-era wallpaper had long since given way to seafoam-green paint. When Nick was a kid, he and his sister shared the room on frequent sleepovers, and then it became his when he'd moved in to help take care of Gramps. Now both exterior walls were flanked by an L-shaped, brushed chrome and glass work center. File cabinets extended the usable space to nearly the eight-by-ten parameters of the room. Printers, computers, faxes and various media peripherals were organized to maximize efficiency. A tiny closet set in the same wall as the doorway they entered through held some of Nick's extra clothes as well as whatever parts and pieces Nick felt might be useful someday. Between the doors a large metal bookcase was crammed with buying guides, technical manuals and a decent collection of science fiction and fantasy.

Nick dropped into a leather executive chair. "I have one bad chip out of thirteen." A hard copy of the EPROM report, the GCB file and the financials obtained from Jake were spread across Nick's desk. As Orozco bent over his shoulder, Nick flipped the corners of the computer printout. "I'm pretty certain that the two I sent back to Duke were bad, too, that it's not just a random download error on the EPROM."

"What do you mean the chip is bad?"

"I think someone wrote it as a cheat. By someone, I mean Duke. It wouldn't make sense if it were going to be used in Nevada. I mean, we've approved the source code and the other dozen are good, but if they put that chip in a machine on the floor of a casino there's a possibility that we'd pick it up during a field test. Not a huge chance, but enough of one that you wouldn't want to risk your gaming license on it. Duke's insistence on getting it back, it didn't make sense. Those two things make me think that there's something else going on." What he'd overheard at the funeral didn't seem worth mentioning, at least not yet. "Now I want to go over what they've told us and what Jake pulled and see if there's something more going on. If they're dirty, no matter how, the GCB doesn't want them in Nevada."

"How do you know it's bad?"

"Well, it started off just as a hunch. I mean, why else would Duke want it that bad? So I ran it, and re-ran it. I was going nuts. I kept thinking the problem would have to be somewhere in the normal places that cheaters would want it; the payouts, the number generators, things like that. The tests were coming out all weird, but not where I thought they would. I finally found it. He gaffed the revenue codes."

"Revenue codes, I don't understand." The desk groaned as the detective settled his bulk against it.

"Taxation and revenue codes. All machines keep an accurate count of the money played. Casinos use them internally so that they can make sure floor people aren't pocketing a few bucks here or there. The count on the slot has to match the count of money at the end of the day, or shift. In Nevada we also use it for tax auditing. All EPROMS are programmed to track money played. That's the big part of my job, testing slot machines, actually the programming for slot machines, video poker, that kind of crap."

"Why?"

"To make sure the programming hasn't been messed with. That the number generators are working properly, that they're within a tolerance of randomness." Orozco was looking at him like he was speaking Greek. Help desk call from hell; he tried to explain as much in lay person language as he could. "See, none of the computer programs that randomly generate numbers are actually random. Because they're all based on mathematical algorithms they can't be truly random, but they can get pretty close, really close. That means that you can hink with the programming. If you knew which particular program was in a certain machine, you could write a program that would identify within a certain mathematical probability when that machine was going to hit big. So we have to insure that the chips are being switched out on a regular basis and that they haven't been messed with."

Orozco was obviously trying to follow. "Okay, so Ducmagian wrote the EPROMS so that they wouldn't accurately track money. So he and whoever he was working with were trying to bilk the IRS. And he knew the GCB would find that and turn them in to the feds. So he needs to get the chip back, so he heads over to the club figuring he'll lean on you."

"Well, yes and no. I mean the EPROM. It's not set to under-report. It's set to over-report dollars played. We're talking for every dollar in it reports two. The problem is when you got to the count room, the money would be off. I still don't get that part of it. Why would Duke write that into an EPROM's code? Plus the financial inquiry I had done on Frontier. They're showing tons of revenue coming out of their cruise concession. Paying taxes on it all seems legit. Except it's not exactly the same thing they told us. Why would they lie?" Drumming on the newest additions of paper, he pondered, "I'm not sure if anything will be in here, but this is from the Frontier-Baron's negotiations and machine trials. I should get the rest of it in a day or so. Maybe he said something, made some slip that will show me what he was up to. Even if it means digging up the dead, I want to know why."

"I thought Ducmagian used to work for ESD?" Orozco's hand found Nick's shoulder. Startled, he looked up into the detective's face. "You'd finger one of your own?"

He sighed. "Look, there are two people who know more about a slot machine than anyone else: the guy who programmed it and the guy who tested it. One Midwestern casino knew this guy was ripping them off on a multi-game machine, but they couldn't figure out how he was doing it. He got five flush-draws in 25 minutes. Every time someone walked by him, he would switch to another game in the machine. They sent a surveillance tape to a testing lab that also consults on possible fraud cases. One of the guys in the lab called back and said, 'we know that guy. He programmed that machine.' After Harris, no one is above suspicion."

Fingering the reports, Orozco asked, "Can I get copies of these?"

"Sure, okay, there's a quickie copy place down the street." While Orozco collected papers, Nick buttoned his shirt. "But the GCB file. If anyone asks, you didn't get it from me, okay? They're supposed to be confidential, as in criminal penalties confidential."

"Warrant could get 'em."

Nick smirked as he pushed back from the desk. "Got one on ya?" He teased.

When Orozco laughed, Nick nodded and stood. "Didn't think so. You drive? Querida's headlight is broken. Got the lamp, just haven't put it in yet; wouldn't want to get a ticket while I'm chauffeuring a cop around."

"My pleasure, Agent O'Malley." Nick grabbed his keys as they headed into a sweltering desert evening. "So you and Detective Carr," Orozco stood on the edge of the porch, hands in his pockets, "everything's okay now?"

"I wouldn't say okay." Files smacked against his thigh. "We're working things out. Guess that's about as good as it can be right now."

CHAPTER TWENTY

Windward's contribution to the Ensenada gambling junket was an older vessel with the obligatory overblown name. The Buenaventura was a smallish, vintage early-80s cruise ship. It had none of the mega-ship glitz...no twenty-story atriums or three-tiered dining rooms. Intimate charm replaced overblown glamour. Greens, golds and tans dominated the palette and tons of pale wood had been used throughout the public areas.

Flyers advertised the standard Vegas-style girly shows, a magician, a comedian, a couple of singers; all the usual crap. On the whole the entertainment package sounded possibly adequate to piss away an evening. Their main dining room and a decent-sized swimming pool were housed on deck seven, a bar with two tiny Jacuzzis on deck nine, and deck eleven was a sunbathing area. None of those things were what sold out the ship. The casino, with black-jack, poker and row upon row of slots, took up most of deck eight. That's where Windward raked them in.

The interior cabin Nick had snagged last minute was on deck five. After a few wrong turns in the maze of halls, they found their room. Mirrored closet doors lined the constricted hall on the right as they entered. The cabin was narrow and dark. Nick suspected he'd been consigned to a dungeon designed by a colorblind Martha Stewart wannabe. The bathroom on the left was pink, like sliding-down-someone's-throat pink. Exposed plumbing hinted that the shower might get you clean. Pale blue walls, chocolate carpet, pink bed ruffles and blue blankets were all offset by a bright orange stripe running waist high around the perimeter. Even if you weren't prone to seasickness, this room might give it to you.

A single full-sized bed had gold-flecked mirrors for a headboard. Twin nightstands and a vanity opposite the foot of the bed were 80s-era white laminate. A TV was mounted on the wall above the vanity. "You booked us a room with one bed?" Brandon's duffle bag sailed across the room and slammed into the mirror. "You used my name and booked a room for two guys with one full-sized bed. What the fuck were you thinking, Nicky?"

"Chill." Nick slid down the nineteen-inch gap between the wall and the mattress. His hand ran along one of the two lozenge-shaped protrusions jutting out from either wall. "These pull down into extra beds." Shoving the bag to the floor before he flopped into the middle, he added, "Hell, we can even play pretend and pull one down in the morning and mess it up so the maid doesn't suspect we're sleeping together. Of course, condoms in the trashcan might give that away."

Brandon crawled up Nick's body and straddled his hips. "You think that's gonna happen, huh?" He leaned in brushing Nick's lips.

"I'm kinda counting on it." As his arm's slid about Brandon's neck, a shudder ran through the cabin followed by a low rumble as the ship got underway. They both looked towards the roof although the vibrations seeped up from below. "Well, yeah." Nick laughed. "We're going to need to do something to wear ourselves out enough to sleep through this."

Laughing, kissing him again, Brandon whispered, "Let me see what I can do about that."

CHAPTER TWENTY-ONE

Saturday morning the Buenaventura docked at Santa Catalina Island, off the Southern California coast. Native Californians shortened the name to just Catalina. There was only one village on Catalina: Avalon; the rest was given over to wilderness habitat. Because of the nature of the harbor, ships docked away from shore. Most of the island was one mountain, dotted with meadows and valleys. In some places coastal cliffs fell sharply into the sea, while in others the hills rolled gently to beaches below. Ferries shuttled passengers in and out of the small marina accompanied by the flashing silver of bottlenosed dolphins dancing in their wakes. Flat-bottom boats and submarines plied the surrounding waters. Flocks of scuba divers swam among the fish. Houses clung to the hills rising from the ocean.

Typical of most West Coast seaside towns, quaint shops hawked everything from wind chimes to surf gear. Brandon and Nick wandered through, poking fun at each other and the merchandise. Not typical were the slew of golf carts parked on the street. Cars were limited in number by city ordinance. Given the entire island wasn't more than twenty-one miles long, they weren't terribly necessary. Ice cream served as lunch while they walked along the sandy beach under the gypsum-white walls of the Casino. The palatial Casino had never been a place for gambling. Its name derived from an archaic term for a dance hall. Six stories above the harbor a huge circular ballroom lorded it over the city.

Only one thing made the day less than idyllic for Nick. No playful hugs, no kisses on the strand, no sitting on the rocks wrapped around each other...no touching at all. What might have been hopelessly romantic was dropped to reasonably fun. Nick might have tried to sneak a kiss or three, but Brandon probably would have bolted if he did. He was obviously nervous enough just being here with Nick; Brandon spent every moment as though someone he knew might turn the next corner. It was almost a relief to get back to the ship.

That night eating required a hike, unlike the previous evening when neither had felt like doing much except crashing and had skipped dinner as well as sex. First they had to go to the aft dining room, the Tropical, accessible only from the rear stairs or elevators. From there they had trekked up a floor, back to the mid-ships stairs and down again into the Vista dining room. The only vistas available were if you happened to be seated to either starboard or port. Somehow Nick doubted the food would be worth the journey.

It was "Captain's Night" so they were supposed to dress for dinner. Nick had donned a collarless black silk shirt, modern-cut black slacks and a black opera coat that swirled about his ankles as he walked. His cop was in a basic black suit, definitely off the rack, white shirt, gray tie. It looked like he was wearing someone else's clothes. Not that they looked bad—a potato sack would look hot on Brandon's body—but he seemed so uncomfortable, constantly messing with his tie and sleeves. Nick couldn't resist teasing Brandon about it as they walked. He'd finally dropped the subject when Brandon had growled, "I only own one. If it's good enough for a judge, it's good enough for a crappy cruise ship."

Yanking open the etched glass doors to the dining room, Nick asked, "What do you do if you have more than one day of testimony?"

"Then," Brandon tugged on his tie again, "I'd be screwed."

Large, round tables occupied the center of the room. A few booths were scattered along the interior walls and long rectangular tables, seating eight, were positioned to take advantage of the windows on either side of the ship. Mauves and bleached wood exuded a Miami Vice ambiance. Two women, either of whom could have been Nick's grandmother, were already seated when they arrived. They introduced themselves as Marva and Elsie. Brandon leaned in and whispered, "See, only old people take cruises." The steward placed them to either side of the elderly pair.

They had just taken their seats when four young women were escorted to the table. Both he and Brandon jumped to their feet, earning Elsie's approval. Brown hair and brown eyes on all of them, the girls ranged from slightly dumpy to California-girl pretty. Nina, Sara, Lidia and Val bubbled their introductions. "Well, they're not old," Nick hissed over the women's graying heads. "Do you think any of them can legally drink?"

"I could card 'em and see." Brandon hissed back. "Still in California after all, twenty-one and all, tag 'em and bag 'em."

Elsie popped in, "Oh, so you're in law enforcement?" It wasn't the best way to start a conversation with Brandon.

At that Nina, or maybe Lidia, burbled, "Oh, my God, are you like a cop or something?" Draping herself on Brandon's arm she cooed, "Cops are, like, so sexy with their uniforms and all." Her skirt was too short and her breasts to large for her braless condition. Whichever one of the quartet she was, she was busting out everywhere. She was also doing her damnedest to make sure Brandon noticed it all.

Marva leaned back in her chair, eyes sliding back and forth between him and Brandon. Finally she choked out a laugh. "Listen princess, take it from an old lezzie, these boys aren't interested in your tits." Already rocky, the dinner conversation went downhill from there.

Nina, it was her, decided that the older woman was pulling her leg. Endless attempts at flirtation were thrown Brandon's direction. Seemingly without a thought he'd started flirting back, and then Nick would catch his eye with a glare. For a time he'd scale it back, and then the cycle would start again. Growing more jealous by the second, Nick hardly ate anything. What he did eat, he didn't taste. When the girls did the group troop to the bathroom, Elsie leaned in and whispered, "Why doesn't he just tell her he's gay?"

Fork halfway to his mouth, Nick glared at the vacant seats. "Because he doesn't want anybody to know."

She gave a startled, "Oh," and then a gentle touch on his arm. "Don't worry, hon, sooner or later he's going to get tired of eyeballing the back of that closet door. And when he turns around he's going to be so surprised that closet was made of glass. Just be there for him when it happens."

Dinner done, the girls decided to head to the casino. Nick started to beg off for both of them, but Nina was already dragging Brandon by the arm towards the stairs. Irritated beyond irritated, he drifted behind them. The three remaining girls were trying to be nice, include him in their fun. When they dropped themselves at a bank of slots, Nick groaned. The neon eye candy and rain of coins was too much for the girls to resist. The only reason he didn't just pull a fit and blow was that they'd chosen the Frontier games...the new ones he'd been testing. At least Brandon was able to disengage himself and slide toward Nick.

Under the rules of the International Council of Cruise Lines, all gaming equipment on cruise vessels was supposed to meet the regulatory standards of the Nevada Gaming Control Board, or some other licensed jurisdiction, on paybacks and software. Translated into human speak: lines shouldn't buy machines from clandestine operations. Since it was a guideline and not a law, it didn't mean jack shit. They bought from whomever had the best sales pitch.

Once in international waters there was no regulation. Big publicly-traded lines tended to keep things really clean. Outfits like Windward operated to do one thing: casino gambling. The industry as a whole was suspicious of the trend, believing that most of these "cruises to nowhere" were pretty shady operations. They had carte blanche to install slots with the tightest payback percentages.

Sleek silver boxes with rounded case tops and backlit bellies; some manufacturers went for box design branding. Frontier wasn't into anything that subtle. A two-inch-high logo was stamped on the belly of each machine. The cabinet tops had the tables of play and odds. A few plays and Nick was now both irritated and bored. He'd seen it. It operated as advertised. Six electronic games to choose from on the touch screen. Keno, slots, a few types of electronic blackjack, and poker; all in all it was pretty innovative. What he wanted to do was crack the case and mess around in the insides. Security would jump him if he even tried. Nick took a swig of water. "You know you'd get the same odds by sitting in a deck chair and throwing coins over the rail."

The reason for the extremely tight games in onboard casinos was pretty obvious. Once the ship was at sea, there was no competition. You couldn't just hop up and head to the next joint over. But slot and video poker players on a cruise ship were apparently clueless. The casino was packed. Nick hoped the girls didn't have any illusions that they were gambling with the odds in their favor. Turning on him, Nina glared. "What are you, some kind of expert or something?" At that Val squealed. It was an ear-piercing child's squeak that reminded Nick exactly why he hated gambling.

She was bouncing and chanting, "I won, look, I won."

Nick leaned in over her shoulder. The screen showed a row of vine-covered bars, all matching, and the strobes were flashing but the jackpot sounds just weren't there. A flicker on the monitor sent Nick's gaze to the LED above the coin slot.

When malfunctions occurred, slot machines generally stopped accepting coins. The lights on top would flash, but in a 'call attendant' code not a jackpot flurry. As expected, the hopper readout on the face of the machine was alternating its display between 0000 and 9999. It'd tilted. "Sorry, babe," he put his hand on her shoulder, "you didn't win, thing's busted."

"No." There was so much disappointment in her voice. Nick almost felt bad for her. He was about to offer something vaguely sympathetic when Nina jumped in with her biting, slightly inebriated superiority. It was late, he was tired and not having fun. Tossing the empty bottle in a nearby trashcan, he stalked from the casino.

CHAPTER TWENTY-TWO

Brandon caught up with Nicky as he was sucking on a cigarette at the rail. Staring off across the blackness, Nick snapped, "I'm starting to think that maybe you play for both teams." He flicked the ashes into the ocean. "It really fucking hurts me when you do this. You know that. I guess you just don't give a shit."

He'd done it again, pissed Nicky off. Brandon really needed to come clean with him. This was going to freak his boyfriend big time. "Well..." He took a deep breath. "Not much since I got divorced." It wasn't an excuse, but it was an explanation.

The still-lit butt tumbled from Nick's suddenly limp fingers. Bright sparks spiraled until extinguished by distance. Black eyes just stared into blue. "You were married?"

"Yeah." He sighed again. "I made that mistake."

"Wow. Oh, God." It sounded like the bottom had just dropped out of Nicky's world. "So, you've had sex with a woman?" Studying Brandon's face like he was trying to make sense of it, Nicky asked, "Did you like it?"

Brandon shrugged. "It's different, kinda fun sometimes." He pulled a pack from his own pocket, drew out a clove and lit it. Then he offered it to Nick to replace the lost smoke. "Don't you think so?"

Absently, Nicky accepted the proffered cigarette. He hadn't stopped staring at Brandon. "I wouldn't know."

After lighting up his own smoke Brandon turned, elbows braced on the rail. "You've never fucked a woman?" Nick was taking it better than Brandon thought he might. Stunned definitely, but not blowing up or freaking.

Stepping away from the rail, Nick wandered down the deck. Brandon pushed away, and followed. "Never. Never had any desire to." Nick fell heavily onto a deck chair. "I've known I was gay since I hit puberty, actually probably before that."

They were alone. Vacant deck stretched fore and aft. And Brandon hated himself that he was checking before acting. One day he might be over it, comfortable enough to not worry. That day was not today. He sat down next to his sexy vampire boy. Knees and hips touching, he asked, "You ever kiss a woman?" Running his hand down Nick's leg, he gave it a squeeze.

Nicky's reply was startled. "Of course I have."

Not specific enough obviously. Brandon could almost see the gears grinding behind Nicky's eyes. It was probably a shitty way to spring that on him. Of course Brandon wasn't certain that there was a non-shitty way to tell someone that. Teasing, he asked, "No, okay, you ever French kiss a woman?"

"Oh, God, no!" Nick recoiled. "So how many women have you slept with?"

"A few. My ex-wife. I slept around a bit while I was trying to convince myself that my ex just turned me off and guys didn't turn me on. Unfortunately, one of those was before Dian was my ex, and is one of the reasons she is my ex. There was a stripper at one guy's bachelor party…that was more if I didn't everyone would think something was up. It's every straight guy's dream that some hot chick who throws her tits around is going to want to jump in the sack with him. If I had turned her down, I would have never lived it down at the precinct."

"I can't even imagine fucking a woman." Nick shuddered.

Brandon chewed on his lip while he thought, *Ah hell, no time like the present.* "It's hard to have kids without the fucking part." Two bombshells dropped in one night.

"You have kids?"

Brandon held up his index finger. "A girl, she's almost eight now. I haven't seen her in seven months." He ran his hand over his face. "Her birthday's in a month. I need to remember to buy her a present in Mexico. She collects dolls, or so her mom says." This was going just be hard. "I'm not going to be able to be with you that weekend. I planned to go up for her party. Ya know, dad duties." It felt like he should invite Nicky. He really wanted to invite Nicky, start sharing his life with his lover. But what would he say to his family. 'Hope you don't mind, brought my gay boyfriend,' just seemed a harsh way to spring it on them. He stood. "Shit, this is killing my buzz. Let's grab another drink, and then go back to the room, stop talking about it, okay?"

"Okay." Nick took to his feet, and tucked his hands in his pockets. They wandered back into the promenade and threaded their way to one of the bars. While they waited, Nicky asked, "Hey, what's your daughter's name?"

Brandon handed Nick his drink after signing off on the charge slip. "Shayna. She's named after my mom."

"That's pretty."

"I thought so. It was probably the one thing Dian and I agreed on." He took a swig of his own drink. "Look, you've satisfied your curiosity and seen the Frontier setup. So now we're basically here to have fun. Let's not ruin it by reminding me that I managed to fuck up three people's lives before I figured out who I was."

CHAPTER TWENTY-THREE

Kicked back, with one knee up and propped against the mirror, Nick was a study in black; boots, slacks, shirt, eyes and hair. Even the warm copper of his skin melded into a dusky shadow in the dim light. The clove sparked as he took another drag. For a moment the outline of his face was bathed in red. Nick held the smoke in his mouth, motioning Brandon to the bed, "Wanna taste?"

"Sure." Brandon slid down, pushing Nick's hair from his upturned face. "What do I get to taste?" Brandon moved in closer, teasing Nick's lips with his own.

"Cloves," Nick sucked in his breath, "rum," and opened his mouth, "me." The last of it was almost lost in the kiss.

Brandon tugged Nick's shirt free and slid his hands against warm skin. "I like the 'me' part of that. Cloves, rum, come...I like the combo." He ground his hips against Nick's leg as he ravaged Nick's mouth with his tongue. "You've been eating candy, too. I can taste it."

Nick laughed against the kiss. "Shithead."

"Fuck you." The words throbbed hot against Nick's neck.

Everything began to tingle. "That's kinda the plan tonight."

"Please do." Kisses were following Brandon's fingers down Nick's body as he unbuttoned the black silk shirt. "Hard, please, and then harder." The whispers against Nick's skin were intoxicating. By the time the explorations reached his belly, Nick was trembling. Brandon was kneeling beside him; his tongue traced little patterns of heat along the edge of his pants.

Nick lifted his hips into the kiss. "What do you want tonight, Brandon?" He fumbled with the button and zipper, fingers shadowed by Brandon's lips.

"I've been waiting a long time for you to ask that, Nicky." Brandon was almost purring against Nick's skin. "I want you to fuck me."

Nick wasn't sure that Brandon meant it. "Really?" He'd just gotten so used to bottoming he'd forgotten that it didn't always have to be that way. It hadn't always been that way. "Then how much do you trust me?" Jake never had. But Brandon was not, thank God, anything like Jake. "You ever play with toys or bondage?"

"I trust you." Two sets of fingers were working on the buttons of Brandon's shirt. "I've done some." Nick's tongue ran over the exposed flesh of Brandon's stomach. As he passed just under Brandon's navel, Brandon gasped. "Sometimes I fuck myself when no one is watching; that's what dildos are good for."

"True." Rearing back, Nick slid his pants off his hips. The cool air caressed his cock. "But I want to hear you moan because it's my dick up your ass, not some piece of latex. I want you to trust me, really, really trust me. You ever been tied up?"

Brandon leaned in, tasting the tip, and Nick hissed. "Once a guy used a set of wrist/thigh cuffs...the kind with Velcro that snap together." One fist wrapped around the base of Nick's cock. There was still more than enough to fit in Brandon's mouth. His lips slid against the satiny flesh.

Oh, God, it felt so good. Nick drifted in the sensations, grinding his teeth into his lower lip. "I like my bondage a little more plain and simple."

Pulling back, Brandon asked, "What did you have in mind?"

"Grab the purple bag on the floor over there." Brandon reached for the bag, his butt flexing under the fabric as he leaned across the bed. "Hmm, you're making me hard...again."

Grinning, Brandon rolled over and tossed the case on the pillows. "Well, that's the plan tonight." Nick, half dressed, knelt on the bed, cock throbbing. Brandon ran his palm down Nick's shaft. Burying one hand in his long black hair, Brandon pulled Nick into another burning kiss. "That's a pretty sight." Twisting his hand around the length of Nick's cock as if to make sure Nick understood just what he meant, he added, "I want all of it."

"Jake wouldn't ever let me." Damn, hot and heavy in bed with Brandon and talking about Jake again. When was he going to get over that habit? "He said I was a fuck toy only."

"What the fuck was Jake's problem? Couldn't take it?"

"Yeah, he said it hurt too much."

"I can't believe he would say that to you." Brandon's tongue was working him so slow. "Well, looks like he missed a real treat."

"He was a wuss sometimes." Nick was sick of the talking, especially about Jake.

For a while he just explored Brandon's body with his mouth and hands. He unbuttoned Brandon's slacks so he could reach down and feel Brandon's cock; the weight of it was imprisoned beneath gray cotton. Thumb toying with the tip of Brandon's cock, Nick stroked him through the light material. "Tell me what you want."

"Be gentle. Do with me as you please," Brandon sucked on the skin behind Nick's ear. "I'm yours tonight."

Nick teased, "Never, I don't know how to be gentle...I wasn't trained that way." Hell, if they were really going to do this, then there had to be some rules. At least the basics needed to be gotten out of the way. It was always so much easier to do that before you were in heavy make-out mode. "What's our safe word?" Of course this wasn't quite a dinner table discussion, not the first time usually.

"Our what?" Brandon's mouth was still buried in his neck, hand still playing between Nick's legs.

Well, it looked like he was going to have to take the lead. It had been a long time. Pulling back and grabbing Brandon's wrist to stop the distraction, he explained, "Safe word. You always have to have a safe word. You say it, I stop and release you." So it didn't seem so harsh, he brought Brandon's fingers to his lips. Brandon's skin tasted like both their bodies. "Any distress, even if you just can't handle it any more, you say it. 'Cause when things get intense, you'll start saying no, but you won't really want me to stop. The safe word means 'I mean it' or 'I can't breathe' or 'I can't feel my legs anymore.' One word that you wouldn't normally say during sex. That's what trust is."

Brandon traced his thumb along the edge of Nick's cheek. "I don't know what a good safe word would be." Although his tone was light, his eyes were serious; good.

"Hmmm." Nick contemplated the possibilities. Reaching back and snagging the bag, he pulled a few lengths of multi-colored rope from inside. Red, black, purple, blue...none were more than ten feet; a good thirty-foot section would have been more useful, but he hadn't been planning for this. It would keep things pretty tame for the night. "How 'bout 'peanut butter'." He always traveled with a little rope. You never knew when you might want a gauntlet or two. Hemp was fun for the feeling of it scratching against the skin. Colored climbing ropes were better for the decorative ties. They'd serve tonight. Blue, he chose the blue to match Brandon's eyes.

"Peanut butter?"

"Yeah, peanut butter. Simple. Easy to say." He laughed. "It's not going to get mixed up with anything else in the heat of passion." He turned serious, threading one cord through his fingers. "I promise you that if you say that I'll stop everything and get you undone. I promise I won't leave you tied up alone. I promise I'll never leave you face down on a bed. I promise to look out for your safety. Trust me."

"I trust you." Brandon hooked the blue cord with one finger. "What are you going to do with this?"

"Tie you up." The rope was heavier than it looked, with a soft nap that caught the skin. "Tie you down. I am a student of Nawa-kesho...Japanese rope bondage. It's been a while since I've had a chance to practice it. Karada is one of the more beautiful katas, a full rope harness...very erotic on a body. It takes a long time to weave, which is all part of the fun. But we should start on a much smaller scale, I think. Will you be my nawa junjun, my submissive one, tonight?"

"Oh, really...you want me to call you Master?"

"Nah, not yet at least; after I train you right you can call me Sensei." He stifled a laugh. Words of submission weren't what got him off. They always seemed contrived anyway. The act of giving in, letting yourself be controlled, that was hot. What someone called him didn't matter if they were willing to be bound. "I think, maybe, something like the pearl...I do that for some of the girls as club wear. You bind under and over the top of the breasts with several turnings of rope, then you can accent and squeeze the breasts into position with shorter lengths." He'd actually gotten hard a few times doing that. Rope on skin, male or female, was just so damn sexy. "Momo Shibari, my junjun kneeling, arms drawn between your legs and wrists bound to your ankles." Nick shuddered with the mental picture of Brandon trussed like that. "Maybe it's too much for our first time playing this way. I have to teach you to really trust me before that. Hold out your arms. Put your hands like this, like you're praying."

Brandon pleaded, "Be gentle, okay?" He knelt on the bed, resting his butt on his feet.

Nick looked down at his hands, winding the rope in his fingers. It was as silky as the skin on Brandon's shaft. He pushed his long, thick hair behind one ear. When he turned to gaze at Brandon, it spilled down the other side; a black satin curtain framing his face.

Brandon held his arms out, palms together. "Like this?"

Nick folded the length of rope in half and nodded. "Yeah, like that." The looped end he held against Brandon's arm, just below his elbow. Running the other end over and around both arms, he licked his lips. Just the sight of the blue cord against Brandon's pale skin was exciting. Loose ends were drawn through the loop and snugged down. Then the wrap went in the opposite direction, pulling against the loop. Three times Nick turned the rope around Brandon's arms. He always worked in threes. It put enough tension on the skin and looked sexy and dangerous without being too bulky. Each movement was slow, deliberate, drawing it out for both of them.

Nick threaded the ends through the loop formed when he reversed the direction of the rope. Wrapping the rope between Brandon's arms and over the other binding formed cinch loops. He ran the ends through the original loop leaving a smaller one and then ran it through that loop, forming a knot. Then Nick pulled it all taut, but not too tight. He didn't want to hurt his lover, just restrain him.

Brandon moaned as it was tugged down. "So this is what it looks like when you're finished?" His cock jumped under the fabric with each tug.

"Oh no, babe." Nick flashed a smile. "This is what it looks like when we're just getting started." Nick ran the end down Brandon's arms to his wrists. Then he wrapped it once around, running the rope under itself. With a tug, because Brandon seemed to like it when he did that, he started winding in the opposite direction. Another moan told him he was right. Again he wrapped three times around before he threaded the ends through the loop that was formed when he reversed directions. The cinch loops between the wrists bound Brandon tighter. Only a few feet of loose cord remained. Nick slid it through the initial loop. Leaving another small loop, he ran the ends under the wrist to elbow rope and back through and drew the knot tight.

Finally, Nick pushed Brandon's bound arms back against his chest. He took the last bit of rope and ran each end up either side of Brandon's tattooed neck. Then he tied them off, making sure that the knot was a little off center; not resting against Brandon's spine or carotid artery.

He sat back and looked over Brandon. Arms bound, hands just below his chin, Brandon was kneeling helpless on the bed. Nick could see his cock bulging under his shorts where his pants hung open. Electric blue rope, white skin, Brandon staring at him, so hungry for it...goddamn, he'd forgotten how charged it was to be in control. His eyes drifted over to the tangle of ropes. It was hard not to want to take it further. Brandon would probably let him take it further. But a full sexual binding was just too much for their first time. Hell, even if both partners came into a relationship with experience, you didn't jump right into it. Trust had to be established first. There was no shortcut to trust.

He fished another cig from the pack and lit it. Nick waited, watching, letting Brandon get more excited while he took his time. Shrugging out of the silk, Nick tossed his shirt on the ground. He took another drag. He stroked himself and ran his hand over his balls. Brandon watched, biting his own lower lip. Finally Nick ground out the cigarette. "Do you want me to fuck you now, Brandon?"

"Oh, hell, yeah." His blue eyes were frantic. "Fuck me hard, hard as you can." That hot, deep voice pleading like that; it sent shivers down Nick's spine.

He put one foot up on the bed. Very deliberately, he began to unlace his boot. Time, waiting; both could be a terrible tease when you were trussed up. Nick was going to make Brandon wait a little longer, make him watch while Nick undressed.

There were twin thuds as first one boot, then the other, landed on the floor. Slowly, he slid out of his pants. Now it was time to show Brandon just how much control he'd given up. Now it was time to teach Brandon that he could trust Nick.

Nick reached over and, with gentle pressure, pushed Brandon back on the bed. Ankles under his ass, knees spread, Brandon bent backwards under the weight of Nick's hand. Then he was over and falling. His arms jerked against the ropes. He couldn't stop himself from falling. "Fuck!" Blue eyes went wide in terror. And then Nick caught him.

Cradling Brandon in his arms as he lowered his lover back on the bed, Nick whispered, "Don't worry, babe, I'll never let you get hurt. I promised you that. Remember?"

"Yeah."

"Still trust me?" This time, Brandon just nodded. Nick reached down and untied Brandon's shoes. As slowly as he'd undressed himself, he was going to draw it out more for his lover. Let the frustration build. Let Brandon's body start screaming for it. Shoes and socks dropped off the end of the bed. He sat back and surveyed Brandon. Touching Brandon's stomach, chest, face, Nick let his hands explore his possession. Brandon was his, only his right now.

He snagged his fingers in the pockets of Brandon's slacks and drew them off the long legs. Each move was deliberate and unhurried. He ran his hand over the bulge between Brandon's thighs. The boxer style briefs Brandon wore were damn sexy on that cut body.

"Maybe I'm getting bored...should I just turn on the TV?" Nick teased, and Brandon groaned. "Nah, I think I want to see what's under here." Now the shorts came down and off. Nick spread Brandon's legs wide. "What do you want me to do?" Nick lowered himself and sucked Brandon's sac into his mouth.

Brandon tried to move his arms. The rope jerked on the back of his neck pulling him up short. Nick laughed inside, Brandon fighting the restraints just made it that much more fun. "Whatever you want." As Nick's teeth grazed the skin just behind his balls, Brandon added, "Oh, gentle!"

"Never...ever." Nick teased. Brandon cringed, drawing his leg up. Nick pushed it back down and nibbled up the length of Brandon's dick. "Beg for it, Brandon."

"Fucking suck me! Fuck me!"

Wow, that was begging. But if Brandon wanted both, he'd get neither...at least not yet. Nick ran his tongue in little circles over the tip of Brandon's cock. As Brandon raised his hips into the touch, Nick pulled back, keeping it as tenuous as possible. "Your ass? Or your cock?"

"What ever you want, just do it, please do it." Brandon moaned in bliss.

Nick drew one finger through the slick shine on Brandon's head. "That's right." Tracing the pattern of the veins, he went lower and lower until he was circling Brandon's hole. "It's whatever I want." Slowly, he pushed in. When Brandon hissed in pleasure, he stopped and waited. Then he moved again, going deeper. Each time Brandon responded, he would stop for a while. The control was wonderful. Seeing Brandon shaking in frustration was wonderful. Knowing just how hard he was going to fuck his blue-eyed captive was wonderful.

Brandon begged for more. "Oh yeah, stick your finger farther up." He struggled against the ropes. Nick could see the rope cutting into Brandon's skin every time he moved. "Let me loose, Nicky."

Nick stilled. "Is there a problem?"

"What do you mean is there a problem? Just fucking untie me, Nicky." Brandon's arms were straining in the bindings.

"You know what to say if there's a problem." He stared intensely down at Brandon. Grazing Brandon's lip with one knuckle, Nick leaned in. In a voice full of smoke, he added, "So no, I'm not going to untie you." He watched as understanding crawled into Brandon's mind. Those sensuous lips parted and Brandon's tongue ran across the edge of his teeth. His breathing slowed. Brandon was a fighter...God, was he a fighter. Nick could tell he wasn't giving up, just regrouping.

A few more strokes with his finger, and Nick withdrew. Brandon moaned his frustration. There were some practical things that had to be attended to anyway. He might as well let the anticipation build for both of them.

Brandon could only wait and watch as Nick slid off the bed. Condom and lube landed on the covers next to his bound lover. Nick climbed back up, "You want me to stick this big dick up your ass...while you can't do anything about it?" Stroking himself in front of Brandon was a real turn on. For both of them apparently; Brandon was so hard his dick was jumping in time to his heart.

"Oh, yeah." Nick could see that Brandon wanted it now. He drew out the torture, slowly rolling the condom onto his dick. "Yeah," Brandon moaned again. Lube gleamed as Nick stroked himself up, getting ready.

Nick pushed Brandon's legs back as he knelt between them. Leaning in over the tattooed body, he grabbed Brandon's face, "Beg me for it!" He reached back and slapped Brandon; hard enough to sting a little. The struggling started again. "Tell me you want it." Slowly, Nick drove his throbbing cock into his lover.

Brandon's body gave into the not-so-gentle pressure. "Ah, that stings." Brandon arched his back as Nick drove deep inside. "Burns so good, pump my ass." The restraints ground against Brandon's skin as he fought them. It was so fucking intense having Brandon like this.

Nick hissed with pleasure. "I'll pump your ass, hard!" He hadn't had this end in a long time. Feeling how Brandon's body bore down on his cock as Brandon bucked beneath him, Nick drove it deep. He'd forgotten how good it felt to be inside someone. Ramming Brandon like he hadn't had sex in ages, 'cause he hadn't fucked anyone in ages, Nick bit Brandon's bottom lip; bit it hard.

"More! Harder!" Brandon tried to move his hands, but it was no use -- he couldn't move anywhere. The more he struggled the tighter his body became. It was so intense, Nick could barely take it. Brandon was pleading. "Pump me, baby! Pump harder! I want you all the way in me."

Palms against the back of Brandon's knees, Nick reared back. Thrusting deeper and deeper, he was pounding so hard he could feel the shockwaves in his brain. "Brandon...I'm going to blow, baby!"

"I want you to come on my face. Let me taste you!"

The hell with being in control; Nick yanked himself out of Brandon's body and crawled up his chest. Somehow he managed to get the condom off in the process. Straddling his lover and stoking his dick, his mind melted out through his cock. Once the circuits started firing again he looked down. Come painted Brandon's smoking hot face, running over his cheek and chin.

Nick collapsed back on the bed. How much more sexy could Brandon get? For a moment Nick toyed with just leaving his lover trussed and frustrated. No, he couldn't do that to Brandon, at least not yet, not here.

He rolled over, grabbing and stroking his lover's hard cock. As he jerked Brandon, Nick slid his lips down over the head. Pulling and sucking, he could hear Brandon's money shot chant, "God, Nicky. Hell, Nicky." He ran the other hand between Brandon's cheeks sliding his finger up and inside. "Fucking yeah, Nicky," rewarded him. Brandon's blue eyes were rolling back in his head. He shuddered into orgasm. Nick pumped and sucked and swallowed as white-hot come filled his mouth. Damn, Brandon was hot.

As he licked off the last bit of come and pulled his finger out, Brandon shivered. "Ah, Nicky, baby."

CHAPTER TWENTY-FOUR

Last night had been intense. Nick couldn't get over how intense. His time with Brandon just kept getting better and better. They'd debated staying in bed for the day, but decided that they'd go nuts if they remained in the cramped cabin that long. You could only fuck so much before things got sore. Ensenada waited. The ship had pulled in early in the a.m. Time to go wander about, grab some lunch; maybe they could take a nap and fool around in the afternoon. Nick liked making those types of plans with Brandon. Anything that included sex and Brandon was great.

The sound of the shower's drizzle seeped out of the bathroom. Nick toyed with the idea of slipping in with Brandon. Unfortunately there was hardly enough room for one person in that Pepto-Bismol shower. Besides he was dressed already. If he shucked his clothes now, they'd never make it off the ship. Not that that wouldn't be fun, but...the water was cut off mid-thought. Ah well, a little anticipation was nice anyway; build-up and all that.

A battered, black cowboy hat went on his head. Silver conchos laced on a red band wound about the crown's base. Dyed leather straps trailed off the back. The brown-blond feather of a hawk was tucked on the left side. A five-year-old Nick had found it in the desert and given it to Gramps for Christmas. Things like that made up for the money his parents never had.

Brandon stepped out of the bathroom, and did a double-take. Thick, black hair braided down his back, the barest relief of muscle showing under a white T-shirt and hips kissed by low slung blue jeans, Nick knew he was almost unrecognizable. "What the fuck?" Brandon stepped in. The T-shirt went transparent wherever his still-wet fingertips landed on Nick's chest. "What's up with the new look? Every time I see you these days it's like I've got an entirely new boyfriend."

Nick snorted "Hey look, Goth and gay are two things I don't want to be advertising wandering around Mexico." Nick shuddered. With nothing but a towel wrapped about his hips, Brandon was completely edible. Damn, he was getting hard again. It pinched. If he was going to keep his uber-sexy, closeted cop around, he was definitely going to have to invest in some relaxed-cut jeans.

"You look like a cowboy, babe." Brandon pulled Nick into his body. "A gay cowboy."

Brandon smelled like soap. "Want me to toss you on your butt, paleface?" Toss him on his butt, rip the towel off and smoke his pole...oh hell, what did they need to go out for?

"Promise?" Sucking on Nick's lip, Brandon swiped the battered Stetson and slipped it on his own head. Brandon's mouth tasted of mint. Strong hands ran down Nick's slender waist and cupped his tight ass. He knew he had a runner's glutes, firm and hard and fuckable. It was nice to know Brandon appreciated them. Brandon rubbed his wrists against denim. Bringing one up, he flashed it before Nick's eyes; a hatch-mark brand wound across the back. "Fuck, I got a rope burn from last night."

"I know." He pulled Brandon's arm to his mouth and pressed his lips against the skin. "It's fucking sexy."

Brandon wrestled his arm from Nick's grip. Finger hooked in his lower lip, Brandon displayed a purple set of dashes running just on the inside. "Where you bit me...is that fucking sexy, too?"

Nick hissed as he drew in his breath. "Uh-huh. It marks you as mine." He ground his hips into the towel and laughed. Brandon was getting hard, too.

A wicked light danced in Brandon's half lidded eyes as he considered Nick from under the brim. "So, where'd you get the hat?"

"Belonged to my Gramps. I wear it when I work outside or go hiking. Wouldn't want to get a tan and lose Goth points." Nick's skin, where their arms crossed, was almost two shades darker than his lover's pale body.

Brandon broke away. He snagged a pair of trunks and fell on the bed. "And what tribe was your Gramps?" He wriggled into the tight fabric, tucking his stiff dick to one side. "Babe, I need my jeans." He held his hand out, and Nick tossed him a pair from his bag.

"Drunken fucking Irish." Watching that sexy biker struggle into his clothes made Nick wish he wasn't wearing any. Black jeans sliding up his hips, ass lifted off the bed...how did Brandon get so fucking sexy? He sighed as he imagined what he could do to Brandon. "My dad was adopted, from a Catholic orphanage in the Four-Corners region."

He'd have to jump Brandon if he didn't turn away. While he couldn't look, he could help. A Harley T with a winged heart logo and firebrand letters should be hot. He tossed it backward onto the bed. If he turned around he'd start ripping clothes off both of them.

He figured talking about family should be enough of a distraction. "You know the kind of place where they used to send wayward young women. The Salvation Army's helping him try and find his real parents. They might be dead by now, but maybe not. Dad's aunt told him when Gramps died." A little calmer and in control, he rested his butt on the vanity and watched as his lover pulled the shirt over his head. "Not that he didn't freak'n have a clue by the time he was ten...I mean, there's no family resemblance between Dad and Gramps. Anyway, she gave him everything she had. The story was that his mom was white and his dad was an Indian. No one knows from what nation. But looking at Dad and looking at me, I'm guessing Navajo. Anyway, they put dad up for adoption as soon as he was born. If they were teenagers when he was born they might still be around. If they're looking for him, the Salvation Army keeps a database and they'll find them."

CHAPTER TWENTY-FIVE

Ensenada jammed itself about the pier. The "Cinderella of the Pacific," she lay south of the international border, just an hour and a half from San Diego by car. No matter how they arrived, it was one of the premier tourist destinations in Baja. Seals packed themselves on the buoys dotting the harbor. Their barking called the ships to port.

Ensenada's downtown area was the largest tourist trap Mexico could support. Just a block from the waterfront, shopping was concentrated along Boulevard Lopez Mateos. Sunny summers cooled by ocean breezes meant open air taquarias that sounded mighty fine for lunch. Shrimp tacos sold for a buck a pop, beer for a little more. Brandon and Nick chose one where more locals seemed to hang out. It was your best bet for finding anywhere to eat in Mexico. Blue-painted picnic tables stretched under metal awnings. Sitting across from each other, Nick's casual, but cutting, comments about other tourists caused Brandon to snort beer out his nose more than once. Yet again Nick focused a predatory glare at the street. Then his face went slack. "Brandon, check out the guy with the tattoo."

That didn't seem like the start of a joke. "What?" He turned to follow Nick's stare.

"The guy with the double Ms tattooed just below his left ear." Nicky spoke at a near-whisper. "The guy by that pottery store, the one with the red door. He was at Duke's funeral."

Holy shit; scrawny, buzz cut marked by La Eme with the full-bloomed red rose and intertwined Ms...Chino. Everything inside went watery. "Do you think he'd recognize you?" Chino was heading their way.

"Hell, babe, you barely recognized me this morning. I was all prettified for the funeral, my hair loose, frock coat; not this." They watched as Chino jaywalked, dodging cabs and cars. Then their view was blocked by the wall of the restaurant. "Plus the guy was convinced I was balling Duke's ex. So, no I don't think he'd recognize a gay cowboy."

"Good." Brandon leaned in. Despite the heat he had shivers. "Because that asshole is one bad-ass dude. You do not want him recognizing you." Over Nick's shoulder, along the rail separating dining from street, Chino appeared.

"Why?"

Waiting until the drug dealer was farther along, Brandon responded. "The MM behind his ear is a gang tat. It says I'm in a gang, this is which one, and I don't care that everyone who sees knows it. Cops, rivals…I'm bad enough I don't care."

"So he has attitude—don't they all?" Nick was whispering. It felt like they were caught up in some low-budget cop flick.

"More than attitude. See how old he is? First off, if you're in a gang and you live past twenty-five you're pretty much a veteran. Then you add an advertisement—come and fucking take me out. That tat at that age equals one seriously bad-assed mother fucker."

"We gotta figure out why he's here."

That sounded like the worst plan in the world. Of course this was Nicky, a guy who dropped probably close to a grand booking this cruise just so he could look at some slot machines. Talking him out of it wouldn't be an option. "Fuck, you ever tail anyone before?"

"No."

"Okay, we're going to relay him." Brandon stood and motioned with his head for Nick to follow. Walking casually, at a tourist's pace, he explained the rules of the hunt. "Stay as far back as you can without losing sight of him. Wander, like you're shopping. You'll blend in better than I will. Don't look directly at him. Think of it like you're trying to figure out whether he's straight or not. You don't want him to know you're checking him out. Act as normal as possible. When you see me, either drop back or pass him up and I'll pick up the tail." That was the first part. "Got that?"

"Yeah," Hat back on his head, hands in his pockets, Nick offered a double raise of his eyebrows for fun. "Don't let him see me, window shop, and scope out straight guys."

There was no way to get Nicky to play things straight. Brandon sighed. "If he does something unexpected, like turn and come back at you, just walk on past and I'll jump on it. If he seems like he's caught me, I'll do the same. If it gets too hot just get something to eat or drink, that's our signal. Anything at all, just stop and quit. If I quit, you quit…that's our deal." Their prey stopped at a corner and dug out a smoke. "You go first. I'll stay here for a minute and then come along behind. If he drops into a building, we stop. You don't follow people inside, got it? Basically we're stalking someone and we're doing it in Mexico. Neither one of us wants to end up as a guest of the Fedarales."

When Nick nodded his understanding, Brandon stopped and let him go ahead. He half considered a tray of silver rings and half watched as Nick drifted into dogging the gangster's steps. Without thinking he found himself holding a large silver ring. The face of a gargoyle, its bat ears would cover the knuckle while skeletal hands wrapped around the first joint of the finger. It was so Nicky. Still watching, he absently asked, "¿Cuánto?"

With a trader's knowing eye, the old Mexican man appraised Brandon's look and Spanish. Then he pursed his thin lips. "Treinta-cinco."

Nick was doing just fine. "Veinte." Brandon said it with the soft 'bv' sound of a California native.

"Veinte-cinco." Good enough; Brandon would have paid thirty for it. He nodded and pulled out a twenty and five ones. Shoving the ring in his pocket, he headed out after his lover. They played the game, hopscotching through Ensenada, heading deeper into the tourist entertainment areas. Sometimes they rode Chino close; neither more than a few steps behind. Other times Brandon would be out ahead and Nick on the opposite side of the street. With all the tourist trade flowing in the same general direction, the mark probably never knew he'd been tailed.

Although Nick had good instincts for active surveillance, this guy was just dumb or overconfident. His route should have included areas that were wide-open or deserted. He walked with the traffic flow instead of against it. There were no attempts at mirroring, trying to catch a tail by looking into shop or car windows. Any one of those would have pick up their rough shadowing tactics. Finally, Chino ducked into a large semi-open cantina. Brandon paused, and pulled out a cigarette, waiting for Nick to catch up.

Nick slid behind him. "Now what do we do?" He reached over and filched the cig from between Brandon's lips. After a deep drag, he added, "You're the expert at this."

"I think we sit at that bar there," Brandon waived the pack of cigarettes toward another patio bar across the street. Using his teeth he pulled out another smoke. "We have a few beers and watch that bar over there. See who our banger talks to."

A table in the back corner of the veranda gave them a decent view of the other establishment while providing them with cover. As they sat down, the ring dug into Brandon's leg. He fished it from his pocket. After ordering, he laid his closed fist on the table between them. "I got you something."

Startled, Nick turned to him. He'd been staring at the door, like he was trying to will Chino to come back out. "Really?" Brandon opened his hand, revealing the ring. Silver glinted in the afternoon sun and flashed in Nick's eyes. "Oh, wow, now that is wicked cool." Tentatively, Nicky picked it up and just stared at it for a time. The gargoyle had feral eyes and a wicked fanged mouth; there was even a little pointed tongue rolled behind the teeth. "I've never seen anything like it." He rolled the heavy piece in his palm. Then he slid it on the middle finger of his left hand.

Beer came and the waitress went. Nick waited until Brandon was taking the first swig before saying anything more. "I really like you asking, but don't you think it's a little early to be talking about engagements?" He laughed as Brandon choked on the beer, and then yelped when Brandon's boot caught his shin under the table.

Chino chose a table street-side. After a bit, two men joined him. Ambrazos, Mexico's formalized business hug, passed all around. It was hard to make out the new arrivals. One appeared older, maybe a businessman by his clothes. In Mexico it was damn hard to tell. The Guatemalan wedding shirt he wore could seamlessly serve in board room or beach house. The second guest was too far in shadow, too hard to make out. The trio sat and drank. Business in Mexico, legitimate or otherwise, was always conducted over drinks.

Thankfully, the dive they had picked carried food, or Brandon would have starved. In case they needed to pull a fast exit, they paid as it came. Darkness descended upon Ensenada as one hour passed after another. He was about to suggest to Nick that they bail when he caught site of Chino coming out of the other bar. "Nick, there he is." The two other men were with him. The older gentleman, visible now that they were under a streetlight, was blessed with thick salt-and-pepper hair, but seriously in need of a Stairmaster. The other guy, the one Brandon hadn't been able to make out, was just as scrawny and buzzed as Chino. Prison screamed from his clothes and attitude. Nick started to rise.

"Sit. We have to wait a bit." Businessman stepped into the road and hailed a taxi. All three climbed in.

Nicky was way too excited that the chase was back on. "Okay, let's grab a cab and follow."

Brandon sucked down the last of the beer. "Up for the cab, not for the following."

"What?" Nick apparently didn't want to let it go. "Why?"

"It's dark. We're in Mexico. We have no idea where they're going." The bottle landed on the table with a thunk. "Besides I'm just a little too drunk and a lot too horny to go chasing around a foreign country after guys who kill people for fun."

Of course Nicky couldn't just leave it. "But…"

"No buts, babe." He slid a hand up Nicky's thigh as he leaned in. "I'm going to haul you back on the ship, strip you nekkid, and blow you like you've never been blown before."

"You planned this, huh? We shouldn't have been drinking, should we?" Brandon grinned like the Cheshire Cat. "Bastard."

CHAPTER TWENTY-SIX

"Okay, whoa, Brandon…" Nick was up against the mirrored closet doors. Brandon's teeth nipped his neck, while those big hands explored in his jeans. They'd barely gotten the door shut before Brandon was feeling him up. When he'd said a little drunk and a lot of horny, he'd damn well meant it. Brandon was rubbing him hard. Biting, stroking, licking—all of it was just incredible. Nick tried to move them further into the room. With his cop all over him he got tangled in his own feet and they went down. Nick landed on his stomach, Brandon landed on his ass. Brandon yanked the white T from Nick's jeans and began licking up his spine.

"You are just a little excited." Nick rolled onto his back as Brandon crawled up his body. Of course with the stroking he'd gotten, he was more than a little excited himself.

On his knees, straddling Nick's hips, Brandon yanked the T-shirt over his head. "No fucking shit, babe." The cotton muffled Brandon's words as he struggled simultaneously with it and pulling off his biker boots.

Flopping back on the carpet, Nick watched as his lover tossed the shirt to the floor. Those baby blues were so wicked. God, he liked to watch Brandon undress. Slowly, the tattooed cop unbuttoned his jeans. He'd pop one button, then wait a bit, licking his lips before working another loose. Nick ran his hands down Brandon's thighs. "Babe, where did you learn to strip like that?" One more button down as Brandon shot him a hungry, burning look.

"Work." Brandon laughed, hooking his fingers on the waistband of his jeans. "Busting lap dancers at strip clubs. I watch how they move since I'm not all that interested in seeing their tits." After a little awkward maneuvering, and a lot of rubbing against Nick, the jeans hit the floor. Muscles, tattoos, the white trunks with blue stitching that clutched Brandon's ass, and athletic socks that hugged tight calves—it was an incredible sight.

Nick worked his own fly, lifting his hips off the floor. "Wait." Brandon caught him as he was sliding the fabric down. "Don't take 'em all the way off." Trunks and socks landed next to the clothing pile.

Stopping when the jeans were halfway down his thighs, Nick asked, "Like this?" Brandon smiled and nodded as he dug the necessities from the bag. One good thing about being on the floor was the luggage was right there. Dropping condom and lube by his knee, Brandon leaned in and ran his tongue across the throbbing head of Nick's cock. Brandon teased Nick, licking just the tip. Then he wrapped his mouth around Nick's cock and sucked down hard. Teeth grazed sensitive flesh and Nick hissed with pleasure.

He'd never had someone blow him like Brandon. Always so intense, it was like Brandon was starving for a cock in his mouth. Going down hard and deep with teeth and tongue, the pressure was brutal and passionate. He'd hit the back of his throat and just hold it there until Nick was ready to die. And it wasn't just that he was eager; Brandon paid attention to every moan, every sigh. God, did Nick like it.

Moaning, grinding his teeth into his lower lip, Nick slid his hand between Brandon's legs. He cupped Brandon's balls, enjoying the heavy weight in his palm. Brandon's skin slid like silk under his fingers. Hard and throbbing in his hand, Nick twisted and pulled, earning moans that vibrated through his own body. Then the blissful contact on his dick was gone. Nick whined. Pulling his knees up with his feet and butt still on the floor, he started to sit up. Brandon's hand on his chest stopped him.

With a laugh, Brandon rolled the condom down Nick's throbbing length. Following with a liberal application of lube, "I'm gonna ride you, babe. Just lie back and enjoy it." Brandon straddled Nick, leaning down to ravage his mouth. Intense kisses burned his skin. Holding Nick's cock steady he worked himself down on it. A little at a time, riding Nick slow; it was heaven for both of them. "God, fucking yeah." Grinding his ass against Nick's hard dick, Brandon braced himself; one hand on Nick's denim-clad knee, the other stroking himself.

Hands gripping Brandon's thighs, Nick lifted his hips off the floor, driving deep. Never had anyone been so into his pleasure. Watching Brandon stroke himself added chills to the fire seeping through his thighs. Half-lidded blue eyes devoured him. There was nothing sexier than one of Brandon's lust-filled glares. "Oh, fuck me, baby, ride me." Sweat plastered the T-shirt to his chest as he thrust. Brandon was shivering, shaking, his body drawing in on itself as he exploded. Hot come spattered Nick's cheek. The thought that Brandon had come so hard twisted his insides in fire. "Oh God! Fucking God!" Nick screamed as ecstasy tore him apart.

Brandon pulled them together, his tongue driving into Nick's mouth. "Oh, Nicky, baby, you're so fucking good."

Fingers played in his hair as Nick ran his own hands over taut muscles. He was about to comment on Brandon's prowess when a pounding behind the closet wall startled them. Chagrined looks turned to embarrassed chuckling and dissolved into riotous laughter. Neither realized that the walls were so thin, or that they were so loud. The only thing that stopped the mirth was more kisses.

Snuggled in bed for the remainder of the evening, the buzz slowly wore off. Canned programming on the TV couldn't hold Nick's interest. His mind was cycling, and recycling everything until he was just confused. There were too many facts and too many missing pieces, and he just couldn't make them all fit right. "I think I'm going to take a shower." Long, hot soaks usually cleared his head. Unfortunately he would have to settle for a lukewarm drenching. It still should help.

Brandon nuzzled his neck, running his fingers through Nick's midnight hair. "Okay, Nicky." Brandon gave a long sigh as he rolled onto his back. "I'm pretty beat though, what with drinking and sexing." His laugh even sounded exhausted. "So don't be surprised if I'm out cold by the time you're done."

Soaping up under the tepid drizzle, Nick tried to sort out the trip. The cruise had netted pretty much a zero. He'd gotten to see the concession, now he could visualize it, but not much more than that. This afternoon's sighting of Chino…well, they knew he was in Ensenada, and they knew he talked to two guys and that was it. What a waste.

No, he couldn't think like that. All of it had brought him much closer to Brandon. It still threw him that his lover had been married, had a kid even. He'd never been in a relationship with anyone who had that kind of history. There would be a lot of adjustments to make in his thinking if they were going to make this work long term. God, did Nick even want to make it work long term? He could imagine that life with Brandon. He wasn't sure he could imagine that life with Brandon and rug rats tearing apart his house. Kids just hadn't ever been in his personal plans. Nick liked kids. He babysat for Miri when her resident asshole left her hanging. Uncle Nick was one of their favorites, because he'd let them play videos all night and make themselves sick on popcorn instead of dinner. They weren't his, after all. It wasn't his responsibility for how they turned out. But if you made yourself part of someone's life, you owed it to their kids to make them your responsibility. He wasn't sure he could handle that.

Toweling off, walking back into the main cabin, he could see Brandon sprawled on the bed, already half asleep. "Damn, babe, forget me so quick?" Blue eyes came to barely half-mast. Absently Brandon waved toward the nightstand then rolled over pulling a pillow over his head. Nick sat on the edge of the mattress and picked up a plastic bottle. Square and white with the ubiquitous safety cap...prescription pills rattled within. "What are you taking?" The label said Zalepon, generic for Sonata. That registered a big fat zero in Nick's brain.

"Drugs..." drifted from under the pillow, "sleeping pills." Apparently, Brandon had downed his dosage while Nick was in the shower.

"Do you take them every night?"

"Every other four, not if I'm on call. They make it hard for me to wake up if I get less than four hours sleep."

"Can't you sleep?"

"Not always."

"Why?"

"Mmm," Brandon's voice was full of slumber, "thinking."

"'Bout what?"

Nick had to shake the pills in Brandon's ear before he got an answer. "Stuff."

"Like what stuff?"

Brandon offered up a response. "Like what was so bad in a twelve-year-old's life that he would hang himself with the dog's choke chain. It took a long time to get him out of that tree. Been up there for a day or so before anyone even noticed he was gone. Had to hold his legs while the coroner cut him down."

Holy shit, Nick's mind could hardly wrap around the image. He shuddered and tried to think of some way to respond to a statement like that. 'Gee, that must have been awful' didn't seem to quite cut it. Brandon's snore saved him from sticking his foot in his mouth. Nick would have needed more than sleeping pills to cope with memories like that. How the hell did Brandon not go insane with those kinds of things running around his head?

Hours later Nick still hadn't figured it out. Each time he shut his eyes a vision of some kid swinging from a tree swam up into his mind. He debated filching one of Brandon's pills but tossed it as a supremely bad idea. Finally, he gave up on sleep and decided to try and walk it off.

Yesterday's jeans, Brandon's leather jacket and one-thirty in the morning found Nick wandering near the darkened casino. A lone occupant was just inside the arch. Ships generally closed their casinos while in port. Curious, Nick stepped inside. Canvas tool case at the man's feet, nail-bitten hands flipping through keys: IT maintenance. Flopping onto a stool at a slot bank near the entrance, Nick watched the tech crack the case on the tilted machine. The guy gave him a once-over stare and then, seeing that Nick had no interest in playing, went back to his work with a shrug.

The place was a ghost town. Probably half the ship was still barhopping in port. Those that weren't into the party scene were too old to be wandering about after midnight. Between personality and lack of sleep, Nick was punchy. "Got a Manufacturer's License?" he shot at the man's back. In Nevada you needed one to legally open the processor drawer, the locked box containing the EPROM. Almost every casino in Nevada had a Manufacturer's License.

Turning and scratching behind his ear with the key he'd used to open the case, the guy replied, "Let me guess, you're outta Vegas?" He looked like many other computer geeks Nick knew. A little too heavy, the wrong clothes for his body, the wrong haircut for his face; not bad looking, but he obviously cared about other things.

There was no reason to distrust this man, but neither was there any reason to trust him. Too much weirdness and too much death was making Nick paranoid. "Nah." Nick laughed. "I do IT for a few of the local casinos in Elko."

"Aha, that explains it." Keys went back to a clip on the tech's belt. "I used to work for one of the resorts in Reno." He rummaged in the ubiquitous black computer tech case. "Bet you never thought your IT degree would get you shit work, huh?"

"True enough. I guess it's better than driving a truck. That's one of those jobs I just couldn't do." Nick shuddered, thinking back. "It's what my dad did while I was growing up." That actually wasn't a lie.

"Almost got roped into selling used cars myself. Managed to land this gig though, pretty cushy. Live in Ensenada, house on the beach, and every so often fix a few slots or vid-poker machines." Nick offered up a vague sound of jealousy. "I have contracts with most of the lines and concessions. They won't let me come in and fix these babies at a normal hour. I have to wait until just before they're ready to shut down the promenade." The tech picked up an EPROM removal tool; it looked like a miniature set of salad tongs. Gently he rocked the chip from side to side. Finally he freed it from the machine. "Somebody forced this one, hinked it all up." The tech held it up for Nick's inspection. Three tines were bent and the ceramic case was cracked with little bits missing here and there. "Shit, not really worth trying to salvage this one. Not with a cracked case. Might accidentally get erased."

"Well yeah, if you left it out in the sun for a few weeks, enough UV might seep in from the side and erase the chip."

They both laughed. "I don't want to mess with the integrity issues. Better to just put an 'out of order' sign on this puppy and let them replace the EPROM when they get back Stateside."

"True." Nick shrugged. "Sucks to have a machine out of commission, but better safe than sorry, I guess."

"Well them's the breaks." The tech bounced the broken EPROM in a sweaty palm. "Now time for my beddy-bye. I'm going to have to kick you out of your chair."

"Yeah right. No worries." Nick took another swig of water and almost spit it out. Like a slow motion movie, the chip tumbled from the tech's hand into the garbage outside the gate. In any land-based casino the chip would be logged and then destroyed. Damaged chips should be purposefully corrupted through the erasing process. Ultraviolet exposure three to four times above that necessary for erasing would insure the chip could never be reused. Then it would be physically destroyed. An EPROM in the wrong hands could be used to reverse engineer the programming, either by a cheat or a competitor. Maybe that was procedure here, too. If it was, thank God the tech didn't follow it. Nick forced himself to wander off a bit, wait as the guy pulled the gate down and snapped the lock in place.

Casting back, he tried to remember his courses on evidence gathering and integrity. Evidence should always be secured as soon as possible in a medium that protected its contents from unauthorized access, corruption or destruction of the data, or accidental omission from an investigation. Shit, no evidence tape or heat-sealed packages. He might have a ziplock in his luggage with some toiletries. There was no way in hell the site could be secured. At least Nick would be able to keep a chain of custody record on the EPROM. The moment the man was safely out of sight, he snagged his camera phone…digital pictures should be taken relating to the evidence being gathered prior to collection. Quick snapped pics of the EPROM on top of the rest of the garbage, and one of the machine it came out of. It was the best he could do. Then Nick's hand was rooting in the trash. He came up with his prize coated in strawberry-smelling sludge.

Congratulating himself, he headed for the room. Lady Luck had kissed him tonight. A one in a million opportunity and he'd had pocket Aces and pulled two more on the river. Maybe he should play the lottery when they hit California. Sighting Chino, getting laid by Brandon twice in two days, and now he had an EPROM to compare code. Nick smiled as he hit the landing and looked up. Nothing looked familiar. He had no clue where he was. With his mind so wrapped up with the EPROM he'd taken the wrong stairs. Okay, that was a small problem; he just had to backtrack the stairwell and start over at the Promenade.

Voices drifted down from above. One of them hit him like nails drawn across a chalkboard. Holy shit, Chino. The chance of being recognized when it was just him was too great. He had to get the hell out of there. There was no place to go but back up or into the hall. Scanning quickly, he could see the corridor stretched off in both directions. Service doors were set at various intervals. It looked like he'd hit a level with cruise offices, maid service, security/count room, and the like. Off to the left another hallway cut in. Moving quick and quiet, he headed there. Just in time he made it; three pairs of feet hit the landing. Throwing his back up against the wall, Nick held his breath and waited. If he moved, they'd surely hear him.

Their footsteps crawled toward him. Then, with a jingling of keys, they stopped. Someone was unlocking one of the doors he'd passed. He'd lay odds it was the count room. "Man, why does it have to be all this pinche meter feed?" It was the squeaky kid's voice from the funeral. "Why couldn't we load it up with C's or G's?" Nick risked a quick peek around the corner.

Two gang-bangers that he recognized stood in the hall. An unfamiliar man in a security uniform was unlocking the count room. At their feet were several large backpacks, the kind tourists carried everywhere. Lines always employed some form of surveillance, but a quick glance at the CCTV camera showed just how lax it was on Winward. Cords went to the wall, but not through it. They weren't plugged in. The retrofit on a ship like this would run into the millions. Instead they faked it. Why did that not surprise him?

"Because, zurramato," the unfamiliar man was speaking, "people don't generally stick hundreds in a slot machine…at least not on these low rent junkets." This was a prime example of why internal oversight was a joke. Ocean-going casinos had detailed internal control procedures concerning counts, cage procedures, and other processes, all similar to licensed jurisdictions. Security was solely responsible for enforcement; the gate keeper for money flowing through the casino. As on land, officers escorted the chips from all the gaming areas and coin overage from the slot machines to the count rooms. Subvert security and you'd subverted the system.

Chino broke in. "Shut up, both of you."

"Why?" The other banger's voice was muffled. He must have stepped into the count room. "It's fucking three a.m., ain't nobody here but us and the cockroaches."

A loud whump sounded, followed by another. "Get the fuck in there; rack it and stack it just like the rest." While he couldn't see it, Nick guessed they were tossing the backpacks into the count room. They were in there forever. Nick's legs were cramping and all the water and beer he'd drunk earlier was manifesting itself painfully. Just when he thought he would fall over, Chino was in the hall. "Okay, let's get the fuck out of here. Get off this boat." Their voices drifted away and up. Thank God. Still, Nick made himself wait until his bladder screamed. Then he made his way back to the cabin.

Several wrong turns gave him time to think things over. He was pretty certain they'd been talking about money; he wished he could know for sure. Gang slang was not his forte. Brandon was a cop; he'd know what they were talking about.

Once in the room, Nick made a beeline for the bathroom. Physically, if not mentally more comfortable, he crawled up on the bed to get Brandon's take on things. Head still under the pillow, his lover didn't even twitch with the disturbance. Light shaking got Nick nothing. It wasn't until he'd damn near wrestled Brandon's arm off that he got a response.

The arm jerked back and an irritated, "What?" was muffled by the pillow.

Nick lifted a corner of the pillow. One baby-blue cracked open. Nick didn't know that you could glare with just one eye. "Brandon, what's a C?"

Brandon sucked on his upper lip before responding. "A bill." He shut his eyes and pulled the pillow back down.

This was getting him nowhere. Nick grabbed the pillow and tossed it on the floor. "A what?"

Turning his face into the mattress, Brandon answered, "Hundred bucks." It came out as more of an animal growl than words.

So they had been talking about money. "What's a G?"

Brandon sighed heavily. "Five hundred bucks, bundled." The words were followed by another sigh.

Folding his legs under his body, Nick considered that. "What's meter feed?" The EPROM was still in his pocket. He fished it out and set it on the nightstand.

Brandon rolled over and looked up at Nick. "You tweaking?" Catching a glimpse of the bedside clock, he hissed, "It's almost three." He propped himself on his elbows and stared at Nick. "What's the matter, babe, couldn't sleep and reading True Detective?" When Nick shook his head, Brandon answered. "I don't know, I've never heard that term. What's the context?"

"I was down by the count room, just wandering." Stretching himself on his stomach he toyed with the rings in Brandon's ear. "Chino was down there, with a guy I also saw at Duke's funeral, and one of the security staff. They were putting something in the count room and I'm guessing it was money." His jacket hit the floor and boots followed before he snuggled into a tattooed side and continued. "So the three of them were talking and one said, 'Man why does it have to be all this fucking meter feed? Why couldn't we load it up with C's or G's?'"

Sliding his arm under Nick's body, Brandon pulled him in close. "Babe, they're talking about drug money. That's how dealers talk about their cash." Brandon swept Nick's hair out of his eyes. "If Chino's on this ship then you're not safe. I don't want to chance him seeing you." Brandon's voice was tense. "We're not leaving this cabin until we hit port. I'll just keep you entertained, get us food when we need it. Hell, both of us will probably sleep most of tomorrow anyway. Don't you worry, babe, I won't let anybody hurt you. They'd have to go through me first."

Half asleep as he was now, Nick just nodded. Things were way beyond what he was trained to deal with. He drifted off, safe in his cop's arms.

CHAPTER TWENTY-SEVEN

A black rectangle about the length of a large paper clip, with silver contact pins bristling along the bottom and a clear quartz window on the top, the salvaged EPROM looked like a ceramic centipede. All of it was just housing for the UV-sensitive silicon chip in the center. Once programmed, an EPROM could only be erased through exposure to strong ultraviolet light through the window. Absent that, a programmed EPROM could retain data for almost twenty years and be read unlimited times. In short, the EPROM was a memory part that didn't forget its program when power was removed. As long as the silicon chip wasn't damaged, the programming should still be accessible.

Cleaning the EPROM was a meticulous and time-consuming task. Strawberry frou-frou drink had crusted on the pins and case of the EPROM. Daiquiri was Nick's educated guess. A toothbrush and miniscule amounts of solvent were the most he could risk. Nick's shoulders ached and his hands cramped. Frequent breaks were required just to keep working. Enough of the gunk had to be removed to allow the electronics in the ZIF to make sufficient contact with the pins.

Arguably, the harder step was bending the pins back to true. This EPROM was a standard Dual-Inline-Package, DIP. Two rows of pins, which matched sockets or holes in the circuit board, ran across the base. The primary advantage of the DIP format was that they were easily removed and installed by humans. Easy was a relative term. Push too hard, don't have things lined up just so, and you'd bend a pin. Whichever monkeys had installed this one had blown one or both of those. If Nick were really careful, he might be able to straighten it back out. If he wasn't, well then it would break, and Nick would be screwed.

Nick slid the refurbished EPROM into the socket. ZIF sockets were unable to bend pins, which was why they were used for programming and reading. You just placed the chip on the pad and closed the handle to make contact. Then it was just a matter of connecting the required supply, and running the proper software algorithm to compare the embedded code with what GCB had on file. One deep breath and Nick set it to run. Lines of green code scrolled down the DOS screen. His ecstatic "Yes!" as he jumped from his seat stopped two investigations personnel in their tracks. Nick just grinned and shrugged. Investigations thought electronic service was full of weirdoes anyway.

Every difference was logged. Wiggling in his chair with excitement, he waited for the report to run. When it was done he pulled the report on the gaffed EPROM originally supplied by Frontier. Line by line by line, Nick compared the two. The same programming deviations were present in both chips. There was no way it was a mistake. Frontier was gaffing the chips it supplied to the Winward line casinos. Mexican Mafia hardliners, drug money and over reported revenue generation; Nick didn't have to be in audit to understand the implications. Even with all the controls in Nevada, money laundering was still the biggest threat in the industry.

Nick jogged down the hall and stuck his head through an open door. An older man, graying, spreading, but with a razor-sharp mind, sat at a battered desk, which had seen almost as many years as Nick. Although GCB was vital to the continued revenue stream of the state, it was still civil service. "Chief, I need to talk to you for a moment." As the head of ESD, the chief had to be part politico and part computer geek, at least enough that he could understand the techno garble that often spilled from his agents' mouths.

"What about?" Chief Robert Black looked up from his computer, and motioned Nick to sit. At least the GCB wasn't stinted on tech.

"Frontier Entertainment." He slid into the chair crammed between the desk and bookshelves filled with regulatory and technical manuals. "There's some issues."

As he turned away from the monitor, the chief's elbows went up on the desk. "Nasty stuff about Duke, huh?" Fingers from one hand drummed on the table. His face was cradled in the palm of the other. When Black had come on board, it had taken his staff a while to realize it wasn't impatience with them, but rather nervous energy seeking outlet that caused the habit. He believed in them, would go to bat for them, and they loved him for it.

The current head of ESD was a big proponent of regulators responsible for overseeing technology being well-versed in that technology. Technological developments moved lightning-fast, but regulations were often hard pressed to keep pace. He also felt that the gaming industry viewed those responsible for the regulations as basically stupid. That was going to change on his watch.

When the whole issue of certifying electronic voting machines had come up in Nevada, he'd jumped at the chance to show his department had a broader application. A processor was a processor, as he often said, only the interface changed. On a slot machine the interface was spinning reels or a video display; voting machines just had different buttons on the outside. ESD's recommendation had won the day. He'd also fought hard against a move to require payouts if the computer didn't indicate one was due, but witnesses saw the reels stop…punctuating his point with a graphic demonstration of various ways cheaters could stop the wheels without actually having won.

"No shit." Nick had never been entirely comfortable in the man's presence. He always felt like he was in the principal's office when he sat in this chair. It had more to do with Nick's experience that most people thought of him as weird rather than anything Chief Black had ever said or done. "I've never known anyone who got murdered. It's awful."

"Yep. So what's the problem?"

Nick fudged the truth a little. "There are errors in the source code script on some of the EPROMS they sent." It wasn't completely untrue. Two were off, the one he was supposed to have sent back and the one from the ship.

"You've logged it? Nothing major?" When Nick didn't immediately respond, he continued, "Why don't you just call 'em up and ask what the deal is." The unwritten policy at ESD was: if you can solve it with a phone call…solve it with a phone call.

"Well, okay, but I've pulled the company's form, and the personal information sheets, and Duke was the only programmer. It's not like I can ping him on a hotline to heaven and ask him what's up. Everyone else is hardware or marketing or admin, I mean it's a small shop -- four key players. I've left messages everywhere and no one's calling back." He shrugged as if it didn't matter. "So, yeah, I could talk to them, but it would be like a help desk call from hell. 'Can you find your desktop, sir?' 'Yeah, my computer's sitting on it.' It's an error that's showing up when they're embedding the code. The initial code is good, but it's not being downloaded to the EPROMS right. I bet it's just something hinky that would cost them a few grand to track. Or, I could go onsite and I can nail the problem in less than five minutes."

"We don't do onsite inspections." Suspicion wound through the chief's tone. It had taken years of searching to find the man that filled the chair in front of Nick. He was as savvy as they came.

"Not because we can't," Nick pressed. "I mean there's nothing in the law that says we can't go inspect how they're embedding. It's just a function of manpower; we don't have any." He laughed nervously, "And hell, ninety percent of the time we can solve it with a phone call, so we never needed to. But this is like a special case. How often does someone's only programmer get killed?"

"I see, O'Malley." Black stared over his desk, "You've decided to go private sector on me. You're going to go out there, pitch for his slot, and make me pay for it."

Nick snorted. "I may like horror movies, but I'm no ghoul. Christ, it hasn't even been two weeks since his funeral. I'd at least wait four before I did that. Besides, Los Angeles, maybe. San Francisco, that I'd consider. Bakersfield not on your life...or in this context, mine."

There were few senior agents in the division. Most people bailed after a couple years of service. Nick's opinion, as a long-timer, carried a lot of weight with the brass. Still the chief teased him. "So you want the State of Nevada to pay you for a mini-vacation in California?"

"Oh yeah, beautiful downtown Bakersfield, my idea of a holiday. Look, if we don't step in, it's going to hang them, and us, up for months getting this fixed. All these guys we kinda know from bigger fish. I'd hate to fucking do that to them, especially after loosing Duke. They're going to have enough issues as it is replacing him." He stared at the ceiling for a moment before continuing. "Programmers you can find, especially after the dot bomb fallout. Programmers who also are fluent in the gaming regulations of the State of Nevada aren't the easiest to come by. If they hire a warm body with an EE or CompSci, we're going to spend fucking hours on the phone trying to explain the requirements to them. And God help us if they get someone with a trade school certification."

As the chief leaned forward, his hands stilled. "I don't like bullshit, O'Malley, and you're feeding me bullshit." An intense set of green eyes considered Nick. "You don't think Duke's death was an accident do you?" This was the reason the man was so good at what he did. He had a cop's sixth sense, a tech's mind, and a politician's facility for getting things done.

"No." Nick's gaze slipped left for a moment. Refocusing his attention, he asked, "Do you?"

"No, I don't think I do. I take it it's not a small problem that you've found." After considering it for a moment, Nick shook his head in the negative. The chief drummed his fingers, palmed his face, and sagged back into his chair. "It's American Coin all over again, isn't it?" GCB had tried to get American Coin's owners on criminal misconduct in connection with the gaffs in their programs. When their chief programmer had agreed to turn State's evidence, he'd been shot in the back of the head. This time Nick's nod was affirmative. "Then let investigations handle it."

Nick sighed. "I'll take it to them and you know what will happen, they'll bring it right back to us. Right now it's too technical. They won't know what to look for onsite. If I go out and there are no hassles, then Duke was probably acting on his own. If I get the run around, well I guess that would be enough for a warrant. Get our AG to work with the California AG, and go in gang busters at that point." It was time to drop the act. "I think they've gaffed the codes, and I think they're laundering money…but not in Nevada. But I don't *know*. We need to know."

"O'Malley, don't pull a Harris on me, okay." Ron Harris of ESD had been instrumental in securing American Coin's programmer's cooperation and had been devastated by the killing. The murder remained unsolved until twelve years after the fact, when the man who'd been tried and acquitted finally confessed to his part, and rolled on his conspirators. "He got way too involved, and when they killed his witness and the investigation went south, he lost direction. It flipped him. You all are too valuable to me. I don't want to lose anybody like that."

"Beware of the dark side, Luke." Nick laughed. His manager didn't. "Okay, I know. It's serious stuff. I won't lose focus and I won't let it throw me if things don't turn out. I'm pretty much a realist on that kinda stuff. Bad guys get away with shit all the time, but we do what we can. I think Duke flipped on us, and I think the guys he was working with on it popped him. Whether all of Frontier is involved, or not, I don't know. But I want to. It pisses me off that someone who used to work here would go south like that."

Black steepled his fingers, obviously thinking. "Okay, but you're taking a couple of the casinos in Laughlin while you're out there. We can push them up on the schedule, I guess; look and see who's due. It should look like 'well, we were just out here anyway, folks.' Everyone will probably still be suspicious, but it'll give you some excuse. How are you going to cover your field assignments while you're out playing hooky on the Colorado River?"

"I'm supposed to be in the lab Wednesday, Thursday and Friday anyway, getting into Frontier's hardware. If we don't get the source code problem worked out," he let the thought hang for a moment, "whether the machine can take a twenty-seven thousand volt shock won't matter. If it's more than just an imbedding error, that's not going to matter at all."

"This is a one timer O'Malley, understand?" Wagging his finger as though he was scolding a child, the chief added, "Don't see this as an excuse to ride expenses. And you're fucking in and out of there in enough time to get your butt home…'cause I ain't forking out overtime on this shit." Each statement was punctuated by a jab. "I'm going to have enough explaining to do as it is. Are we clear on that?"

Nick clapped his hands together and raised them to his forehead. "Got it. Cheap room, fast food…in, out, butt home."

"Remember you're taking one of the State of Nevada's vehicles into the insanity of Cali-forn-ni-aye. Be gentle with it. I've seen how you drive."

"Chief, if it's okay with you, I'll take my bike and expense it out." This could get him in a little trouble. He hoped the chief would buy it. "I've got some friends in Cali. I thought I might head over to see them Friday night, spend the weekend. It's all part of the story if anyone asks."

"Aha! The ulterior motive comes out." They both laughed. "I expect you in with a full workup on Monday. If there's something wrong, we have to step on it quick. I want to go to the board with this as soon as possible, preferably *before* people start asking why, after all these years, we chose to do an onsite. Good, bad, mildly indifferent…I want it all double-spaced and spell-checked."

Taking his feet, Nick assumed they were through. "Always." As he headed to the door the chief's next comment caught him.

"O'Malley, be careful." The chief sounded genuinely concerned. "If your hunch is right, you could be walking into something messy. Promise me that if it smells wrong, if your gut tells you things aren't right, you'll get the hell out of there. I don't care if you get to the front door and something about the sign on the building turns you off, walk away. You don't have to find anything. What you've got is probably enough to justify making them jump through hoops, and probably exclusion if they don't have a good explanation."

"Duke used to be one of us. If he was in on it we need to nail that down quick. He's dead. I can't ask him, so we'll never know a hundred percent. But if someone did something to shut him up we need to try take them down."

"Promise me, O'Malley."

Hand on the door frame, he understood that his boss really was worried. "I won't do anything stupid, I promise."

CHAPTER TWENTY-EIGHT

Casino inspections were awful. Nick often took what other agents considered shit jobs, gas stations, dingy local bars, just so he wouldn't have to subject himself to the torture. Lights whirling, bells ringing, electronic music blaring from slot machines; add the constant sound of metal rain as the coins hit trays, and Nick's shoulders were wound tight in the space of five minutes. There was too much of too much on a casino floor. Maybe if you worked it nine to five you got used to the sensory overload. Somehow he doubted he ever could. Even with earplugs, eight hours of the fun-houses on crack had Nick's nerves screaming. What was worse was he'd asked for this.

The quiet of his motel room was almost a physical relief. The bed was hard, the air-conditioning barely passable, but it was calm. He probably wouldn't even turn on the TV tonight. Half a ham sandwich, a Diet Coke, and a run by the river stripped a few more layers of insanity from the day. He wolfed down the remaining ham and cheese while he flipped on the laptop and stripped. A long, hot shower followed by a little net surfing...the plan was to be in bed by nine. With an estimated five hour drive to Bakersfield ahead of him, Nick wanted to hit the road early.

Toweling off, he glanced at the laptop on the nightstand as he walked out of the steaming bath. No desk, but plenty of hot water. An IM from Brandon was flashing on his screen. Two system messages displayed: an invitation to a voice chat and an invitation to view web cam. Accepting both, he dug out his headset. Feedback on the laptop's internal speaker was awful. Out of habit, the little crappy web-cam was already clipped to his screen. Reciprocal invitations went back across the net.

When the video started he could see Brandon's sexy face half-covered by the soup cup he was chugging from. As he set his dinner down, the dark haired man leaned in toward the computer. 'BranCarr567 has accepted your invitation' popped in the box. "Heya, Nicky." Even over the net that smoky voice turned Nick to butter. When the video transmission started, Brandon's face went into shock. "Whoa shit, you're nekkid." Eyes narrowing, Brandon leaned in toward the screen. "You're not at home, are you?"

"Nope." Nick dropped prone on the mattress. "Just got out of the shower…just me in a towel, babe." Nick pushed his wet hair behind his ear so the headpiece would sit better. He dragged the extra pillow over to prop himself up. "I'm at a Super-8 in Bullhead City."

"Where?"

"Bullhead City, Arizona, across the Colorado River from Laughlin. I had field inspections at the casinos there."

"Then why didn't you just stay in Laughlin?" Soup finished, Brandon chucked the microwave cup behind him. A plastic-against-metal clatter sounded. "I've been to the River Run there, gotta be better places to crash than a Super-8."

"This place has free DSL. Actually I'm here because the only places to stay in Laughlin are the casinos. If we have to do an overnighter, we're supposed to avoid staying at a casino. Sometimes you can't help it, but you're supposed to try. And by try, I mean bend over backward and stay at a place that rents rooms by the hour instead of a decent bed in a resort with slots. Anyway, babe, tomorrow morning I have a site visit at a manufacturer. I was going to call. Since ya pinged me, I'll ask now. I thought maybe we could get together tomorrow night for dinner in Los Angeles, maybe do *other* stuff afterwards."

"Oh, trying to get me excited, huh?" Brandon leaned back, almost out of frame. "I got to work on Saturday, ten hour shift." He smiled. "I could probably manage a run to Lala-land Friday evening. As long as you don't get pissed if my phone rings and I got to bail on you 'cause I get called back into work…Sunday I'm off. You gonna stay the whole weekend?"

"I was kinda planning on a Saturday/Sunday thing." Nick shifted his shoulders. This was not the most comfortable bed he'd ever been in. "There's a place called Cat & Fiddle on Sunset in Hollywood. Nice, quiet, little booths kinda tucked away in cubbyholes for privacy, want to meet there? A friend gave me the names of some decent hotels in the area where we could go afterward. Spend the mornings eating room service, maybe go wander around Venice beach?"

Brandon gave him another brilliant smile. "Sounds great. Hey, give me a sec, be right back." Brandon rose and walked from view. An empty apartment stared back at Nick. When Brandon returned, his T-shirt was gone and his fly was half undone. Those abs, with just a hint of a six pack, were damn sexy. "So, LA—why LA? Where's your inspection?"

"Bakersfield."

Dead silence answered him. Brandon's tongue rode the outline of his lips, and then his jaw went hard. "You're fucking going to Frontier aren't you?"

"Yeah."

"Don't you dare, Nicky!" With the look Brandon shot him, Nick was so glad he was talking over the internet, and not in the room with Brandon.

"Hey…it's my job." Nick leaned in, as if he could appear more sincere by getting closer to the camera. "Something's wrong with their code, and I have to go figure out what it is. Duke's dead. No one's returning GCB calls. Their code is fucked up. It went up the chain, and they decided I have to go." It wasn't terribly far off the truth.

"No, you fucking don't." Brandon was scolding him like a child caught shoplifting. "Stay the fuck away from them. It's dangerous fucking shit."

He answered defensively. "I have to. Frontier's my assignment. I told the chief what was what and he said, go onsite and clear it up."

"What the hell did you tell him, Nicky?"

"That there are problems. Exactly the same things I told you."

"Why do I doubt that?" God, Brandon was pissed enough Nick thought he might kill the conversation. After a few moments of stewing, Brandon spoke again, "You're going in solo?" Brandon's voice was as tense as his expression.

Nick laughed. "It's not a military operation, it's a site inspection. Going in solo, shit."

"Don't fuck around with this, Nicky." Brandon was back to parental protective. "Do you have a gun?"

"No! Are you nuts? I'm ESD, we don't use guns…we get computers."

"You are not invulnerable Gaming Control Boy. Just 'cause everyone runs scared in Nevada doesn't mean it's that way out here. There is some wicked shit going on with Frontier. One guy's dead, probably because of what he was involved in there. You got to be careful, real careful. Let them know that everyone in the world knows you're supposed to be there. I don't want you hurt…I don't want you dead."

"Well, necrophilia is just disgusting, especially when the body starts to rot…"

"It's not a fucking joke!" If Brandon could have wormed through the internet, Nick bet Brandon'd be shaking him about now.

"Okay, okay, I know." He tried to calm the situation down. "This is scary shit, I understand that, really." With a deep breath, he drew his fingers through his still-wet hair. "I'm nervous as all hell. I'll be careful. If anything strikes me wrong, I'll be out of there quicker than the Road Runner. Promise."

"You better. I'm going to be freaked all day worrying."

"About me?"

"No about the fucking president. Who the hell do you think I'm talking about?"

"Gee, I didn't know you cared." If Brandon was being sarcastic, it meant he was calming down. Nick hadn't got all his lover's cues down, not even most of them, but that particular habit he'd picked up on early. "Besides, I'll be scarier than them…pull up in Querida and all that."

"You drove the hearse?" Now Brandon just looked perplexed. "Don't they have state vehicles or something they can give you for a trip like this?"

"Well, I wanted to take the bike on the road, but then it puked itself all over the driveway and I'd already turned down the car, so I'm going broke filling the tank." His last swig of the Diet Coke was warm. Nick grimaced as he tossed it in the trash. "You'll get to see the new stereo speakers I've got tricked out in the back."

This time Brandon laughed. "Drive it to the beach, park, and maybe fool around to some rivet-head jams?"

"Now you're going to get me all excited." Not that Nick minded Brandon getting him all excited.

"Want excited?"

"Sure, what did you have in mind?"

"Well," Brandon stood and finished unbuttoning his fly. "I figure you're nearly naked, I might as well be, too." Oh, baby, strip show via web cam—better than anything available on local TV. Nick's body began to throb. When the jeans slid off Brandon's hips, Nick hissed. Every time he saw that toned body and beautiful cock, his body was set on fire. Especially since Brandon really knew how to draw out undressing. "Like that, huh? I was in the mood for playing dirty tonight." Wicked lights sparked in Brandon's blue eyes as he sat down and leaned in towards the camera. "Thought maybe I'd use my vibe for you. Would you like to see that?"

Nick melted on the bed. "Oh fuck, yeah. You need to be fucked up the ass hard." Stroking himself through cheap terrycloth, he murmured, "I'm getting a serious hard-on. Why don't you bend over and let me watch?"

"I bet. I had a different position in mind." Brandon put one foot up on the desk and pushed the chair back. The other leg followed so that he was spread eagled in front of the camera. Damn, Brandon's balls and ass were cut off from view. "Are you watching?"

"Oh, yeah. Move the cam just a bit lower." Brandon leaned in and adjusted the frame, and Nick nodded. "Much better." Clean-shaven balls and sexy tight ass. Desire wicked through Nick's cock, moving from the tip down, coating the inside of his thighs, the back of his legs, and the ridges of his spine with a clawing heat. "God, what a fuckable ass. Cock is nice, too."

What did Brandon have in his hand? It was red and thin. "What an interesting vibrator, you naughty cop you." Smiling, Brandon held the toy next to his own hard dick and dripped lotion down the latex. "Looks like it's covered in come; it's kinda hard to see 'cause of the lighting. Shit, you're wearing a ring, aren't you?"

"Yep, let me adjust the light. The ring vibrates, too." Brandon moved slightly out of frame again. Cheapass piece of shit; the viewing area was so limited. Nick decided Brandon's birthday present would be a better web-cam.

"You moved the camera, I can't see your whole cock now." There was more fiddling. "Better and *much* better light." Rubbing the toy across his balls, toying with himself, Brandon's eyes were half closed. His teeth bit into his lower lip as he shoved the jelly vibrator in his ass. Excess lotion pooled around his tight hole. Nick whimpered. "That's such a nice view. God, I like the look of that lotion on your ass…looks like you've been creamed. Man, I wish that was my fucking come running out your ass."

"God, yeah!" Brandon's other hand was moving along his cock.

Bright red latex, white cream, pink skin, Nick wanted to reach through the net and drive himself in between those legs. "What a show, fucking your ass and stroking off. Got anything bigger to put up there?" His own hand moved between his legs as the towel fell open. "How 'bout my fist?"

A deep laugh, "Seven, eight inches better?"

"Hell, yeah! You got one that big?"

Brandon pulled the toy from his body, moved back to sitting in the chair and then leaned in. Lust fogged his voice. "Yeah, it's jacking itself off in a hotel room in Arizona." He stuck his tongue out to punctuate the joke. "Hold on, let me grab it." Brandon disappeared below the desk for a moment, and came back up with a more naturally-colored dildo. Elbows resting on the desk, holding it up before his face, he poured more lotion over the surface. "You know what the best thing about busting hookers is? They get real detailed on what the best toys are and where to get 'em on the net." Another velvet laugh broke. "The lotion trick is from one of my regulars…every other weekend I used to bust this tranny on the same corner. She'd get real detailed on why lotion was such an important prop in a visual show. I guess you agree?"

"Uh huh." Nick was loosing the ability to talk coherently. Thank God they weren't trying this stunt with text. As Brandon got himself back into position, Nick's pace on his own skin increased. "Let's see what you can do with that."

Far more slowly this time, Brandon slid the dong inside his ass. All the way in and then slowly back out. Watching was heavenly torture. "Shit, that's hot. Wow, I don't think I could take that much up my ass."

"Bet you could give me that much." Brandon's breathing was getting ragged.

"I could give you all I got." Nick was hardly faring better. "But I would pound harder and faster. You need a real cock up your ass?"

"Do you know where I could get a real cock?"

"I bet I could find one for you. Fuck, I wish that was my mouth instead of your hand."

"So do I." In between moans, Brandon begged, "Tell me more. Tell me what you're going to do to me."

Nick watched as his lover's chest muscles twitched under his skin. His face was contorting into that pained look of ecstasy Nick loved. "How 'bout I kiss and lick and bite all the way from the bottom of your ears down to the back of your knees? Run my fingers down and across all those really sensitive parts of your body. Goddamn, I want to suck that cock, suck it for hours."

"Hell, yeah, you give such good head. I like it when you suck my cock."

"It's such a lickable cock, suckable balls, too. I could lick it right now. Wrap my mouth around it and suck it deep, licking all over. Take your balls in my mouth and suck on them. Swirling my tongue all along the length and sinking it back in all the way to the base. Letting my teeth gently scrape their way up while I'm playing with your ass." Talking about it, watching Brandon pump himself while he rammed his hole with the dildo, it was so dirty and exciting. "I'd suck on you, using my own come to lube you up and sinking first one then maybe two fingers in, all while just sucking your cock, biting at the base of your balls, sucking kisses all along that narrow space between your hip and your cock, fucking you, like I want you to be fucking me. Fuck I wish that was my dick instead of that toy…"

Brandon shuddered and then convulsed, his body drawing up into almost a fetal position. Come exploded between his fingers, droplets spattering his stomach almost all the way to his chest.

"Ah crap, I came all over myself." Going limp in the chair, he pulled the dildo from his body and dropped it on the floor. Half-lidded blue eyes stared at Nick over the net.

"That's what I was going for, and it was fucking hot." Nick's breath hitched in his lungs as a cold shiver shot through his dick. "Would have liked to see the money shot a little clearer."

"Well, I tried, but it's hard to get a good pic on the web cam. How close are you?"

"Close," Nick hissed. "Damn close. Talk to me."

"You want me to throw you down on the bed, fuck you hard?" Oh, there was the voice, slow and deep and easy.

"Oh yeah, whip me, beat me, make me write bad checks."

"You're fucking weird, Nicky. I like you weird. Fucking gonna throw my legs over you and ride you hard. Grind my hole all the way down that huge dick of yours. All you have to do is lie there and let me ride you."

Nick stretched out on the bed. Hopefully he hadn't moved out of frame. "Better than a motorcycle, huh?" He took two slow pulls, and then a series of fast strokes along his skin. Damn he wished he was inside Brandon right now instead of in a damn hotel room.

"Way better. You can feel my tight hole just grabbing your cock." That velvet voice, what Brandon was saying, it was driving ice under his skin. Especially after watching Brandon fuck himself. "God, I like watching your hand on your dick. Wanna pound my ass with your big dick?"

"Damn straight," Nick hissed. Damn, it was going to happen soon. "Slam into you hard." His stomach muscles were twitching. He could barely talk. "Make you scream."

"Moaning out your name…Nicky, baby. Ride you hard, slam my ass. Come on, baby, come for me. Let me see that spunk shoot from your dick."

"Ah, God!" His body shook as he blew. Come spattered his own chest and stomach. He squeezed and pulled, forcing a few more drops from his head. "Goddamn, that was hot."

"You bet it was hot. You're always hot."

"I'm beat." He panted. "I wish I wasn't beat. Stay up and talk dirty with you all night."

"Hey, Nicky. Look, call me tomorrow. Call me when you get to Bakersfield, and call me when you're on your way to LA, okay. Where are you going to be?"

"I'll be fine. Frontier Entertainment." Brandon's glare said it all. "Sorry, they're located on the 98 just outside of Bakersfield. The place is called Marlow Industrial Park. I'll be in and out in a couple of hours; I don't need a safe call."

"I know. I just need you to do it for me, so I won't worry."

He yawned widely. "Alright, if it makes you feel better. I'm going to have to sign out. I'm wiped."

"Yeah, I know." A deep sigh—it sounded like Brandon was pretty sleepy, too. "Get cybered and roll over and go to sleep. Bastard."

Nick chuckled. "See ya tomorrow."

"Tomorrow, Nicky, baby, we'll do it for real." The cam went dark, but one last thread of velvet drifted through the headset. "Sleep tight, don't let the bed-bugs bite."

CHAPTER TWENTY-NINE

Bakersfield in the throes of summer was brutal. Bakersfield in the throes of summer in a car with no air conditioning was worse than brutal. It wasn't quite past ten a.m. and the temperature was already in the 90s. It was a major pisser that the Kawasaki had chosen to blow a valve this week. Repairs would be a bitch when he got back. The hearse was a bitch now, even with both windows down.

At least this gave him a chance to really test out the new stereo. Almost five hours of drive time, few cars on the road, and no Highway Patrol in sight; time to crank up the tunes. Some *House of 1000 Corpses* and *Living Dead Girl* should keep him from going insane. As Nick spun the volume knob, the plastic broke off in his hand. Fucking cheap-ass piece of shit...he was going to kill Sean when he got back to Vegas. Hardcore, Dark-Rock thundered at full force from the back; *Hellbilly Deluxe*, *Sinister Urge* and *Past, Present & Future* courtesy of Rob Zombie were racked in the CD changer. The sub-woofer massaged his butt with low-line base. Needles highway to the I-40, to the 15, to the 58 would put him in Bakersfield just after lunch. By then, he'd be deaf.

One stop for a bag of chips and gas—the Caddie barely got ten miles to the gallon—and he was back on the road. Between a V-8 engine and no traffic, he made good time, rolling through the city at about half-past noon. Frontier Entertainment Industries was housed in an industrial park just outside the city limits. Farms and vineyards stretched toward the horizon to either side. Bakersfield proper was somewhere behind him, hidden in the folds of the land. Ahead lay the Tehachapi Mountains, the gray strip of CA-99 crawling up into the pass.

With dead air and a dark interior, the hearse would be an oven by the time Nick was finished. Past the buildings, at the farthest end of the lot, a few weary trees threw shade at their feet. It was midday; by late afternoon the shadows would be cast across the asphalt. Slipping the M-M in sideways, hogging three spaces in all, Nick killed the engine and yanked the driver's window to half-mast. If anyone had a problem with his parking they could take it up with the GCB. Shit, the lot was empty anyhow. A few trucks, some junker cars, an older Mercedes and a purple Toyota hatchback with gold rims were the only other occupants.

Time to keep his promise; he felt like he was checking in with dad after a date. Saying Brandon's name and holding down the button on the Bluetooth headset activated the auto-dial. One ring and a clipped "Carr," sounded in his ear. Phone etiquette was not high on the list of Brandon's priorities.

As Nick pulled the laptop case off the floor, he replied, "Hey, what's up?" Somehow he doubted he'd need his computer, but he couldn't very well leave it in an unlocked vehicle. Besides, while his badge conveyed his authority, Nick's laptop, much like Brandon's gun, let everyone know he had the power to back it up.

"Working, that's what's up," Brandon snapped over traffic noise in the background. A faint ringing in Nick's ears made it doubly hard to hear. "Make it quick."

Irritated, he slid out of the hearse. "You told me to call you when I hit Bakersfield." It came out sounding pissy instead of annoyed. He slammed the door. "I'm here."

"Okay great." There was a long pause. "Look, I'll call you when I'm not busy, okay."

"Okay, whatever." Man, Brandon could be such a jerk sometimes, telling him to call and then getting angry when he did. His sunglasses barely cut the glare from the high desert sun. As he headed around the building, he added, "Don't get pissed at me 'cause I'm doing what you asked." Damn he sounded like a whiny pirate. Nick didn't want to end a conversation that way. He eased his tone back. "Miss you, talk later?"

Another gulf of dead air. "Yeah, me too." Just before the line cut off Nick caught the whispered, "later, babe." Wow, he rated a babe outta Brandon today. Things were looking up. A nice dinner with a sexy guy who called him "babe" was a promising start to what he hoped would be a hot evening. Since he was in the hearse, he'd brought more rope this time. A little wine, a little bondage, a lot of naked Brandon in bed; the thought shot shivers through his hips. No sense getting all hot and bothered before work was done; there was plenty of time for fantasy on the drive into Los Angeles.

Dark wood paneled the tiny lobby. A phone, a yellowing thirteen-inch monitor and an IBM keyboard covered in plastic sat forlorn on an unoccupied maple wood desk. Two guest chairs, upholstered in stained mustard-colored fabric, seemed stolen from the 70s. For a company allegedly rolling in dough, Frontier certainly gave off a cash-strapped feel. Maybe it was the whole 'we're a lean, mean, upstart manufacturer' image they were trying to portray. It certainly wouldn't inspire Nick to invest in the company.

"Hello?" The query echoed emptily. The door behind the desk was ajar. He called out as he eased it open, "Hell-oo!" Dingy carpet lined the hall—once blue or maybe gray, it was hard to tell now under the accumulated grime. On the right, the hall ended in two closed doors. A break room-cum-supply closet was directly ahead. On the left, another door and a turn. Nick figured he might as well see where that led.

Light spilled through the open fire door at the end of the hall. The carpet abruptly died at the edge of poured concrete. Two men were conferring at a battered metal desk. "Excuse me." Both wore a work casual uniform of Khakis and polo shirts.

"I'm sorry." The oldest of the pair looked up. Once-deep-brunette hair was flecked with gray. A bright smile and intelligent eyes eased the impact of an acne-scarred face. "Didn't you see the no-soliciting sign out front?"

What, did they think he was selling day-planners? Then it hit him, the laptop case on his left side. "Not selling anything today, folks." He swung it back so that the badge came into full view. "I'm Agent Nick O'Malley, with the Nevada Gaming Control Board. I'm here for a surprise inspection of your facilities." The surprise was they were actually doing an inspection. "Is there someone I can talk to about the embedding software and your programming?"

"No one told us about an inspection." The other gentleman stood. Dark green shirt, tan out of a bottle, hair just a little too red…he was probably close to the same age as his partner. It didn't appear that he was accepting the growing old issue as well.

Nick ran his teeth over his bottom lip. "That's why they're called surprise inspections instead of advance notice inspections."

"Oh, yeah, no shit." Running one hand through the salt-and-pepper mass, he extended the other to Nick as he came forward. "I'm Tom Ukropina…president of Frontier, marketing guru and general scapegoat. This is Conner Ambrose, vice president and general manager." Hand shakes went all around. These guys seemed nice enough. Of course, according to Vegas legend, Moe Dalitz was a pretty decent guy, at least when he wasn't ordering hits on people. "We tend to wear a lot of hats around here. Small shop and all."

"Just four principals; well, three of you after Duke's death." The name was familiar. He ran through the files in his head. "You used to be in Marketing at Imagiteks right?" That memory linked up to another. "I liked the Keno program you guys had. Too bad more casinos didn't pick up on it."

"They weren't aggressive enough with it. Too busy focusing on traditional slots." Tom eased back, resting his butt on the desk. "It's a dying market, at least with the new video and touch screen interfaces. They missed the boat on the voucher payouts. Couldn't ever get them to pick up the ball and run with the new technology. They said people wouldn't be comfortable with the video game interface, not having chips in their hands."

The laptop case was starting to pull at Nick's shoulder. "Younger people seem pretty comfortable with video interface." Sliding it to the floor at his feet, he jammed his hands in his pockets. "Most everyone likes the voucher payouts. Hard for people to steal your quarters when they're tallied on paper. As long as they keep the audio coins hitting the tray on payouts, it should work fine."

"Yeah, but the video generation is not the majority playing slots yet. Imagiteks just couldn't see the future coming." Tom shrugged. "Can't beat 'em, leave 'em, and start your own company. It's still a little strapped around here, but we're making it work."

"Give it ten years and the touch screen interface will be the only thing you see." Again reality wasn't jibing with the paper trail. Nick expected a bustling enterprise. Not big, you didn't need a huge operation for slot manufacture, but busy. Instead, the factory floor was dead. A few guys were working on a bank of slots and poker terminals. Guts exposed, wires tangled on the floor and electronics piled to one side, they weren't new machines. "Not much going on here." It just didn't feel right.

Connor spoke up. "Well, we're kinda stalled waiting on GCB approval to launch our new line. We've lined up the Winward concessions, but the only builds we'd do for them is replacements or refurbs. That was Duke and Laura's bailiwick. She used to work some of the casinos on the big lines, convinced Winward to let us run the slots on contract. Works well for us since we have a captive market for our games; keeps us from starving while we get going. Although we use a lot of competitor's machines as well in those. As small as we are, there's not a lot of variety in our product; players would get bored on just our slots."

"Come on back into the offices." Frontier's president patted his shoulder as he walked by. Shooting his next comment over his shoulder, he asked, "So that's why you're here? Our Nevada approval?" Tom apparently was a master of the obvious.

"Bingo." Connor waited for Nick to collect his gear, and then followed him down the hall. "I left messages for both of you and Laura Schmidt. But no one returned my calls."

"I just got back from back east. Trying to drum up some business in Atlantic City. Met with some programmers out there, ya know, to fill Duke's shoes. Hard to find someone willing to leave a cushy job for a promise of a cut of the action. Especially after the dot bomb fallout, stock options just aren't that attractive."

"Hell, I didn't know what to tell you. Wanted to wait for Tom to come back." Connor shrugged. "I barely know how to turn these damn things on. I was a pit boss, not a techie. That was Duke's business. Laura isn't in the office much. Maybe she didn't get the message, or wanted to talk with us first. Both she and Duke worked outta their houses for the most part. She and her husband, they live in San Diego. Bills and payroll are done online. Maybe once a month we would all get together to go over things."

"We've got to run to catch a flight to Sacramento." They headed past the break room and reception area, to the farthest door. It opened onto a largish office space. Four desks were arranged haphazardly in the room. Two looked like work was actually done at them. As he dropped into an ergonomic executive chair, Tom suggested, "Connor, why don't you call Arturo in? He does a lot of the repairs and such; worked with Duke a lot, was helping him with the programming. I'd bring him up, but he doesn't have the regulatory background. Any questions you have you can ask him. We'll set you up in here at Duke's terminal."

Connor snatched the phone from its cradle. There was a muffled echo from the factory floor on the other side of the wall as the page sounded. "Don't you want to be around while I'm here?" While their agreement in seeking Nevada approval guaranteed Nick unobstructed access, he was surprised they'd let him have it unsupervised. GCB agents, if they announced themselves, were generally chaperoned. Of course, who was there to play daddy?

"Why? Is there something wrong? Something we should know about?" When Nick shook his head, Tom continued, "We wouldn't be much help anyway. Arturo knows more about what they were doing than either of us."

Arturo arrived, an older heavyset man, and introductions went around. Tom brought him up to speed while Nick settled in. Unfamiliar with the role of the GCB, why the principals were letting Nick just wander about was explained over and over to Arturo. He was suspicious, but finally shrugged and headed back to fixing machines. His role was mostly hardware, although the few questions he'd asked gave Nick the distinct impression that he was pretty programming-savvy.

He had Tom sign off on the "ticket" stating that they chose not to be present and were okay with having any results mailed to the company. All Nick had to do if he needed anything was page Arturo on the floor. It was feeling more and more like Duke was on his own in this mess. If they had something to hide, it seemed doubtful they'd just let him have free range on their computers. Or it could be that the really incriminating stuff wasn't kept at the corporate offices. Finally alone, it was time to start digging.

When he flipped on Duke's computer, instant messenger activated. Nick was about to shut it down when an IM popped up. Lori Baby was pinging.

Who's this?

An avatar of a woman in her mid-to-late thirties, brunette and obviously taken by a web cam, displayed. Some people should really think about their avatar choices. She could have done with a more flattering picture. Lori… Laura, she was the fourth in this little enterprise. And Lori "Baby," huh? Well that was just interesting.

Two seconds and he committed himself. *Tom.* RadGamble identified as the user. Duke had chosen an avatar of a king of spades pinned to a dart board. A pistol in the foreground was the source of the bullet hole in the center of the card. Why did that so fit him?

Why are you on Duke's computer?

Think fast… a quick glance across the office and the four workstations, one for each principal. The docking stations for Tom and Connor were vacant. *Laptop's packed. MapQuest emergency, running to the airport. Can't talk.*

Ahh, good luck with the AG meeting.

Thanks. He waited a few minutes; enough that he could have actually run the search and then switched IM to invisible mode. The phone rang at his elbow, startling Nick. After two rings it stopped. Probably was set to ring on the floor as well. Nick started fiddling.

The IM sparked an idea. People were often careless about their messaging habits. In fact he reminded himself to go wipe the archive of his little session with Brandon. Wouldn't do to have another GCB agent stumble onto that; misuse of government property and all. He popped the messenger control panel up, mousing over to contacts and down to message archives. Bless you, Duke, for not cleaning out your IM folder. Lori Baby and Duke had been really fond of chatting.

Between his business partner and his ex-wife, Duke had been a pretty popular guy. Sometimes there was just no accounting for taste. He wondered what Lori's husband would have thought of her extramarital activities on the net. Besides the fact that they needed some lessons in cyber-sexing, they were a busy pair. What bits he read were fairly incriminating. Duke wasn't in it alone. Days could be wasted reading through all this. Nick didn't have days.

CD burner, blank CD scrounged from Duke's desk, and a 'print to file' command. What the hell; he dove into the word-processing and database programs. Since he didn't have the time to do a full file backup, Nick switched the file view to arrange-by-date mode. A quick and dirty drag-n-drop threw it onto his disk. Six months of memos and internal documents should give the GCB enough to look at and see if a full-scale computer seizure was in order. The only files that were password-protected were Duke's gaming programming files. Nick didn't have time to sit there and hack the passwords. After a few moments of thought, he was off to do a rampage through Duke's backup CD's. Older versions of the same program would show it wasn't a glitch. Anything that looked remotely useful went into his briefcase. It wasn't an illegal seizure. Two of the three principals of the company had given him unfettered access.

Now to make it all seem legit. He paged Arturo and asked for a tour of the factory and access to the electronics responsible for the imbedding process. Nick could probably draw that out for a few hours and be ready to blow by three thirty, four o'clock. Dinner by seven, and tying up Brandon by nine; more days should be this good.

CHAPTER THIRTY

Brandon and Weaver clambered out of the un-marked. An extra forty pounds on Weaver meant he needed the assistance of the door frame to haul his bulk out of the car. Once on the sidewalk, the heavy-set man hitched up his pants. "Now, my little baby D, why are we doing this scutwork follow-up?"

Brandon ditched his sunglasses onto the worn upholstery. "'Cause we were in the neighborhood?" Drug seizures had expanded the range of vehicles used for un-markeds beyond the once standard American-made four-door. Still, in Riverside that tended to mean ten-year-old shit cars previously owned by tweakers. Today they were in a red Toyota Celica with crapped-out air and a slipping transmission. Scanning the battered 70s-era box that called itself an apartment complex, Brandon figured the car pretty much fit the area—low rent and run down.

The nasty glare told him that Weaver was not amused by his feeble attempt at humor. Brandon sighed. "And the park where this witness saw something go down is under some big-shot city councilman's district. Which is why there is a 'task force' to clean up the park. And since none of the 'task force' managed to pick up on a group of underage prostitutes using the swing-sets as their street corner, but an eight-year-old girl did, we get the short stick so we can prove that 'all available efforts' are being given to his pet project."

In mock benediction, Weaver's hand waved a half-assed cross in the air. "Thou art learning well, grasshopper."

From his hip, the intro to *Bela Lugosi's Dead* sounded. That was Nick's ring. It was a little trite, but it fit. Flipping open the phone, he barked out, "Carr." The other detective threw him a don't-waste-my-time-in-this-shithole look.

"Hey, what's up?" Nick sounded way too upbeat. Time to check that boy's meds; he was out in the middle of Bakersfield, walking into possibly a front for the Mexican Mafia and he sounded like he was headed for MouseWitz.

"Working, that's what's up." Weaver was a DII pulling Field Training Officer duty, and technically his supervisor more than his partner. Pissing him off was not a good idea. Shit like that put you back on the beat. "Make it quick."

There was a pause. "You told me to call you when I hit Bakersfield. I'm here."

"Okay. Great." A half shrug and a roll of the eyes told Weaver he'd keep it short. "Look I'll call you when I'm not busy, okay?" It came out sounding short-tempered.

"Okay, whatever," Nick's tone was exasperated. Well it wasn't as if he hadn't gotten the run down when they started this relationship. He'd just have to deal. "Don't get pissed at me 'cause I'm doing what you asked. Miss you, talk later."

Softer this time, "Yeah me, too," and softer still, "later, babe." As his thumb jabbed the disconnect, he caught Weaver making a kissy face. Damn, he'd caught it. Responding by flipping the older man off as he walked around the car, Brandon asked, "You ready to play politics, boss-man?"

"See, now that," Weaver pointed to the cell phone, "is the triumph of hope over experience." Cracked walkways littered with broken toys and bottles made their walk to the entrance an obstacle course. "How long you been divorced now?"

Brandon scanned the rusted call box for names, there were none. "Seven years...I was, like, twenty-two when we split, been on the force a couple of years maybe." The alleged security gate gave with a push. Beaten dirt, hemmed by a few dying shrubs, pretended it was a center garden. Iron stairs led off to the right. Twelve doors on each floor meant twenty-four units total. "Which apartment are we looking for?" Five meaty fingers wiggled, then one shot out to point left. Weaver's hunch was sound. The first door was marked one, the second two, the third was missing a number, but by then they figured they were on the right track.

"So..." Oh crap, the interrogation was about to begin. "You got yourself a new girlfriend?"

Brandon really didn't want to talk to Weaver about his personal life. You did that with partners. It was expected. But hell, juggling half-truths and lies was hard. They'd had the partners talk the first shift and he'd managed to get by with "not seeing anyone" and "divorced." Which lead into the discussion of the wreck Brandon's married life had been. Past history was easy to deal with. Other cops just assumed it was because your ex couldn't handle being married to a cop. A lot couldn't. Then he'd asked Weaver about his kids and hadn't had been able to get a word in edgewise for two days. "Yeah."

"And," Weaver prompted.

"And what?"

"What she look like -- stacked? Fat, skinny, glasses…come on give, Baby D. Your partner's gotta know these things. Departmental regulations." Weaver laughed. "Not a cop groupie, is she?"

If Brandon didn't give Weaver something he'd keep at it. "Definitely not a cop groupie… actually freaked a little when I said what I did." He tried to keep it vague while not too vague. "Tallish, long hair, dark eyes and athletic…runner. Trains for marathons." Hopefully his partner would drop the subject.

Door number five's brass number was hanging upside down. Weaver jerked his head towards the entry. "Looker?"

Brandon nodded. "I think so." As he stepped up on the concrete stoop, Weaver moved right and back so he'd be slightly out of the vision of anyone who answered. This was a dance you learned with partners. Brandon turned, keeping Weaver in the edge of his vision while presenting as little target as possible to the occupants. You just never fucking knew what was going to come out of an apartment at you: dogs, trash, bullets…

As Brandon raised his left fist to knock, Weaver threw another question. "Is she one of those Goth freaks you sometimes hang out with?"

His answer was wary, but relaxed. "Yep, a freak." The knock echoed.

"And you met her?"

Brandon pounded again. This time he could hear footsteps. A single nod let Weaver know the show was about to start. "While I was in San Diego."

Both waited, tense. Brandon actually was less threatening in this environment, which was why he was at the door. This was a witness interview, not busting someone's chops. So a white-trash boy for a white-trash neighborhood. He hadn't been raised that way. Time on the streets did that to cops; they inexorably slipped towards the level of their prey. *Azoic* concert tee tucked into jeans, Big-Boss boots with their waffle treads so he could run without slipping on his ass. The gold shield hung on a lanyard around his neck. Weaver was more conspicuous. Khakis and polo shirt; you didn't try and fake a look you couldn't pull off. Both wore sturdy leather belts with holster and sidearm. Weaver's badge was on his belt as well.

Dingy overalls and a blonde mullet answered the front door. It took Brandon a moment to realize there was more to the man than just bad taste. Sleep or drugs, or both, fogged the glare. "Yeah?" It was delivered in a tone that asked why his chops were being busted today. Couldn't expect less here…it wasn't a middle-class neighborhood where people answered their doors with *can I help you officer?*

"I understand your daughter witnessed some suspicious activity in the park."

"Don't know what you're talking about." A thin arm snaked around the man's leg. Large, doll-like eyes peered from behind his hip. Brandon gave the little girl a toned down version of his come-hither smile. Maybe nine or ten he figured, a few years older than Shayna. Of course his point of reference was a little off. Every time he saw his own daughter she seemed to have changed into another person.

Dishwater blonde hair hadn't been brushed, and jelly stained the edge of her mouth. She wore cheap pink flip-flops that were probably bought at some discount store. Her dirty toes curled and uncurled as her gaze crawled over Brandon. Finally she grinned in response. "Uh-huh, I did daddy." She wiped her nose on the sleeve of her too-large pajama tops. "I called them from the payphone over there."

Nodding, Brandon reached for the notepad in his back pocket. Weaver stepped up. A nice, easy witness interview; they'd take a few notes and file a report. In, out and done. And then he felt it…something was wrong. Suddenly tense, his eyes jumped to those of the father. He saw it, the hate, suspicion, disrespect. "Weaver!"

The man drew his hand up and back. "I told you, you little bitch, never to talk to the cops." As he spoke the fist came down.

"Holy shit!" Brandon grabbed the man's arm and spun his back into the wall. Weaver jumped in and pulled the child out the door. There were nut jobs on the force that went looking for fights, jabbing suspects with pins to make 'em jump. More than enough fights came looking for Brandon to suit his taste. Like this guy. He hit the wall, bounced off and fell down. Spewing a torrent of hate, he lashed out with his steel-toed boot, aiming for Brandon's knee. In that moment he was guilty of the worst crime, one not written in any law book…contempt of cop.

Brandon grabbed the guy's leg, trying to flip him up and over. A handful of shirt tangled in the idiot's fist. They both went down. The drilled-in mantra played in the back of his mind. Keep him away from your gun. The guy wasn't giving up. A knee meant for his groin caught Brandon's thigh. It would hurt later; adrenaline was running now. Basic training said you never hit a suspect with a closed fist. Time on the streets taught you to do it where they wouldn't bruise up. Three hard, quick rabbit punches landed in the guy's beer-gut. That beat a little respect into his punk ass. Somewhere behind him, Weaver was yelling for backup.

Once he managed to flip the man, he used his own weight to keep the guy down. Digging the handcuffs off his belt, he wrestled a grimy arm behind the tweaker's back. Just to teach him some manners he pulled it a little farther up than really necessary. *Ri-iick* went the cuffs on his wrist. With a knee on the guy's spine and one hand captured, Brandon could ease up a little. He yanked the other arm from beneath them both and locked it down. None too gracefully, Brandon untangled himself from the pile. Using the short length of chain as a leash he pulled the idiot to his feet. "Okay buddy, time for a ride."

A less-than-cooperative child was the result of arresting her daddy. Weaver and Carr spent a broiling afternoon waiting for the uniforms to show up, then waiting for child protective services to show up, and then waiting to speak with their diminutive witness who spent most of the time crying. The social worker promised to call them if the girl decided to talk, but not a one of them held out much hope. Had to love the job…if you didn't, you'd end up screaming.

Of course something like this meant reports to complete. And reports to complete translated into reports for Brandon to complete. Both were hoping the tweaker didn't open his big mouth. A lot of guys on the street just took it if you didn't go overboard. You wanted to fight with cops, cops were going to fight back. No one expected less. If he did start mouthing off, they would have to stand on subduing in a manner consistent with training. Fucking Attorney General had slapped Riverside P.D. with a consent order a few years back. Some of what it contained was good shit, like going back to the daily roll calls that had been abandoned because of "budget," and paying for advanced training…before anyone who wanted it had to eat the cost themselves. Other items were complete bureaucratic bullshit.

As they made their way from the abysmal heat of the outdoors into the torpid confines indoors, Weaver stopped in the hall. "So, about this afternoon…"

"Don't worry. I may have roughed him up a little, but I'm the one with the bruises."

"Fuck no, Baby D, that's covered." Weaver leaned against the wall and crossed his arms over his barrel chest. For a moment Weaver just considered his partner, a sappy half-assed grin on his face. "No, Carr, is this one *The One?*"

Partners learned how to push each other's buttons early on. "Get bent." Relationships were Brandon's button.

Weaver laughed. "Come on, admit it. There're only two women in this world that have your cell…your step-mom and your ex. That's some pretty exclusive company she's keeping."

"Maybe." While he was on the beat, he'd had a sex-friends relationship with the night admitting nurse at the local county psych ward. For three years it was great. Drop off the squirrel, dude would rush the processing and then they'd get their rocks off in the back room. Brandon had backed off when nurse boy had started whining about something more significant. Even he had never gotten more than Brandon's pager. It let him decide if he wanted to call a guy back. He hadn't even thought twice about giving Nicky his cell and his home numbers. Nicky didn't even have to ask for 'em…Brandon had grabbed his phone while they were joking around and programmed them in. "Maybe it's The One."

Weaver grinned and threw Brandon the sign that he was going for coffee. He was the kind of guy who didn't press when he was serious about things. That answer was good enough, at least for now. "Want anything?" Although Legal Grounds, the coffee shop across from the historic courthouse, had arguably the best coffee in town, how anyone could drink coffee in this heat was beyond him. Brandon declined with a shake of his head and continued on into the sweat shop; literally a sweat shop on a day like this one.

The Ds were all gathered around the TV. A few overworked fans were passing drifts of hot air about the room. One of the detective sergeants, Harcourt, snapped his fingers and pointed to the screen. "Hey, Carr, you got to see this."

Brandon waved him off. "I got paper work."

"Ah, come on, take a moment, come here and watch." Okay he could give up a few minutes. This wasn't going to be the hardest report to write…idiot tweaker decided to beat child in full view of two detectives, and then decided to try and beat detective…that ought to sum it up nicely. Harcourt pointed to the bottom right corner of the TV. A well-manicured lawn was caught in a four-way split from a security setup. The top right was an off-centered shot into a kitchen. The other two were the front entry and a darkened den area—typical Nanny Cam set up. It was mid-day by the sun patterns in the outdoor shots and the time stamp. A large German Shepherd bounded in and out of the bottom left frame. "Sex abuse, caught on tape."

Put that on top of the afternoon's entertainment and you started to lose your belief in humanity. These were the kind of cases that made Brandon wonder why he'd become a cop. "The au-pair bring the kids home early for a little fun?" If you didn't joke about it, you'd just end up blowing your brains out.

Another detective broke in. "Nah man, watch the yard." Brandon knew him, but didn't, the guy wasn't vice, maybe juvie.

Into the shot walked a man in a baseball cap, torn jeans and work shirt. Given that he was carrying a rake, he was probably the gardener. Although there was no sound, Brandon could tell the dog was barking, drumming his paws on the ground, tail wagging. The shepherd wanted to play. The gardener picked up a ball and threw it a few times. Then, he unzipped his pants. "Aw fuck, he's gonna do the dog!" Riotous laughter peppered the comments. "Ya think he used a condom?" and "Isn't this the jurisdiction of Animal Control?" Most were laughing so hard they couldn't breathe. A few had tears rolling down their faces.

As the tape rolled, Brandon realized just what was happening. "Holy crap, the dog's fucking him!" He was laughing as hard as any of them. It was sick. It was sad. It was just so obscene it was funny. Given the really horrid stuff they dealt with every day, watching a grown man getting pounded by a dog cracked the hard exteriors and hit them where it hurt. When things like that happened, a cop's only retreat was finding the humor in the situation—whatever little bit there might be. "Where? What? Why do we have this?"

"The guy called dispatch and told them somebody was messing with his dog. Patrol goes out and tells him, can't do anything about it 'cause there's no evidence. The guy's seriously pissed and they tell him 'get it on tape and then we'll have evidence and we'll do something about it.' So the fucker did."

"Fuck man, you fucks are sick." He retreated to a desk to start the paperwork process. As he did he caught sight of the clock. Damn, it was almost four. He really ought to call Nicky back. Forms could wait a bit. Time for a smoke anyway; he'd call Nicky from the alternate office at the top of the garage.

As he lit up, he retrieved the number and hit send.

CHAPTER THIRTY-ONE

Querida sat forlorn in the lot, her only companion the pimped-out Toyota. It was late afternoon, but Nick was still upbeat. How could he not be with the prospect of seeing Brandon? As he popped the door his cell phone rang. Touching the button behind his ear, he answered, "Yo! It's Nick." Long, productive day and a long, sensual night ahead; things couldn't get much better.

"Well, hello, sexy you." That smoky voice brought a smile to his lips.

Four thirty-five, by his watch. "Hey, I was just thinking about you." Tossing the laptop case on the seat, he caught a glimpse of the broken radio. Really, he should fix it before he headed out. LAPD was notorious for 'excessive noise' tickets. A distracted-driving fine was not something he wanted. "So we're on for Cat & Fiddle, about seven." Nick headed toward the back of the hearse where he kept a small box of tools. Three things you always carried in a classic car: water for the radiator, gas just in case, and a tool box with at least the basics.

"May not make it until seven-thirtyish or eight. I'm not going to be able to blow out of here until about six." A pleasant laugh carried over the connection. "Plus I have to run by the apartment and grab a bag. Unless you want me wearing the same clothes all weekend."

Now it was Nick's turn to chuckle. Popping the back gate, he purred, "Babe, I don't want you wearing any clothes this weekend." He crawled into the casket compartment and scrounged the tool box for a pair of pliers. The first he found was small set of needle-nose he kept for wiring projects. That would work for getting in to the tight face of the radio where the nub from the broken knob was hiding. "I'll hang out and have a drink. Just keep me posted." Worming backward, his feet hit the pavement. A hard jab in the ribs caught him when he stood. Slowly, he looked back over his shoulder. Arturo was behind him.

Given everything, he didn't doubt that the hard piece of metal grinding into his backside was a pistol. It struck Nick just how vulnerable he was. Out in the middle of nowhere; the freeway was blocked by the building. All the other employees of Frontier had left by the time he'd finished the inspection. There didn't seem to be any other ongoing business in this industrial park. He knew he was fucked. His only hope of salvation was the open line and Arturo not knowing there was an open line.

"Arturo, hey, watcha doing?" Brandon said something in his ear, but Nick ignored it. On the periphery of his vision, another man approached. Now his gut went cold. It was the guy they'd been following in Ensenada. Like a bad card, Chino seemed to show up in every deal. Nick slid the small pair of pliers so that the grip was almost hidden up his sleeve. Trying to pretend he wasn't holding anything, Nick relaxed his arm and fingers. The only indication was his thumb pressing the nose into his palm. Arturo started to speak, but his companion put his finger to his lips indicating silence. Chino tapped the side of his head then pointed to Nick's ear...the one with the Bluetooth headset.

Thumb and pinky spread, the other three fingers bent over his palm; Chino wiggled his hand. Then turned it upside down, indicating he wanted Nick to hang up the phone. Shit, here he was in the middle of nowhere and his only safety line was about to be cut off. His only hope was to buy some time. Thinking at breakneck speed, "Hey, ya know what, babe, I think I'm actually kinda tired." He wanted to convince the pair that this was not a good idea. Make them think someone was expecting him soon. "I'm just going to head back to the hotel room. We'll meet there in what, fifteen minutes?" Again he ignored Brandon's confused comments. "You, me, some peanut-butter and some rope, it'll be fun." Another jab, the pair was getting impatient. "Gotta run." This could be the end of everything. Nick had no delusions as to how fucked he really was. He wanted to say it once, just in case. "Brandon...I love you." Hoping against hope that it was enough, Nick hit the disconnect.

Chino stepped in, took the phone off his belt and popped the battery off the back. Both went sailing through the open casket compartment to land somewhere in the front of Querida. Everything was cold for Nick, like someone was dripping ice water down his spine. He swallowed. "I don't know what you think the problem is here, but ya know, I got people expecting me. You really don't want to do this."

"Calle te Mariposa." Chino's torn voice grated. "So you're the mula Nick O'Malley we couldn't find. Looking for some Irish guy and you're fucking Indio, goddamn figures. And here you come, walking into my hands. What you think, Tio, think he needs to go on vacation for a while?"

Well now he knew who Tio was. "People know I'm here. You won't get away with it. When I don't come back they'll put Arturo's ass in the fire. What's he going to tell them?"

"S'okay, Tio here is on the phone with Laura in San Diego, right now. Probably an hour phone call about all sorts business." Somewhere back in the factory there was probably a phone lying on a table with an open connection to San Diego, building an alibi. "All he knows is you left, got in your wicked-ass ride, and headed for the grapevine. Last he ever saw of you." Chino's laugh was worse than his voice. It shredded every nerve down Nick's spine. "And, esse, we talked to Laura, she says Gaming Control don't do no site inspections like this. Ain't got the cash for it. So you're bullshitting us, cabron. You're here on your own. Reg says we take you out. Tio will clean up shit here. Then if anybody asks, that missing chip was just something Duke was fucking with. Laura says that Duke said you don't hang with other agents. Don't talk much, just do your job. You wouldn't have told nobody what was going on."

"You're so wrong about that." He could tell they didn't believe him. They probably figured he was just stalling. Well he was, but not with that thin of a lie. "And what about you?"

"See esse, I'm in Mexico right now. There's ten people who'll swear it." Another soul-tearing laugh sounded. "You and me, we're taking a ride, a long, long ride."

They were going to kill him. Nick was certain of it. If he could make the freeway there might be a chance. Obviously, Arturo would shoot him if he tried to run. That would have to be taken care of. Moving his thumb slightly, the tool dropped into his palm. One deep breath to prepare was all he could afford. Then Nick rammed the needle-nose pliers into Arturo's arm. Dropping the gun, Arturo screamed, "Pinche Cabron!"

There was a bang as the pistol hit the ground, discharging. The bullet whizzed between his legs and chewed into the asphalt at Nick's feet. Nick kicked the gun under the chassis and took off towards the highway.

Two steps and Chino tackled him. Driving Nick's face into the pavement, he slammed his fist into the small of Nick's spine. God, did it hurt. His one chance was gone. "You're going to pay for that, puto." Wrenching an arm behind his back, Chino pulled Nick off the ground. With another nasty laugh, he slammed Nick into the side of the hearse. Something popped in Nick's shoulder and pain screamed down his arm. "Tio, I think I saw some rope in that ride. Let's make sure el mayate don't try nothing stupid again." Death was laughing and cursing behind his back. Nick was so terrified he couldn't even breathe. At least he'd gotten to say *it* once to Brandon.

Chapter Thirty-Two

Brandon clutched his cell as he listened to a sea of dead air. Oh crap, he was so not ready for the "I love you" statement. It hit him hard and in all the wrong places. His stomach was rolling as he made his way to the stairs, boots banging on the metal treads as he dropped through the well. That was just too much to deal with on the heels of such a weird-ass conversation. It was like Nick hadn't really been talking to Brandon at all. Twice Nicky'd just ignored him. Sometimes Nicky was plain weird. And then the peanut-butter and rope comment, what the hell was he on? Stepping into the street and the muddy-brown glare of the sun, all the wind was knocked out of Brandon's chest. Oh, fuck, the bondage and safewords thing...he barely touched the steps as he vaulted into the station screaming for Weaver.

Skidding past the entrance to vice, grabbing the frame to stop himself, Brandon caught sight of his partner. It was a long shot, but the only shot he had. "Weaver, I need your help." Jeff was at his desk filling out more reports. There was no time for long explanations. "Look, I got a contact in Vegas...the guy's also a friend. He was out in Bakersfield and something's gone way wrong. I need you to pull a favor out of your guy at the CHP."

His partner just stared, pencil raised halfway to his lips. "You're fucking nuts, Carr." Deliberately, slowly, the older man set the pencil on his desk, folded his hands across his gut and leaned back in his chair. "First off, what are you smoking up there, 'cause whatever it is I need some. And what makes you think I'm going to waste a favor on your sorry ass?"

"Look, anything, man." Drumming his fists on the fake wood grain he tried to think. "The guy's in trouble, real trouble." He had to make this work. "I think he's stumbled into something." Slow down, Brandon told himself, he had to sell it to Weaver. "Okay. Okay, this guy, Nicholas O'Malley, was with me when that shit went down in Vegas. The reason I've been getting calls from the dick in Vegas is my guy was friends with the vic. I've been doing a smooth-over, making sure Nick is up front with Vegas Metro, and they're being really good about keeping me in the loop. He is, at this point, still a person of interest in their investigation."

After a deep breath where Weaver just continued to stare, he kept going. "He's in Cali right now. He had to do an onsite investigation up in Bakersfield today. There's word out that the place he had to inspect might, might just be a front for La Eme. The lab Narc busted, the Nevada murder I told you about, and there's some stuff I heard through LA's OCID...there's an ongoing investigation which has targeted some guys who are in deep with the place he had to be at today. It's all wrapped up together." Jeff's face said he still wasn't biting. "Weaver...Jeff, look the guy's a brother, this is an official investigation."

Weaver was skeptical. "A brother?" Probably the oldest tradition in law enforcement, brothers in uniform came first. It didn't matter if it was the gal who drove the meat wagon or a guy handing out parking tickets, they were all brothers. Marriages failed and kids turned against their parents, but if you fell down there'd be a dozen boys in blue to help you back on your feet. The only people you could ever truly rely on were other officers.

"Yeah, O'Malley's an Agent with Nevada Gaming Control; he's like the guys in photo or latent...not front line, but a brother all the same. You took his call a few weeks back."

"A state agent." Massaging the bridge of his nose, Jeff looked up through his fingers. "And he's in trouble?"

"I think big trouble." Brandon swallowed and pulled at his earrings. "I told him to keep checking in with me, just in case. They sent him out in the field all by himself..."

"I sense an 'and' here."

"And I just got off the phone with him." Crossing and uncrossing his arms he paced before Weaver's desk. "It was one of the weirdest conversations I've had. Everything's screaming at me that something's gone wrong and he's landed in deep shit."

"So, your point is?"

Brandon knelt so that he was nearly eye to eye with the older detective. "Call your guy with the Chippies. Maybe they could just put out a look-out alert for him." Knuckles going white against the desk he tried to give Weaver something to hang it on. "A person of interest is in California, up near Bakersfield. You're doing a favor for Vegas Metro who just wants them to keep an eye on the guy. Please dude, for me. Anything you need ever again it's yours for the asking. Every chit I've got…yours."

There was more face rubbing as Weaver considered it. Finally he put his hands in his lap, "There's no fucking way."

No, Brandon wouldn't accept that. He couldn't accept that. "Anything you want," Brandon begged. "You need something, all you got to do is ask. Anything at all, man. Just help me a little."

"What do you want?" Weaver leaned in. "How much do you think my guy can do? Especially right now, he ain't gonna bend over backwards for us." Brandon couldn't keep the terror out of his eyes, and he could tell that Weaver'd seen it. "What's this guy to you anyway? Why you going to lay so much out for him?"

Fuck, he couldn't. But Brandon knew that he'd never forgive himself if he didn't do everything in his power. Even if it failed, he had to try. It had to be worth it. "Jeff." He swallowed his fear. "You asked me today if this relationship I'm in was the one…well it is. And the chick I've been seeing, the one from San Diego, she ain't no gal. I can't lose Nicky. I'm going to lose him. I got nothing if you don't help. You've got to trust my instincts. Something is seriously wrong up in Bakersfield."

His partner's face went slack. Staring at Brandon, Weaver finally hissed, "Christ on a crutch." It was hard for him, Brandon could see it. One of those you-think-you-know-a-guy moments was passing. "You're such a good cop, you can't be…"

"I am a good cop. You know that." There wasn't time for a Hallmark moment. "And I'm gay and the person who means everything to me is in real trouble. I don't have anyone else if you don't help me."

Weaver closed his eyes and turned away. Brandon slammed his fist into the desk. His partner wasn't going to help. All of it wasted. At least now he knew where he stood with Jeff. Getting to his feet, he dug for the keys in his pocket. He'd go fucking find Nicky himself.

Then Weaver spoke. "You are so going to owe me for this, Carr." Weaver was reaching for the phone. "Who are we telling them to look out for?

Brandon almost fell over he was so blindsided. Catching the edge of the desk, "Guy's name is Nicholas O'Malley. Five-ten, about one-sixty-five, black eyes, black hair…waist length…he's Native American decent. God knows what he's wearing, 'cause he's working. He had to take his personal ride. His car is a '68 Cadillac Miller-Meteor Endloader."

"A what?" The detective stopped dialing and stared again.

"A hearse man, guy drives a fucking hearse." Shaking his head in disbelief, Weaver resumed dialing. It was probably the least strange thing he'd been hit with. "Dark-blue with missing rear wheel-well covers and a split front grill. The hubcaps on the driver's side are missing."

Hand over the receiver, Weaver growled, "You will so owe me, Carr, 'cause I'm going to owe my soul to this guy. Give me ten minutes and I'll let you know."

"Ring me." Brandon was already running for the door. "I'm heading up to Bakersfield."

"You so fucking owe me, Carr!" Weaver yelled at his heels.

CHAPTER THIRTY-THREE

Querida bounced along the highway. Every pothole the hearse hit vibrated in Nick's bones. Her V-8 rumble was nearly drowned out by throbbing bass courtesy of Rob Zombie. The stereo was still blaring at full blast. He'd gotten to listen to Chino curse the radio through the first half of the CD. After roughing him up, Arturo had hog-tied him and thrown him in the back of the M-M. Then he'd gone off on an unsuccessful hunt for a tarp. Almost twenty minutes was blown that way. Upon his return, an argument had ensued in Spanglish.

Between Nick's limited Spanish and the peppering of English slang, he figured they wanted to throw something over him, just in case someone passed the hearse on the highway. Chino finally had the idea to pull the curtains in the back windows. It wasn't perfect, but it would keep casual lookers from seeing anything. Then more time was wasted while the banger tried to figure out the gear pattern on the column shift.

During all of it, Nick was messing with the ropes. Someone needed to teach these goons how to hog-tie properly. Kneeling, arms pulled back through the legs with wrists bound to the opposite ankles…that was a hog-tie. Arms pulled to a U behind the back and ankles bound to that… that was a hog-tie. This was just amateurish. Arturo had tied his hands behind his back with figure eights. Even when the rope was wrapped between it left Nick room to wiggle. Ankles were bound as well and tied to his wrists. But if they'd been really serious, the ankle rope should have been looped around his neck; since they didn't care if he strangled himself, it would keep a prisoner from undoing the bonds.

Everything ached. The blinding pain in his shoulder had dropped to a dull throb. If he could untie himself…well, he had no clue what he'd do if he untied himself, but there were more options at that point. Nick rolled his shoulders back until his biceps protested and the left one screamed. His arms dropped just enough to give him some slack. Arching his back and bringing his heels as close to his butt as possible, Nick rubbed his legs together trying to pick up some slack. As he writhed the casket roller shifted, thumping into the gate. He stilled. No reaction from the front seat. Chino couldn't hear it over the death-rock thunder.

One of the many problems with granny knots was that they weren't very strong. It took some doing, but he managed to loose the bonds enough to free his feet. His hands were another matter. The pain shooting down his arm every time he moved bubbled bile in his throat. They hit another bump. The casket roller whumped the gate and Nick heard it; metal grinding on metal. Arturo had shut the back gate and he didn't know how to make it latch.

Well, that could mean a way out. Of course it still didn't solve the fact that he was tied up in the back of his own hearse. He kept working his hands. Only when the pain got to be too much did he stop. All the strength in his left hand was sucked out by the pain. There was no way he was getting his hands undone.

Electronic footfalls backed by a backwards calliope boomed from the speakers. The intro to *What Lurks on Channel X?*, the sampling of the old horror flick, a scream then the drumbeat thunder and a bass overlay. This was the song to do it to. Breathing, concentrating, he waited though another sampling. Then another blinding bass-drum riff swept through Querida. Nick thrashed. The roller slid into the back of the hearse.

Over the next sampling a string of profanity in Spanish spewed from the front seat. A couple times he caught the words pig and policia. Fuck him raw, if the curtains hadn't been in the windows maybe he could signal to someone. He had to do this himself.

Wait for it; it would come again. Acoustic strings throbbed in minor keys. Wait, wait. The bass flash of the drum beat hit. Nick lashed out with his feet. The casket roller banged against the gate. Again he kicked. Again the roller slid. Hinges whined. A siren wailed. It took a moment for his mind to click. That wasn't part of the music.

This interlude was shorter. It seemed like forever. Patience, the next riff will come. Music thundered. Querida lunged forward, floored full bore. Again he thrashed. Bang went the roller, colliding with the gate. A screech of old metal and the gate dropped. The hearse bounced across chewed asphalt. The roller shot back. The gate flew open.

"What the fuck!?" Chino's grinding voice screamed from behind him. The table shot out a third of its length. Then it jerked from under Nick's body. Pain seared across his scalp as his head grazed the edge of the gate. Nick spun in empty air; for moments he knew what flying was. Preparing for impact he closed his eyes and balled his body the best he could. Then pavement slammed him. Gravel burrowed under his skin. No pain. That was odd, there should be pain. Nick rolled. Tires screamed. The black burned smell of rubber and copper filled his nose. He looked up. Above his nose was the rusting chrome of a bumper. Nick started to laugh. Then the injuries bit into his body and he screamed.

CHAPTER THIRTY-FOUR

As Brandon slid from the rented Jeep, Detective Orozco clambered out of his unmarked. The heavyset man jogged across the street and down Nick's drive. "Detective Carr," Orozco stuck out his hand as he slowed to a walk. "So how is the prince of darkness fairing?"

For a moment Brandon just looked at the other cop. "He's doing okay." The man hadn't dropped his hand. Uncomfortable, Brandon switched the groceries to his left side and took the proffered shake. Orozco's grip was firm and friendly. It made Brandon suspicious. "He's pretty drugged up right now. A cracked sternum and ribs, separated shoulder, some scalp lacerations, and he busted the shit outta his tailbone. Otherwise just pulls, strains and sprains; shook his brains around in his skull some, but no concussion. It could have been a lot worse."

God, it could have been so much worse. Brandon had barreled out of the station, taking a uniform and his coffee down to the pavement. Insults followed his heels. Hell would break loose when Weaver realized Brandon had jacked the unmarked. His Harley didn't have a police radio. What should have been almost a three-hour drive, Brandon managed in just under two. There wasn't a speed limit he didn't break, or a traffic law he didn't violate.

Riverside PD used ranges around 460 MHz. California Highway took the bands in the lower 40s. Constant scanning of the frequencies gave him discordant updates on the situation. A cracked transmission started it all. Picked up on the outskirts of Los Angeles, "All units 10-42 possible code 20. Nevada Gaming Control Agent investigating a 330 has not checked in." In civilian speak an officer was missing, find him. He owed his soul to Weaver. "Be on the lookout for male, late 20s American Indian descent, 5-10, approx 165. Officer was last seen in the vicinity of Marlow Industrial Park off I-98 driving a blue 1968 Cadillac Hearse."

A random voice cut in. "10-9 that vehicle." Brandon wouldn't have believed it either if it came across the air.

"10-4. 1968 Cadillac Hearse, dark blue, front end damage, missing hubcaps on driver's side."

The dog and pony show reverberated with cop gibberish. He knew when the CHP picked up the hearse. He heard the scream of the officer when he damn near ran Nicky over. Police chases, suspect arrests, emergency service calls, all of it coming across the air in the 10/11 code language of law enforcement. Emergency vehicles and police activity hit the edge of his vision as he blew over the crest. Somewhere in front of him an ambulance had Nicky. He didn't have the frequency to pick up their chatter. On the back end of the grapevine, first gear disappeared. He trashed second and third getting the Toyota into town.

A bright white tower screamed Memorial Hospital. Inside it was all whites and grays and blues. Pastel nurses parted like the red sea. A badge was an entrance to anywhere and everywhere you wanted to go in a hospital. Long, over-lit hallways of glass and chrome led him to Nicky.

Brandon's bones pooled out through his boots. Highway Patrol, Kern County Sheriffs, Bakersfield Regulars; the corridor to the emergency room was littered with uniforms. Word got around. It always did. A brother was down in a strange place and they wouldn't let him be alone. He'd done it, they'd all done it; the switch off so that there was always someone to lean on, someone to grab coffee for a wife or a candy bar for the kids. And because Nicky was alone, they were his family right now.

Brandon caught one of the nurses by her arm. "Agent O'Malley, his dad lives in Utah. Give me his cell, I'll make the call." Fear echoed hollow in his words.

Experienced eyes searched his own. She sensed he was more than just another cop here for support. "CHP's already made it. Had emergency contact information in his wallet." Fingers encrusted with silver and turquoise lent him their strength. "You work with him?" The staff knew Nicky was law enforcement, and not from California.

"Some, on some things," Brandon lied. The next sentence was as close as he could get to the truth. "He's my best friend.

Have someone call Vegas Metro Homicide. Detective Emanuel Orozco needs to know about this. They're, ah, working a joint investigation. Orozco will know how to get a hold of his chief." Before the last of it dripped from his mouth, a deputy was on the phone. With cups of bitter dregs the nurses brought him updates. X-rays, cat scans, stitches. Hours were spent just picking gravel out of Nicky's skin. Some time around nine he finally answered Weaver's calls, and then held the phone as far as he could from his ear. It didn't help dampen the vitriol.

They gave Nicky a private room, with a narrow hospital bed and power strips running chest high across the walls. Bruises crawled across Nicky's face and mixed with yellow iodine stains. Everything was too bright, too sterile. But it wasn't the ER, and it wasn't Critical Care.

The Chippy who'd almost had Nicky for a hood ornament came and went at regular intervals. He said he'd almost passed them by when the call came in. But the hearse caught his attention. How many could there be on the road? So he'd dropped behind, tailing the Caddy. Nothing had seemed strange other than the music blaring at top volume. He figured he'd pull them over on a Rolling Terry Stop. If it wasn't connected, he'd hit the driver with a citation for the noise. He'd flipped the light bar. Blue and red flashed on chrome. No reaction. He turned on the siren. They sped up. The CHP had picked up the mike to call for back up. That's when Nicky came flying across his hood.

Things could have been a hell of a lot worse.

Orozco coughed, breaking Brandon from his memories. "Yeah, it could have. It still could get bad, I understand." Orozco wasn't talking about Nick's physical well being.

"It could. He's suspended indefinitely without pay while they figure out just how hard they're going to fuck him. Although his chief is standing behind him; he won't let them hang Nicky out to dry without a fight."

"And you?"

Brandon shrugged. "I got yelled at and a couple days without pay. And I took some vacation time at my captain's suggestion to let everyone cool off. They weren't thrilled that I toasted one of the cars. It certainly didn't hurt my case that Nicky was beaten up, tied up and in the back of his car, and that the goons who did it to him were armed. The whole exigency thing put a nice spin on it."

"There isn't a cop I know who wouldn't have done exactly the same thing if their girlfriend was in trouble. They should all understand."

Two days ago he'd sorted some things out with his partner. It had gotten pretty nasty, but between them things were out in the open. Only between them, however. "I really don't think I'm going to be bringing that comparison up at the department." Jeff was still debating whether he would ask to have Brandon reassigned. He claimed it didn't matter to him. Brandon actually believed that Jeff meant it. His problem was what if someone else found out. Having a gay partner was as bad as fucking guys yourself in a lot of officers' eyes. "Ever."

"What I'm wondering is, how did you know he was in trouble?"

Looking off in the fading sky, Brandon thought for a moment. He didn't have to tell the guy. But shit, professional courtesy almost demanded that he did. Cops hated loose ends, not knowing things…it's why many of them became cops. He sighed. "Peanut butter."

"Excuse me?"

"Look, you and the missus ever do anything a little kinky to spice up your marriage?" Orozco's eyebrows shot up. "Okay, well, Nicky's kinks run kinda deep. And in certain types of activities you have to have a word that means 'stop, I'm in serious trouble.' It has to be a word that is completely out of context so you're not confusing it with something else. We use peanut butter as that word." Curiosity, but not disgust or hate or any of the other things Brandon was expecting crossed Orozco's visage. "Anyway, we're having a nice little conversation, making some plans and he comes outta left field, changing everything and talking about peanut butter. I knew he was in trouble then."

"Learn something everyday." Shaking his head, Orozco added, "Well, if it gets real bad and you decide you want to move to Vegas and go through qualifying, let me know. I'll put in a good word for you."

"Yeah, right."

"No, I mean it. And I want you to know that nothing about you and he got written down anywhere. It's all," Orozco tapped his middle finger to his forehead, "up here, nowhere else."

"Thanks."

"No, thank you. We'll probably never be able to charge them with Ducmagian's death, but with the kidnapping, money laundering, and federal drug charges, they'll be vacationing at Club Fed for quite some time. Tell Dracula that his little stunt closed a case I figured would be open until hell froze over. Of course if he ever does it again, I'll personally finish the job la Eme started."

"Want to tell him yourself?"

"Nah, you can convey it." The older man sighed. "By the way, I wasn't just watching your boy because I thought he might be in on it. Actually at first I was, but when ballistics came back…" He paused.

"Then why were you?"

"I knew something was wrong with the whole thing. The only connection the deceased had with the club was Agent O'Malley. But ballistics came back with a match to the gun we found in the car. It was registered in California. It was registered to Mike Ducmagian. They shot him with his own gun and tossed it on the seat next to him. Cute that."

"Why would his gun be there unless he brought it with him?"

"Exactly."

For the second time that week Brandon nearly died inside. "You're thinking…"

"Yeah, I'm thinking." Orozco shrugged, stuck his hands in his pockets and kicked gravel at his feet. Looking first to the sky as if searching for answers, he turned his attention back to Brandon. "But the guy's dead so we'll never know for sure; probably lucky for Agent O'Malley that he got hit when he did. Ducmagian was in debt up to his eyeballs, and looks like right in the thick of things. I think he was probably pretty desperate when he showed up. Desperate men do stupid things."

"Don't tell Nicky that…ever."

Rock-a-Billy Miri was stashing her shears and razors in a black cosmetic case when he entered the kitchen. Red canvas tennis shoes, black pedal pushers and a Halloween close-out T-shirt with wax red vampire lips and the caption "bite me," pretty much said it all. Looking up from under blunt cut bangs, she warned him, "Be careful in there. He's pretty pissed, you know."

Brandon dumped the groceries on the counter. "About fucking what?" Hot dogs, tortilla chips, mac'n cheese, frozen pizza, all of it was quick and dirty comfort food…the kinds of things Brandon's dad used to make when his son was feeling down. They'd sit on the back step and eat polka-dot-casserole; two forks fishing the cut-up franks out of a pan of cheese and noodles. They never talked, just sat and ate. He'd have a Coke. His dad would down a couple of beers and both would try not to think about what it would have been like if mom were around.

"His hair. Where they shaved it to put in the stitches, there wasn't a whole hell of a lot left to work with."

Shoving the milk into the fridge, he asked, "How short did you have to go?"

"Not short, Hon…" Miri rested her butt on the kitchen table and lit a cigarette she fished from a pack. "Gone." The smoke floated about her head for a moment. "I left him a little on the top but I couldn't even get a Mohawk out of it." She shook her head. "Maybe when the stitches heal I can tip it in red or purple, but…" the thought trailed off. Lipping the cig, she tossed her bag over her shoulder. "I'm out. You get Tigger."

"Tigger?"

"You know…'a not-so-bouncy Tigger. A thank you for rescuing me Tigger'… Winnie the Pooh." Miri waved him off. "Okay, you obviously don't have kids." At the door she stopped. "Listen, Nick's one of the sweetest people I know. I've known him since we were in high school, and he can be a little intense sometimes, but he's really sweet. And he hasn't said anything, but I can tell. He likes you more than just friends. Be nice to him, let him down gently, he deserves that…"

"Miri." Brandon cut her off. "I like him more than just friends, too." He slammed the fridge door. "And if you ever breathe a word of that to anyone, you will never cross the state line without getting a hundred tickets." He advanced on her. "Never, ever, ever!"

"Ah-ha! I knew my gay-dar wasn't off!" she shot back, drawing the screen door shut between them.

"Blow, fag-hag, before I come out there and beat you silly." Behind the thin mesh barrier she stuck out her tongue. Brandon emphasized his point with his middle finger. "Not a word. Got it?" Miri drew her index finger and thumb across her lips in zipping motion. Twisting an imaginary key, she tossed it in the garbage as she dropped down the back steps, laughing. Shit, another person he was outed to. At this rate, by the end of summer the entire force would know.

He snagged a beer for himself and a Diet Pepsi for Nicky and headed for the sound of the TV. Dude would be mad, but alcohol and Vicoden just weren't meant for mixing. The living room was dim, late afternoon sun filtering through the half closed curtains. Strains of *This is Halloween* drifted from the surround sound. Nick was on the umpteenth viewing of *The Nightmare Before Christmas*. Well at least it was better than WWE Smackdown. Why anyone would actually own wrestling tapes was beyond him.

A lanky shadow stretched along the couch. Nicky groaned and slid to a semi-sitting position. He wasn't actually supposed to sit on his butt yet. Sweat pants hung loose about his hips. Brandon had to help Nick get dressed; it hurt him so much to move, even with the drugs. His left arm was in an immobilization sling and the whole shoulder looked like it had been scoured by a Brillo pad. The doctors predicted that Nick would suffer loss of pigment in the area because of the trauma to his skin. A six-inch-wide swatch of elastic, ridden by the blue band of the sling, covered his ribs. A large green bruise bloomed under the compression dressing. Various spots of sickly yellow dotted his face and arms.

It took considerable will for Brandon not to laugh. The waist-length black fall had vanished. In its place was a reverse wedge. The longest section of Nick's hair hit about mid cheek. Everything else from just above his ears to his neck line was buzzed. One line of stitches ran across the back of his skull, the other just above his right ear. It didn't look bad; it just didn't look like his Nicky. Well, the stitches and bruises looked like shit.

"Look what they fucking did to my hair." Nick whined, tugging on a hank of bang. The pain meds slurred his speech. His pupils were micro-dots in his black eyes. Dude was doped up good.

Brandon deposited the soda on the coffee table and knelt down. A stiff neck made it hard for Nicky to look up at him. "It's fine." He used his soothing-victims voice. They were on permanent replay of this conversation. Querida was in CHP impound. GCB was pushing his investigation through finer and finer sieves. Suspended from his job, unable to breathe without intense pain, the minor issue of his hair gave Nicky something tangible to focus on. One of the reasons for Miri's visit was to get Nicky off that track. "Trust me."

Nicky pouted. "No, it looks like goddamn shit."

That was it, drugs or no. "You asshole—fuck your hair!" Brandon exploded, "You're lucky you're not in some goddamn ravine in the middle of the National Forrest with a bullet in your skull! I busted my ass getting to Bakersfield, knowing, just fucking knowing, I was going to spend the rest of my week fucking knee-deep in poison oak, beating the brush for your body!" Every pause was punctuated by Brandon's fist slamming into the arm of the couch. "Don't you ever think you have the right to put me through that again!" Head against the velvet, Brandon got himself back under control. "I ran into Orozco outside, he says if you ever pull this crap again he'll beat you senseless. And then, you know what? I'll fucking kill you!"

"I'm sorry." The apology was whispered in a little boy's voice.

Shit, why did he say that to Nicky? "No I'm sorry, I didn't mean that." Sliding down to the floor, back against the couch and hands dangling between his knees, Brandon tipped his head back touching Nicky's hip. "It's your job, you had to do it. I just kinda freaked a little, okay. Don't worry about it. Forget it, I didn't mean anything."

Jack Skellington stood in a snow-covered cemetery and belted out lyrics in Danny Elfman's voice. Christmas was saved, normalcy reigned, flurries fell on Halloween Towne while vampires played icy hockey and zombie kids threw snowballs. "I like this, Brandon."

"What? Nightmare…it's your DVD you should like it."

"No, shithead. You being here." Nick's voice was soft behind him. "Going to bed with you at night and just being together." Nicky stroked Brandon's skull with his knuckles. "Waking up and hearing you singing in the shower. Just knowing that you're around the house is really nice."

Cold crawled down his back and set the tightness in his gut roiling. Too soon, it was way too soon. The last time anyone had said anything like that, Brandon had left tire tracks in their drive. Problem was, it did feel really, really nice. And since Nicky had said it, the big three words, he'd replayed it over and over in his mind. Never mind that he'd said it because he was thinking he was going to die, he'd said it. Brandon liked that he'd said it. That scared him more than he was willing to admit. "I'm not ready to talk about that, Nicky."

"Okay." Nicky's fingers traced the tattoos on Brandon's neck. "I'm just saying that it's kinda nice."

Wrapping his hand around Nicky's, Brandon drew Nick's palm to his lips, "Yeah, it's kinda nice, now shut up and watch TV."

About the Author

James Buchanan is an award winning author of, primarily, gay erotic fiction. James grew up in a small Southwestern town, hours away from any other small Southwestern town. A stint at the State University, where he ostensibly majored in English, garnered him a degree useful for being someone's secretary. The absolute lack of employment opportunities led James to Southern California. After a stint in County Mental Health (administration not client) he ran screaming into the field of Law. James has been practicing for nine years and someday he might even get it right.

James has published several short stories and novellas as well as six novels with various publishers. You can visit James on the web at: www.James-Buchanan.com.

Stimulate yourself.
READ.

www.manloveromance.com
THE HOTTEST M/M EROTIC AUTHORS & WEBSITES ON THE NET

Printed in the United Kingdom
by Lightning Source UK Ltd.
134706UK00001BA/3/P